Lioness of Broceliande

Gloria J. Prunty

Copyright © 2024 by Gloria J. Prunty

All rights reserved. No part of this book may be used or reproduced without written permission from the author except in the case of brief quotations embodied in critical articles or reviews.

Disclaimer

Lioness of Broceliande is a work of fiction. All incidents and dialogue, while based on historical events, are not intended as a factual portrayal. Where real-life historical figures appear, the situations, incidents and dialogues concerning those persons serve as a backdrop to the characters and their actions, which are wholly imaginary. In all other respects any resemblance to actual persons, living or dead, events or locales is entirely incidental.

Interior design by Booknook.biz

For

My husband and my brother, I dedicate my book.
I thank you for the encouragement I needed to
complete The Lioness of Broceliande.

To my Illustrator, Terri Shay,

Thank you, for your beautiful illustrations.

TABLE OF CONTENTS

Chapter 1: The Forest of Broceliande, 1779	3
Chapter 2: The Terror	10
Chapter 3: The Tunnels	15
Chapter 4: London, April of the Year 1792	32
Chapter 5: The Meeting	73
Chapter 6: The Family	85
Chapter 7: Discovery	113
Chapter 8: The Red Dragon	132
Chapter 9: The Marriage	146
Chapter 10: Prison of Quimper	151
Chapter 11: The Tunnels	156
Chapter 12: The Inn of Quipen Bay	177
Chapter 13: The Beginning of the End	182
Chapter 14: Sagath	187
Chapter 15: Quimper	192
Chapter 16: Full Circle	194
Chapter 17: The Game that Never Ends	196

Chapter 18: Return to Broceliande	209
Chapter 19: Muzillac	213
Chapter 20: The Serpent	218
Chapter 21: David and Ariella	225
Chapter 22: One Hundred Demons	238
Chapter 23: Good and Evil	241
Glossary	251
Sequel	255

Lioness of Broceliande

Exeter
Bournemouth
Newquay
Plymouth
Torquay
Poole
Truro
Falmouth
English channel
Cherbourg-en-Cotentin
Guernsey
Jersey
Caen
Lannion
Moriax
Brest
Saint-Brieuc
Saint Malo
Forest of Broceliande
Rennes
Laval
Quimper
Odet River
Lorient
Venville
Bay of Biscay
Concarneau
Quiberan
Quiberon Bay
Angers
Saint Nazaire
Nantes
Loire River
Vendee
Cholet
Challas
La Roche-Sur-Yon
Niort
La Rochelle

CHAPTER I

THE FOREST OF BROCELIANDE, 1779

Broceliande is timeless, an ancient, primeval part of the earth. It is a living thing far beyond the power of man. It existed before man, before wars were fought, before the serpent crawled from the darkest pits of hell bringing sin and temptation into the world. The first to claim Broceliande were the Celts, and then the Romans came. For a thousand years, valleys of the forest pushed back the earth to cover bodies of fallen warriors who slept covered by light of day and wakened with the mists of night, waiting, watching, knowing soon the serpent would rise again, and men would once more pick up their swords for battle. Great stones were raised to mark the passing of centuries, and the moss grew thick and green as more bodies were covered by the living forest of Broceliande.

Years before the Reign of Terror came to France, the dead beneath the earthen shroud heard the serpent, felt his evil, and knew soon the cries of the wounded and the dying would fill the air. A freezing wind from the North Seas brought mists thick and heavy. They covered every stone and mountain stream, the meadows and the lakes. Nothing would be free of knowing what was to come.

"We should go back."

Laura's voice was thin as a whisper, a transparent refrain, barely heard in the twilight of the misty morning. As she closed her eyes and steadied her breathing, she summoned what courage she could and then reached out into the thick darkness surrounding her, blindly searching for the familiar form of her friend. A hand, small and slender, reached back; warm, familiar fingers interlaced with hers. Laura squeezed ever so slightly, finding courage from the softness, the warmth wrapped tight. Perfectly fitted, this hand with hers was something only those who loved one another would understand, memories building and binding one to another. She hoped the princess wished what she did: to return to the safety of the demesne. But she knew Ariella would not leave, not without the wolf cub.

It was Old Nan, a stout and fierce Highlander, from the same clan as Ariella's Mama, who Laura blamed. Her stories of druids with magical power and of knights long dead had filled Ariella's childhood with superstitious fantasies. Their spirits, according to Nan, remained in Broceliande, lingering, attaching their own memories to those of the living. These were the stories that filled the princess with a love for the forest and for all things wild and magical. For Laura it was not the same. She had heard them just as Ariella had, but the difference between her and Ariella was that she wished to have nothing to do with such imaginings. She feared the dark premonitions such stories precipitated, filling her with dread and making her skin crawl. Laura had no desire to speak to the dead long buried in the woods of Broceliande, nor did she understand why they seemed to seek out Ariella. At least, according to the princess, her dreams were filled with images of magical beings that lingered close to her, protecting her.

With laughter and mischief barely contained, the princess attempted to pull Laura into her own happiness, her own musings, as she thought of how wonderful she would feel cradling a newborn wolf pup in her arms.

Holding her friend's hand, fingers intertwined, Ariella guided Laura forward into a sea of mists and shadows where each step seemed a guess. The ground fog was thick and only the best divining steps found solid footage.

"It's easy, Laura. Just brush your feet softly, with small steps. We are on the deer path. Feel the soft ground trodden down. This is where the red hind passes with her fawns. Sometimes they stop to taste the yellow daffodils or the red berries on either side of the path. Soon the morning light will be bright enough to see the chateau just behind us, and then you will not be so afraid." Ariella continued to speak to her friend, continued to warm her cold fingers, knowing they were close to the branch where Philippe had seen the pup. She knew Laura would not desert her, but she needed to repeat the words that she felt bound them, which erased all doubt of how important their friendship was. She lifted her voice, for she wished to sound sincere and because she loved her friend.

"Always and forever, friends first. I am not a princess, nor am I a Noblesse of the Royal Family, not first, not before you! I am your best friend, and you are mine. You are older. I will listen to you sometimes because you are older, but my blood is bluer, as Papa says, so that means I can also command when I must. So, for now, Laura Soveneau, you must, as I command, stay with me until I am ready to return to the chateau."

"Ariella, you do not see time is vanishing! The mists are lifting, and the early morning light is behind us. Everyone will be awake, and your Nana will be looking for you!"

Ariella turned toward Laura, lifting her gaze upward, finding the beautiful cornflower-blue eyes she knew so well and then, with an impish grin she could no longer contain, replied,

"Are you afraid, Laura, that you will be blamed?" Ariella had managed to keep her smile hidden beneath an innocent, heart-shaped pout, but inside she bubbled with excitement, wanting nothing more than to tease her friend, to force her to let go of her silly superstitions, to be her friend and forget for a moment the risk they were taking.

Laura, a tall beauty at sixteen, ignored the presumptuous tone of Ariella's response because Ariella was the daughter of the Duke and Duchess of Venville and because she loved her, even if she was a bit insufferable at times. She knew her friend's teasing was a form of affection, but she also knew Ariella would challenge the Devil himself if he threatened her freedom, and she would love every moment of the challenge. She loved to touch just a bit of danger for no other reason than to feel its forbidden burn. As a princess who was judged perfect due to her own angelic beauty, she kept her true spirit secret. Underneath the guise of refinement, she wanted nothing more than to be wild, to never have to listen again to what it meant to be the heiress of a demesne as immense as Venville.

Laura watched the petite hoyden swirling in the morning mists that danced with her, slowly vanishing, magically transforming from the thickened air of morning to the soft transparency that light began to bring, and all this seemed to happen as the fingertips of the Princess touched and released the softness of the air surrounding her. Her voice sang with the joy she found within the elements of the forest that claimed her as their own. Laura listened and heard the lilting teasing in her friend's voice that she had expected.

"I think you are afraid of the spirits of the dead that still walk at night in the woods of Broceliande."

"And! I think you, Ariella, are a mischievous changeling, not a princess at all! Your head is too full of the stories your Nana tells you. I have heard them all as well as you. What if it were true that the druid Merlin rests here in Broceliande, his bones buried by the sacred stone just beyond the meadow? Or possibly Vivienne, a water nymph, lives in the Lac de Diane. All the rest you know of the sacred stones, monoliths and crystal caves, *C'est la vie*! So, what!"

"I have seen them, Laura! I have seen the dead of Broceliande!"

Laura knew it. Ariella would not be happy, ever, until Laura admitted that she too believed the stories of Broceliande. *That* Laura was not ready to do. She was an innkeeper's daughter and her father the son of a peasant. Some things, secret things, belonged to her class, the peasant class, and what she knew about the tunnels and the crystal cave was not to be shared with the noblesse, even her friend Ariella. She turned back, annoyed by Ariella's persistence. Her own voice did not hide her frustration, for she heard her own words as they echoed, too loud, in the quiet morning light of the forest.

"*Mon Dieu!* You have what you came for. Better see to your wolf pup and stop your teasing. Besides, Ariella, I know more of Broceliande than you think. My mama loves the old stories, but my brother Philippe knows even more than Mama. Even you, *ma petite lionne,* must admit the only reason you have such a beautiful pup is because of Philippe."

Laura did not give time for Ariella to answer, for she wanted to push the little hoyden a bit more.

"We are almost to the edge of the woods, for I can just see the chateau now. It is there beyond the garden shrubs and statuary.

"So I think it is past time to make up the story you must tell your papa when he sees you have brought home a wolf cub."

Ariella thought a moment, then pulled a small coal-black pup from underneath her velvet cloak where she had been holding him to keep him warm. She held him high above her head and then, just like a fairytale princess of exquisite beauty and entitled pleasures befitting her station, she announced,

"He is mine and therefore a *Noblesse of Venville. As* such he requires no explanation and is under my protection. I will name him and consecrate his spirit to the gods of Broceliande, just as Father Jacob blesses my soul in the name of the Holy Catholic Church. When Papa asks, I will say he was given to me to protect since Papa's own gamesman slaughtered his mama and left him to die."

Even knowing Ariella would be forgiven for everything by her papa and would even be allowed to keep this wild wolf pup, Laura continued to see how far she could push her friend. Only their affection for each other made such familiarity possible between an aristocrat of the Second Estate and an innkeeper's daughter. Laura's lack of noble blood placed her squarely at the bottom of the social hierarchy, in the Third Estate. Those of the lowest social order owned little other than the burden of taxes and duty to their lord and seigneur, for that was the way of it.

"I take it back. You are not a changeling. If you were, then there might be more sense to you. You, Ariella, have never heard your papa ever say no, and you know nothing of how others may live. What if I tell you that your wolf pup will be better fed and cared for than some of the peasant children that live just beyond the outskirts of Venville?"

"Then I would say to you, Laura Soveneau, that you are truly fortunate indeed, for you do not live beyond Venville. You live under the rule of the Lord of Venville, and I think even you are glad for the freedoms and love my papa and mama give to those who serve within the Lantenac demesne."

It was all said now, and the words lingered – "those who serve" – and that put Laura back to where it all had begun. She was newly a maid, one who had reached her sixteenth birthday, so six years older than the princess, the princess she had never once refused to serve. Some said she was lovely, though she knew she was not nearly as beautiful as Ariella. She was blonde. Ariella's hair was the color of a raven's wing, so black it shined with a purple radiance, her skin was cream, and her eyes dark but touched with violet. The villagers, Laura's own friends and neighbors, never ceased to speak of Ariella's beauty. Some compared the color of her eyes to the deep purple diamonds that came from the mines of Russia, others spoke of the fairness of her skin, but the point of all, when it centered on importance, was that they loved her, and they knew that she, like her father, had a kind heart.

Laura glared at her friend, then she, unlike any servant in all of Brittany who served by the leave of a princess, stuck out her tongue with such devilish humor that both she and Ariella burst into childish giggles, and then both knew the argument and teasing were done.

Their laughter and faith in their own safety were reflective of all who resided within the protective walls of the Lantenac Chateau, as well as the villagers and farmers who served within the duke's demesne. No one had ever anticipated the devastation that could befall their "fairy" kingdom, for they believed their lord, Duke Lantenac, was indomitable. They believed he would always keep them safe.

Once the soul-wrenching screams broke the silent morning air and the thunder of guns fired vibrated throughout the forest of Broceliande, all who could hear knew that the worst of nightmares had taken hold of the Chateau de Venville.

The two girls froze in terror, for there was nowhere to run.

Chapter 2

THE TERROR

With both anger and heartrending pain, the Duke of Venville forced the muscles and sinews of his rugged body to tighten like cords of iron as he pushed himself beyond the endurance of any ordinary warrior. That he would break in both body and soul was what Count Faucher hoped as he watched Lantenac's masterful dignity and pride turn to ashes. The duke's strong features of refined control and noble breeding transformed as a primal hatred tightened every sinew, every muscle. His facial muscles hardened, forming a mask of unbearable pain, but this did not come from the blood-raw skin beneath the leather straps that bound his wrists nor the broken bones and crushed ribs from repeated beatings; it came as he witnessed the atrocities of evil that Faucher had commanded.

Just beyond his reach, next to deep purple clusters of hydrangeas and spring roses covered with the remains of the morning dew, close to the granite fountain carved from the stone cliffs of Brittany, was the bare and bruised body of his wife, Katherine, the sustaining blessing of his life. Brutally murdered and violated, she yet remained in his eyes the most beautiful woman he had ever known, a gift he had not once felt he truly deserved.

Five of the guards and their leader Count Faucher circled him with pistols drawn as though they expected this dying man would break loose from his bonds and attack them. The remaining fifteen guards had gathered all who resided at the Chateau de Venville into the courtyard. None of the servants had escaped injury, but their final fate was not yet known. The prettiest, a fresh young maid from St.-Malo, Katherine's lady's maid Jeanne, had been brutalized, evident from her ripped gown and tear-streaked face. She could no longer move forward to the courtyard without help from the others. The cook, scullery maids, and house servants all held onto each other. With cries and tears they begged for mercy. Some of the men had been cut by swords, others beaten. All the servants of Chateau de Venville, some having served the family of Lantenac for three generations, were forced to witness the villainy of Count Faucher. This was a man they knew, a man who had once been a common tradesman of the Third Estate like them. Now, as a result of slavers' money, he had filled the coffers of King Louis XVI, and for this he was rewarded. He not only had vast wealth but a title and enough power to do whatever he desired.

Faucher turned to face the men and women, the servants who had lived in the Lantenac Chateau most of their lives. His right hand held tight to his gold-hilted sword, the other hung tightly-fisted by his side. A fierce glower of warning was evident in his piercing stare. Before speaking, Faucher's thin lips tightened and then managed a slight turn upwards, a devil's smile as he indulged his intentions. Murdering the present Duke was his first step, to be followed by taking the massive chateau for himself. Later he would take the village, the monastery, and all the farmlands.

Knowing he was not a tall man; he had learned to intimidate through the force of his stance. His huge shoulders and massive arms gave him credibility and had gone a long way to help him survive in the treacherous underbelly of the vilest of slave ships. Drawing himself to his full height, Faucher shouted his words and filled every intonation with ferocity and cruelty. He burned with hate as he thundered his accusations.

"This man is a traitor to His Majesty, King Louis of France. He, his family, and any who swear allegiance to him are hereby sentenced to death. By order of the King, all lands, all chattels, the village of Venville, the monastery, and the chateau are now subject to rule by His Majesty's Crown." As he spoke, Count Faucher had sheathed his sword and now held a pistol primed, ready to fire into the heart of his prisoner. Faucher would have been handsome if his features had not been so hardened and his face less scarred. Boots of the best leather with three-inch heels compensated for his shorter stature, and a flowing wig held in place by a black tricorne gave him a presence of authority, but nothing could compensate for the scar that ran from center forehead to his outer right jaw. Jagged and angry, it gave evidence of what he would show his enemies, just as it had been shown to him: *"No Mercy!"*

Faucher's plan was not to kill Lantenac quickly; neither had he wished the death of Katherine to be without prolonged pain. What he did – the torture he inflicted and the lies he told the King – rested with him alone. The men with him were his to command, and they would swear to his word, whatever that might be. Whether the Duke was hanged outside the chateau for all to see or gutted here in the courtyard, the end would be the same: torture and a death without mercy.

Faucher's steel-grey eyes were without emotion as he turned to watch his captive. He wished to see the handsome face of his captive agonized in a mask of pain, to see his cerulean-blue eyes achingly empty of all the love they had known.

Lantenac's head was bowed. He looked only at the ground, his wrists securely tied behind his back.

Faucher wished this moment, the moment of defeat for Jean Paul Lantenac, Duke of Venville, to be preserved within his memory. He thought,

He must think he is as invincible as his soldiers do. They have made him a legend, but that great man is gone, buried by witnessing the death of his beautiful Katherine. Soon I will find his daughter, and she will not die so quickly . . .

Faucher's eyes darted without control, erratic, revealing madness, but still his thin lips continued to smile. He was pleased to see this giant man brought to his knees, but, growing impatient, he commanded the five mercenaries who circled the duke to move closer and cut him with their knives to force him to look up and accept defeat.

Even though their knives gave them courage, and they relished the obscenities and insults they were able to expel, they hesitated as though they feared this legendary soldier might possess the power to shred the ropes that held him.

Yet they did move closer, for the five men also feared Count Faucher.

The moment they moved within an arm's reach of this warrior was not their moment but his.

Lantenac had waited, knowing their impatience would bring them just within arm's reach. His grief had broken his heart, but it had not unmanned his hatred, and for that he pushed himself to live for just another moment, another hour, just long enough to send the devil Faucher back to hell, for such an evil man could not have been given birth on God's green earth.

All I need is one sliver of stone, a perfect piece of granite broken free from the courtyard. His fingers bled as they forced themselves between the cobblestones of granite, digging into the splintered edges. The metallic smell of his own blood was welcome, for blood was thick, slippery, a way to move the ropes. Once it was found, this sliver of hope, he sliced at his ropes, at his own wrists, over and over. The cuts bled and the ropes loosened.

Lantenac, by will alone, cut his way through, enough, just enough so his fury could manage the rest, and when he broke the last of the bindings, he gave the most blood-curdling yell any of the soldiers had heard before or would ever hear again. With his bare hands he twisted the arms of the two closest men before breaking the neck of the first and smashing the head of the second into the stone floor of the courtyard. Two pistols fired, one sending lead tearing through his side and the other missing its mark. He would not die, not until he ripped the heart from the bastard whose lies and deceit had brought ruin to those he loved. Armed with a saber from one of the dead men, he slashed the throat of the third soldier before the man had even gripped his own sword. The two last mercenaries blocked his attack, but to Lantenac the only kill that mattered was the one that would take the life of Faucher. He was close, so close, and then the last man fired. He felt the force of it, knew death had come, but not before his eyes met those of his enemy.

What Faucher saw within the eyes of Jean Paul Lantenac caused his blood to freeze. He could not turn away from the message written clearly in the dying man's very soul. His own death would come, not today, but it would come, and the Duke of Venville and those he loved would be avenged.

Faucher turned away. For a moment he thought he might be ill. He staggered, trying to gain his composure, trying to dismiss the promise he had so clearly seen in the eyes of Lantenac. The fear he felt became so great that he struck out at the nearest soldier, the one who had shot the pistol, saving him. This did not matter. All that mattered was regaining his own strength. He struck him over and over until the man fell and blood matted in his hair, covering his face. Then he yelled with ruthless anger as he continued to batter the Hessian mercenary, the man who had probably saved his life.

"You! I should kill you! Why did you not fire on him sooner? You will pay. The men lost are on your head!" Then Faucher commanded, "Kill the servants, leave no witnesses. Kill them all and then find the girl! Find Ariella Lantenac. No witnesses! No recourse! What was done today was done in the name of the King!"

CHAPTER 3

THE TUNNELS

The screams of Jeanne and Ariella's Nana were deafening. Yet she had not heard the voice of her mama. Her mama's tears were gone, she no longer cried, but her papa, the keening sadness from her papa was more than her own heart could bear. She felt it break. She gasped for breath and tried to move, to run, to die beside her mama and papa, but she was frozen, and lying there, she still heard the guns and screams of children and then there was only a bottomless pit of darkness, a place where she now tried to hide.

Heart pounding, body flattened against cold, rough underbrush, she lay frozen, invisible to Count Faucher and the mercenaries. No one had considered that she would have left the chateau, or that she was hidden only a few feet away in the dense cover of brushy hedges. Hedges, where the manicured lawn of the chateau ended and the forest of Broceliande began.

She had watched as everyone she loved was brutally murdered.

She could do nothing to stop what was happening, nor could she close her eyes and make the terror go away. Her body and mind began to go into shock, and she held to the earth as though it were her lifeline, the only solid thing that could stop her from falling into an abyss of darkness. She had only a vague awareness that someone held her to the ground. Their voice came from so far away, from another world, for in the place she now waited, all substance had disappeared, and she only seemed to be a shadow lingering, waiting for the light to end and take away all semblance of who she had been.

"Shhhh, quiet, please. Shhh, I am here. Very quiet, very slow, only on your stomach, back, very, very slow." She listened to the voice as if her mind imagined this and wondered if she could respond, could move. The voice did not stop, so quiet. Then firm hands began to pull her back, back toward the deer path that led into the forest. Still, in her mind, she watched as her mama was carried into the courtyard. Her mama was so soft, so beautiful, her soft ivory skin was like satin. Her breasts, her lovely body, bare. Ariella thought, "She is cold. My mama is cold. Where is Nana to bring Mama's warm fur? She is so warm when Papa wraps her in the white sable."

Lovely silk hair fell over her mama's slender shoulders, and then she was dropped like a rag doll close to Papa. He only stared at the ground.

"Get up! Papa, get up! Please help Mama," and then as though he heard, he stood. He was so huge, a mountain who stood, breaking the men who had broken Mama. In her mind Ariella fought alongside her papa, killing, cutting, wishing to destroy all of them. Her heart burst over and over as she imagined blow after blow raining upon them as they had done to her mama. Crimson streaks covered the chest, the arms of her papa, but he did not stop. The men were not jeering and laughing at him now. Papa took the saber from one. "Yes! Papa, kill them, make them bleed!"

Her hands shook, her body was immobile, lead-weighted, and her mind was within a place of such blood rage and despair that she could not see the truth of death. Both her mama and papa lay on cold stone, eyes glazed by death, and no one and nothing would judge the evil done. Ariella could not leave.

Her eyes could not close, and even as she was pulled back, death stayed all around her.

"Look at me! Ariella!"

Laura's voice trembled, and yet the forest remained as it had for a thousand years: sedate, calm. Many had entered here before them: lovers, warriors, some for the beauty of Broceliande, others for its sanctuary. The mists of the forest slowly ascended, revealing summer moss and lichen-covered stones. A nearby brook added its own song to that of the tall pines, whispering a gentle melody as lazy winds touched their low-hanging boughs. Here, where the girls now stood, was a small clearing. Nothing in this secluded place seemed other than a small bit of woods in the vast forest of Broceliande.

Yet Laura knew this part of the forest like the back of her hand, and she knew the secrets that rested here just beneath the earth. Laura had prayed as her tears fell and she had pulled Ariella into the forest. Now, standing here where she intended to find a place for Ariella to hide, she prayed for the Blessed Mother of Christ to help her reach her friend, to bring her mind back enough to listen, to understand what they must do.

She knew her prayer had been answered when she heard the small infant pup cry for food. He was no longer alone in the world, without a mother or father. The cry was weak but heartrending, and Laura knew without a doubt why she and Princess Ariella had been called to the forest this morning.

The wolf pup may have been a very doubtful dream in the night sleep of a princess, but now the proof of his existence and the timing of his rescue with the deaths of everyone her princess loved could only be a thing of fate orchestrated by the forces of Broceliande. Gods, spirits, sleeping druids or the *One True God*, something wished her to live.

Laura began to speak softly to the princess, removing her own trembling hands from the small shoulders of Ariella, unaware of how tightly she had been holding her, shaking her with desperation, as though she were a ragdoll without feeling, without pain. A weak, stifled cry came again, soft as though she were aware of the danger that was still close. Laura now remembered why she had worn her brother's jacket: for the pockets, one large enough to hold a newborn pup. Laura began again with her friend, desperately needing her to find her way back to at least a bit of reality. Nothing had changed in Ariella's dark midnight eyes, usually the color of deep violet; they were still as impenetrable as the darkness of night without the gift of even one small light, one forgotten star to guide her.

"Ariella, remember why we went into the forest. Remember the small, sweet orphan you wished to save. Ariella, we did save him. Can you hear his tiny cry? I put him safe in my pocket. He is warm there. The gamekeeper will not find him now. Remember, his mama died in the steel trap. My brother knew what had happened, and he saw the baby trying to nurse but it could not, so it snuggled against its mama, waiting to die. Ariella, we saved the baby, and if you will hold it and do as I say, then I will go fetch some milk and a nursing cloth."

Laura lifted the dark furry creature, so tiny she could cup him in her two small hands. She held him to Ariella's cheek. A lifeless slumber had shrouded him as though he had given up, but now a new energy took hold. He lifted his head, tucked deep within the protective curl of his body, and arched toward Ariella. As weak as he must be, he reached for her.

Laura remained very still, keeping her own fear hidden beneath a façade of courage. If she could not do this, both she and Ariella would be captured. Desperately, she prayed for a glimmer of light in the sad dark eyes of her friend. A lifetime of knowing the Princess Ariella and still she thought with unselfish awe, *She is so beautiful. Such sadness does not seem to belong on such a lovely face.*

"Ariella, please." Laura's voice was beseeching, filled with tenderness enough to warm the heart of the coldest of villains. "Please, you must listen. You must fight whatever has bewitched you. I know you can hear me! Please, Ariella, please hear me."

Ariella felt the words of her friend, knew her presence, but she could not focus, could not find her way through the darkness that was growing so strong within her. She seemed to be slowly falling, unable to separate herself from the terrors she had seen. An inner voice she knew to be her own spoke clearly, blocking that of her friend: *Let go, just let yourself fall away and then nothing will matter ever again.*

A fragile thread of life clung to her, refusing to let her go. It was a tiny cry she could not shut out because it came from an orphan like herself. She felt the touch of warm fur and a wetness touching her cheek. There was a bit of roughness like a tickle, over and over, as it licked and then the cry, "the mewing," a cry that brought her back. *You will die, my little one, if I do not help you. I am one such as you. If we live, my little foundling, we will find a way to make our pain a little less.*

Laura did not breathe. She sensed Ariella's response to the pup, and she watched as its small pink tongue touched Ariella's cheek. Ariella tilted her head ever so slightly, to feel more of the sweet touch. Long black hair, fallen free of the velvet ribbons that had tied it, now covered the pup. The tiny black creature was safely hidden behind the silken veil, darker than a raven's wing, more beautiful than the blue aura of midnight; Ariella's ebony hair became a protective cloak.

Laura took a deep breath, trying to speak with a calmness she did not feel. She pulled back the soft strands of Ariella's hair.

"Ariella, can you look at me?"

Ariella, not moving her cheek from the warmth of the pup, tilted her head, listening to the familiar voice.

"Ariella, think of the pup. Without your help I cannot do this. There is only one place the two of you can hide, and to go there you must be very brave. Where I am going to guide you is very dark, and it will be cold and maybe a little frightening, but it is the only way." Laura's hands trembled, and her heart raced with fear, knowing they had little time left.

Eyes of compelling sadness looked up. The beautiful veil of silken strands had fallen back, giving way for Ariella to see her friend. When Ariella spoke, her words were stronger, more confident than Laura could have imagined. The voice was not quite that of the princess she knew.

"I will take him. He is too helpless to be forsaken, and there is no loving mama to hold him. If I had stayed, I would be curled next to my beautiful mama, my cheek resting by her soft breast, naked like Mama, and covered in crimson. In her arms I would close my eyes and rest with my mama forever."

Laura knew her friend was somewhere in between two worlds, one of dreams and nightmares. She wondered if Ariella would ever return to being the capricious hoyden she had grown up with.

Laura wasted no time. Later she would explain the tunnels, a long-guarded secret of Broceliande, a place where the dispossessed found sanctuary from villains, from warlords, and sometimes from those who were their own countrymen. They were subterranean mazes existing under the forest since time immemorial. The first to dig such tunnels under the earth were thought to be the Celts needing to escape the Romans. Later the Bretons fled from the Normans and, in final desperation, hid in the same underground chambers. It was not just war that brought the desperate to hide underground. The Huguenots hid from the Catholics, and smugglers hid from tax collectors.

The tunnels were forgotten by the Noblesse, who never considered a time would exist when they would hide from their enemies, but the secrets of the tunnels were sacred to descendants of those who had found safety here. For them there had been no refuge other than the ancient tunnels of the earth.

Now Laura thought: *If the Good Lord favors me, I will save one of the Noblesse. For me she is a sister, and for my papa there is a blood debt we owe to the family of the Lantenacs. Please, Dear Savior, in all that is holy, help us.*

A gentle breeze began to stir, drifting as though directed by a ghostly presence, ruffling the dark strands of Ariella's hair. She quivered in startled reaction, her heartbeat fluttered, but she did not feel afraid. Her thoughts were no longer silent but whispered words so real she did not know if they were truly her own or those of an invisible presence. *Give your fears, your hate, your anger to me. Grow with me and I will make you strong.*

She did not flinch as ghostly hands touched her scraped and bleeding legs or when unseen lips kissed the bruises on her tender skin from the many times she had fallen in briars or on remnants of branches. Ariella blessed the tenderness of their caress. Her satin dress was ragged and covered with dirt, and her soft velvet shoes were ruined, yet there was something of Broceliande that soothed her, as though kindred spirits here understood. *After all,* she thought, *the forest floor here has been covered a hundred times over with the blood of innocents and I think maybe their spirits still linger here.*

Ariella pulled her pup closer. He was her Sagath. She had named him the same moment she had taken him into her arms. In her arms his soft fur, pure ebony beauty, tempted her fingers to touch him and to let herself imagine how big, how powerful a wolf pup of Broceliande might grow.

She remembered words her Mama had used, not French, but those from a land she had never seen, her grandfather's home, Scotland. The words came to her as she held the small wolf pup.

> *Such a wee sweet bairn, but I know, sweetness and meekness are not the nature of a wolf, and I think if I live through all that will be, through death and violence that I feel even now surrounding me, I will need the fiercest beast Broceliande can give me.*

"Sagath, the name my mama whispered to my papa in her own brogue, her own word passed from a family, a land far, far away. 'Sagath,' she whispered in my papa's ear before she kissed him so tenderly and whispered once more, 'Mine, protector mine, you are my love, for now and forever more.'"

The name Ariella gave the pup made her smile, and as she touched Sagath's ebony fur, she knew that she was forever changed and forever aware of how the heart feels once frozen with pain.

Laura had been desperately searching through stones that were partially covered by moss. They were arranged at the base of what remained of the stump of an oak. The dark soil was rich from long decaying vegetation; ferns grew thick and tall; and lavender bergenia with heart-shaped leaves covered the ground.

Ariella watched, thinking, *Someplace, hidden here, there must be a thing of value.*

Her senses were returning, bringing her back to a realm of reality she did not want to remember. She pulled Sagath close to her bosom, enfolding him in the small circumference of her arms. Her heart beat louder, stronger. *If they came for her, the monsters who murdered women and children, she would be nothing against them.* She wished for the soft touch of the ghosts, imagined or real. Their presence, their soothing had diminished her overpowering fear. No breeze as before, no soothing touch, but a soft haunting whistle came, faint at first, and then more distinctly captured a melody. So familiar, she thought as she formed words to imitate the echo-like tones.

Oh, holy, holy,
Ah, purity, purity.
Eeh, sweetly, sweetly.

The song ended before she wished it to and just as suddenly began once more.

"Oh!" she said, now talking to Sagath, feeling he must share in this special memory. "My papa called this the 'whisper song,' and he said that when the harvest thrush shares his song, always remember to thank him, for this is the most beautiful melody you will hear in the forest of Broceliande." Smiling, she remembered her papa. His presence was there with the magic of this enchanted forest. Stronger now, she began to focus on Laura.

Close to Laura she saw the tiny melodious warbler, no matter that his brown color concealed him as he scratched among the decaying leaves. His red tail as well as his beautiful song left no mistake as to his identity as he foraged on the forest floor. Just as he decided to take flight, she heard Laura's excited voice.

"Ariella! Hurry! I found the entrance to the tunnel. I knew it was here, where Papa showed me and Philippe. It used to be a well, but long ago it dried up, and now it is part of a place Papa called a *carnichot*."

On hands and knees, she was pushing dead and cluttered bushes away and, underneath, Ariella could see ancient oaken planks tied with rotting string made from vines and hemp.

"Help me, Ariella! Help me lift the door." Laura's voice was urgent, almost pleading as she called to Ariella. Even though it was unspoken, they both knew their time grew short. Faucher and his mercenaries were searching for the princess, and until she was hidden, every shadow that moved, every unidentified sound of the forest could easily be one of the murdering brigands who knew many ways to use a sword as well as how to torture and kill with grim satisfaction.

Ariella placed Sagath on a bed of soft green moss, listening as he made a sad little whimpery sound. She reached out, tenderly stroking his fur, reassuring him first with her touch, then her voice. She remembered her mama's words and how they had soothed her when she woke frightened from a bad dream.

"Rest, little one. I will not leave you." Her voice reflected the tenderness she felt for Sagath but also despair, knowing she would never again feel her own mama's touch.

Together the two girls, children still in terms of years, pulled at the ropes and vines binding the ancient wood. With an unexpected release the door lifted, releasing an odor of decay as well as a foul, rotten stink left from those who had inhabited these subterranean tunnels many years before.

Both girls shrank back from the heavy, dank odor. Ariella stared at her friend, her beautiful dark eyes flooded with tears of confusion. Biting her lip to keep from crying, she asked tremulously,

"Laura, how will I breathe? It smells so much worse than a pigsty, and it is so dark, like a bottomless well. How will I take care of Sagath? Where will I take him for his *pipi*, his toilette?"

Laura reached for Ariella's hand and intertwined her own fingers with the smaller ones of the Princess of Lantenac. With words that could have been carved in stone, she spoke with a voice that left no margin for doubt.

"I will never desert you. No matter what I must do, I will take care of you." Gently pressing Ariella's fingers to her own lips, she kissed their cold and dirty tips before continuing.

"You will breathe because the tunnels were dug by men before you who also had need for air, and they left enough shafts, enough well-hidden openings for their purpose.

"There are smaller tunnels that run in many directions from this one shaft. Sagath will learn where to go when he needs to, and he will always come back because he does not need to see. He can sense your smell no matter where you are. I also have a way to give you light. You will not ever be alone in the dark, and you will always have a way to make a flame. Every day I will bring milk for Sagath and food for you."

She studied Ariella for a moment, catching the light in her eyes, making sure she understood. Not until then did she let go of her hand and begin to search through moss-covered earth and decayed leaves. Pulling aside vines, she scrabbled through layers of composted debris, collecting stones, and examining them with particular attention.

"What are you looking for? Can I help?"

Laura answered with a reassuring smile as she held a large flat stone.

"This. I am looking for something to scrape back the mud and dirt, to help me dig through the webs of rotting vines. I was here once with my papa, but the forest never waits. Always there are new seedlings, new layers of green over the old." Her sky-blue eyes did not even try to hide the message they conveyed. It was obvious from the look she gave Ariella that Laura knew this forest, knew it very well. Almost as an afterthought, Laura added, "Broceliande never waits to cover its secrets."

Laura did not waste another moment on explanation. With the flat stone she had found she began to scrape back caked mud and molded rotting vines from underneath the ancient door covering the hidden shaft. She gave no notice to the spiders and other vermin that had inhabited the underside of the planks, but she dispatched them without care.

Within minutes she had found the small leather pouch she had silently prayed would be here. Unwinding a leather tie, she pulled out a flint, a small round of steel, and some tallow dips.

Ariella's eyes, lovely in their innocent trust, darkened as she watched in stunned disbelief. When she spoke, her voice revealed both admiration and surprise.

"Is there no end to what you know, Laura? Who has shown you so much?" Her eyes were focused on her friend and clearly revealed the trust she felt but also her bewilderment. *How does Laura know these things?* Wanting to help, to try to believe that she might truly live and escape the monster Faucher, she asked, as her lips trembled ever so slightly,

"What should I do?"

"Go get Sagath. We will carry him down in one of the pockets of my brother's coat. In the other one I will take the leather pouch. It has what you will need to find your way in the dark, at least until I can return with a proper tinderbox and tapers."

With Sagath snuggled tightly in the pocket of Philippe's coat, Laura began to look for the rope ladder she hoped would be hanging close to the top of the shaft's entrance. She knew this entrance to the tunnels had once been a well, remade and secured with wooden planks. Lying flat to allow her arms to reach into the well, Laura began to rub her hands along the inner surface.

"*Morbleu!*" She gasped and jerked her hand back as though she had been bitten by a snake. "Ahh! How I hate spiders and bugs, crawly bugs with legs, lots and lots of wiggly legs. *Pardon*, I can do this," but first she closed her eyes, gritted her teeth, then looked at her dirty fingers, some scratched and some covered with partially dried blood from her falls in the forest. Then she thrust her hands back to search the inner wall of the well. The uneven wood, worn and covered with rotting vines as well as hidden vermin, made her hold her breath, waiting, anticipating being bitten by any number of nasty spiders.

Ariella sat on the deep carpet of moss next to her and tried to see into the well to guess its depth or measure the distance to the bottom, and she wondered when her friend had learned a word such as she had used: "*morbleu*"? *Ladies did not use such language.*

"Ariella! I have it. Thank our dear Lord! I have it. The ladder is here tied to a nail wedged between stones of the old well." Laura began pulling, readjusting her position and standing for better leverage. As she pulled the ropes free from a myriad of coils and flung them back over the mossy ground, Ariella also began to pull and yank at the ropes as well until the entirety of their length was up. Laura began checking the ladder rungs, making sure they were strong enough to bear their weight.

"I will go first. You will follow me down, holding onto the ropes. Feel for the rungs of the ladder and place your feet carefully."

Laura stopped to listen.

Inhaling a deep breath, only then did she realize how scared she was. Whether it came from her imagination or a changing energy in the forest, she had a crushing need to work faster.

"I have a rushlight I found in the leather pouch. It has been covered with pig's fat, and with luck and Our Blessed Holy Mary's guidance, I will have a light you can follow." She gave the rushlight to Ariella.

Ariella took it automatically but not without wrinkling up her nose and scowling with displeasure. The rushlight was the greasy, smelly pith of one of the grass-like plants that peasants sometimes used for light.

With flint and steel Laura lit the fat-covered pith, releasing a rancid odor of foul-smelling grease that, left for eons, had eventually turned putrid. Laura heard the unmistakable sound of a gag come from Ariella and knew she was withstanding, as best she could, every impulse she had to retch. Laura was attempting to clear her own senses from the overwhelming odors of decay and long-lingering putrid air.

"Ariella, it will get better. Opening the shaft will help, and I will bring back a bag of sweet-smelling sage grass and handfuls of honey-suckle."

"It is worse than a pigsty! Bring me a small pillow of lavender, Laura." Ariella tried to think of something to help her take another step toward the tunnels where she and Sagath would be left alone. Holding her breath, slowly trying to force herself to strengthen her will, she thought of what had once made the two of them laugh, laugh so hard they had to run to Laura's bedroom and hold the soft goose pillows to their face, for they could not stop, and the mischief in their laughter every time they looked at one another made stopping impossible.

"Laura, remember once you and I, we visited your papa's pig man, Juliette's papa. He gave us a bucket of his most foul-smelling pig *caca*." Ariella started to giggle. Sagath must have heard, for he mewed enough to remind both girls he was still there, still waiting warm and snug in Laura's pocket. The giggle found was honeyed medicine, and Laura grabbed it.

"How could I ever forget? The horrible bucket – we put it under Philippe's bed. I was so mad at him for all his teasing. He was sound asleep. We hid just beyond the open door, quiet as mice, and watched. He sniffed, then coughed. His eyes watered, then he came awake like thunder, gagging. He yelled to Mamma, and he screamed over and over, "*Mon bleu, mon bleu*! What has that hoyden done?" We ran before he knew and locked the door to my bedroom. Oh, his face and how he yelled! My brother, he can be such an imbecile."

Both girls broke into welcome giggles as something, anything, to help them remember the whole world was not made up of blackness like the tunnels below.

"We will go on now. The smell may not be so bad if we try to see the face of Philippe." Still smiling, she secured the leather pouch in her empty pocket. With one hand she carefully carried the rushlight in a horizontal position so the flame would last longer; with the other she held the rope ladder and descended into the earth.

Ariella's faith in Laura and the need to protect Sagath pushed her forward. She took one rung at a time, always keeping the light Laura held in sight. The stench was overwhelming as was the darkness, breached only by a spectral glow that touched the walls of the shaft. *She must find a reason to do this, to believe she could survive. There was no noise under the earth, no air that swept through pine needles, no sweet thrush to calm her with a familiar melody. She whispered her thoughts in the darkness, praying for some kind of solace.*

"If I die inside the earth, will anyone know?" Desolation forced her to speak, as a penitent is forced for the sake of salvation to bare his soul. "If I lose my way, who will come for me? Oh, my dear Lord, I am so alone. Why did I not die with my mama?" She expected nothing, so she dismissed the brush of air, the sound of a distant melody, and a fragrance more akin to heather than stale decaying earth.

The immediate presence she felt surrounded her as a vortex might; she was the center. Within the dark, someone or something heard her whispered words. First, she felt a touch, soft silken fingers gliding down her cheek, pulling back strands of her ebony hair, and then a kiss before a response.

Why are you here in Broceliande? Remember, Ariella, remember the dream that called you. Ariella, you would be with your parents now if Broceliande had not called you. The spirits here have need of you, and they do not call the living to serve without reason. Do as we bid. Take your small gift, a small token to remind you of the forest, and follow where the hands of fate take you.

There are many who will live and some who will learn how to love because of you, Ariella. Choose life. Choose to do whatever is necessary, no matter the difficulty, the risk. Live, Ariella. Live so others may also live. A war is coming. The winds blow with a fierceness that will not be stopped. Prepare, Ariella. Prepare...

The words wrapped around her like a blanket of silken dreams. She accepted what she had heard and felt, for at this moment it was real. If she lived now only in a world of dreams, then they were preferable to the terrors. As she descended into darkness – or was the darkness claiming her, deceptively pulling her into an abyss? She did not know the real from the imagined.

Until the moment she stepped off the last rung of the ladder she did not believe anything but darkness existed. She was surprised to feel a carpet of moss beneath her feet, dried from age, but which had once been soft, placed here for comfort. A few steps more, and where she had anticipated wetness or slime, there was neither. As she reached out, seeing only in the dim glow of Laura's rushlight, she felt walls extending beyond parts of the oaken shaft. They were hard, made of clay and sandstone. The space was no longer the small circumference of a well. As she walked, she determined it to be more of a chamber. She sensed air flow and spaces extending from this main chamber.

Ariella knew Laura must leave, to make arrangements for her and the pup, but before she left, Ariella had to ask a question she feared with all her soul to ask. With her heart bare and her voice filled with doubt, Ariella broke the silence and asked her friend,

"Laura, before you go, please answer my one question."

Laura placed the light just close enough to see Ariella as clearly as possible. Still, even in this strange artificial light, she thought, you are *so beautiful. Ordinary villeins such as the ones who live here, in the village of Lantenac, have no comparison. In the great palaces, the grand chateaux, and mansions of the Noblesse, there, I think, is where such beauty would be a most sought-after prize.*

Ariella seemed lost, there was no brightness in her lovely eyes, for she had seen her world destroyed and she had watched without recourse. She appeared to be barely breathing when she asked Laura the question that pushed hardest on her heart.

"Who will come to save me, Laura?"

She did not expect an answer, for she knew no one who could save her. Without a pause, with words filled deep with fire and without a shred of doubt, Laura answered,

"Your grandfather will come." As she continued, her voice trembled with the certainty, the conviction she felt. "He will prepare to cross the North Celtic Sea with the first breath he takes once he hears of your mama's death.

Laura shifted the rushlight, looking directly into eyes that started to tear as a grain of hope began to form. "Ariella, your grandfather is the most powerful, the fiercest lord of Scotland. By his leave men may live or die. No one turns from him, Ariella. He will be here."

Ariella was stunned. She pulled Sagath close to her heart and wondered if this was a man she would also fear.

Sagath had protectively and for warmth curled up, forming a protective shell, before Ariella did the same and drifted into a strange and painless slumber. She shared her last thoughts with Sagath, her little wolf. She had known from the first moment she saw him he was too beautiful, too pure, to be born anywhere other than the forest of Broceliande. She felt a presence within the pup and believed he would grow to have a spirit that could never be subdued. Pretending that Sagath was indeed her champion and protector, as her sleepy eyes slowly began to close, she asked in a bare whisper, expecting nothing,

"Why did my papa name me? Mama did not wish him to, but he said, 'She is my Ariella, the last heir of my family, and so she must be Ariella, my Lioness of God, mine to love and to bequeath, for better or for worse, the last right to rule.'" How strange, she thought, as she and her pup drifted into a welcome sleep, that she and Sagath, orphans and alone in the world, could ever become so fierce and strong as to defeat those that had stolen everything she loved.

Chapter 4

LONDON, APRIL OF THE YEAR 1792

A date marking the first use of the guillotine in Paris

In this room a thousand candles burned. Crystal chandeliers reflected their brilliance ten-fold, and aristocrats from London displayed the gaiety and opulence expected from the wealthiest and most ennobled of British society. They moved in swirls of golden beauty, regal and so far above the common cares of the world that it seemed as though they were akin to the gods, those who once looked down from the mountain of Olympus and occasionally bothered with the fates of ordinary men and women.

Lord and Lady Chandler greeted their guests, doing little to hide their self-satisfaction in knowing this event had a very distinguished guest list of London's wealthiest and most influential noblemen. Chandler House was a mansion in the St. James area in the west end of London, close to St. James's Palace. The newly-designed ballroom, which now welcomed over two hundred guests, was inspired by Lady Chandler's visits to Paris. Very vivid in her memory was the famous Hall of Mirrors, created to please the French queen, Marie Antoinette.

Within her home Lady Chandler had replicated the impressive design. Mirrors were everywhere, trimmed in gold and reflecting images of the most distinguished gentlemen and ladies of the *Beau Monde*. The opulence of wealth and its visual display could not have been more openly apparent, and this was the very observation that lingered in the thoughts of Lord David Grayson.

David Grayson may have been absent from the *ton*'s last five seasons, but the stories concerning him still made titillating gossip. All of the young debutantes attending knew his name, and a few had been the recipients not only of his charming smile but of his rakish flirtations. David possessed a sexual attraction so apparent he was simply known, at least by the ladies of the *ton*, as "the Prince." Why this appellation? Speculation suggested it came from personal experience of those who had known his sexual pleasures, but to confess such firsthand knowledge was not the wisest choice for a young lady of the *Beau Monde*, so the truth of just how libertine he was remained cloaked in secrecy.

The mothers of the *ton* knew enough to keep their daughters at hand if Lord David Grayson attended. Fortunately for them it had been five seasons since Lord David had been seen at any of the seasonal balls. Yet his name and his physical charm had evidently not diminished. For he was still an incredibly handsome man, well over six feet, with shoulders a woman could cling to and know the meaning of male virility. His hair was rich auburn, with thick waves that promised to yield to a woman's touch, and his lips were exquisitely large, promising sensual engagement difficult to resist.

He was a man who knew women, knew how to seduce them, to make them long for his kisses and the pleasure he offered. Yet he played by the rules: never virgins and always truth. He was not and wished never to be sought after for his title or wealth, for he had neither. He was a second son. His oldest brother was William Grayson, Duke of

Summerville. God willing his brother would have a long and happy life, and David would never be a duke. Even more to his credit, at least from his deceased father's point of view, David had already fulfilled his obligations. As a second son he had, by way of limited options, served his King and Country. Four years in the King's army had taken him to hell and back. Now he stood far back and did what he had been trained for: watch and memorize who was in attendance and to whom they spoke and with whom they chose to drink. Tonight, should be simple enough. He would be given contact information, and soon he would know exactly what Pitt had in mind for him.

His positioning was perfect. He had managed to find a secluded corner away from the reflected gaiety and, for him, tedious swirls of virginal silks, white, pale rose, and soft blues vying for attention, each chosen with meticulous attention to the rules of decorum applying to first-season debutantes, all secretly hoping to be noticed and to shine above the others.

It was easy enough to dismiss a world cocooned in a chrysalis of its own invention, seeing and believing only what was perpetuated within itself. He too had once lived such a finite existence, but all shattered once he emerged from the life he had known and awakened to the horrors of war. He witnessed his brothers-in-arms virtually hacked to pieces in the redoubt he held under the command of General Cornwallis. When he crawled out, he crawled out of hell, not knowing who he had killed as he fought to escape the bloodbath. Redoubt Nine at Yorktown was the scene of a strategic victory for the Colonies. Once it had been taken, defeat of the British shortly followed.

Now he was fit for nothing, it seemed, making his way through the bleary and ill-defined world of subterfuge and counterintelligence. Whether he gave anything back to his long-dead comrades he did not really know. Still, he could not pull himself out of the pit, the nightmares persisting. Seventy British soldiers held the last line of defense inside a guarded redoubt large enough for one hundred and twenty men. Four hundred French and Germans stormed the parapet. In the darkness his men struck to kill anyone dressed in blue, anyone who did not wear the red of the King's army. But the dark night and the moonlight had rendered the colors indistinguishable. Who lived and who died was lost in the blood lust to survive.

A melody by Strauss filled the room, gently retrieving him from the lingering terrors that all too often filled his thoughts. Like a sweet balm it quieted the pain wrapped so very tightly around his heart and gave him the moments he needed to regain his composure. He beckoned to a servant, who reached his side within seconds. The silver tray presented to David had several glasses of the finest French champagne. He started to take one of the crystal flutes, then hesitated as he saw the unmistakable figure of the very regal Duke of Summerville walking straight for him. He paused for a moment, then chose two glasses of the very exquisite wine and waited for his brother.

His brother had changed in the last four years. The death of their father had jolted him so hard he had been overwhelmed by the tremendous responsibility he faced. David, as well as their three siblings, speculated whether he would actually stay down, disclaim the title, and risk the loss in wealth and security this would mean for not just himself but the entirety of the family, estates, and those supported by the vast wealth of the Summervilles.

He had risen to the occasion but in a new persona. Real or a well-crafted façade, the result remained the same. The man who walked toward him was no longer the carefree and jovial brother he had grown to love and emulate with pride. He seemed to be a stranger, yet a stranger of immeasurable forbearance. Every inch of him was a duke, from the perfectly fashioned attire to the presence and stature he conveyed. David waited for his brother to speak first.

William Grayson's dark green eyes, a distinctive Grayson trait, held back any emotional response that might give light to what he was thinking. His voice was neither strained nor angry when he spoke, more like that of a stranger than a brother.

"So, my brother, I see two years, or has it been longer, have rendered war heroes a bit passé. Even so, it seems your lingering reputation as a decorated officer still adds to your charms as a rake and a hellish devil to drink or gamble with."

Dark sea green eyes transfixed in a mutual challenge, both daring the other to pull away first. It was a characteristic of the Graysons to always try to be the last man standing, the last to give way. The beautiful Strauss melody continued, and the peers of the *ton* floated by on the dance floor, pretending not to watch the two exquisitely handsome men engaged in this moment of confrontation.

There was no question of the insult. David's jaw tightened, and his eyes grew notably darker. His first impulse was to deck his brother hard, the same as he would have done if they were still boys or at least still brothers in any real sense. Instead, with an admirably steady grip, he held out his hand, presenting the Duke of Summerville with the wine he had been holding.

The duke, in accordance with the expected bit of arrogance his position commanded, took the offering with entitled indifference. The white lace sleeves of his silk shirt fell back, adding a fashionable touch to his personally fitted tailcoat, made of the finest Valencia brocade.

As David watched him, slowly sipping his own wine, he thought, *What a pretentious prick! We Graysons know too much about each other.* Their survival in a household commanded by a father who was a devil in his own right required that.

You care, my brother. You care about me. Swearing allegiance – that was our means of survival. "All for one, and one for all."

We made it our pledge in order to beat the devil at his own game! Our father's manipulations never ended. His goal was to beat each of us into nothingness, for us to believe that without his approval we were nothing. Best you rid yourself of that useless emotion, that caring for me, that remembered pledge of allegiance we made as boys. For I have lived up to my father's expectations. I am nothing! To you, to the men I commanded at Yorktown, and certainly nothing to the high and mighty Graysons.

David's intense memories had rendered him frozen for a moment. Regaining composure by pretending to watch the crowd, he turned back and began to redirect the conversation.

"Yes, then, it is a toast, and here I am at a loss. For there is much I would care to say that I deem inappropriate for obvious reasons. Foremost is that we are in a fishbowl surrounded by the *beau monde*. What better occasion to greet my brother but in the presence of the *crème de la crème* of London's wealthiest and most politically powerful echelon?"

The sarcasm voiced was cold, wrapped in long-endured regret. For much of their former love had been forgotten since their paths had led in quite different directions, neither knowing what the other had suffered.

The duke paused slightly, only long enough to once again make a conscious effort to cool his temper. The anger he had felt seeing David after two years, not at Summerville estate as he had requested repeatedly but here, had been an unexpected jolt. He responded to David's attempt to soften the moment.

"If we do not wish to be the evening's entertainment, it would be prudent to limit our words here and now. Unfortunately, at least regarding my own position, many who attend tonight serve in the House of Lords, and they watch all of us with keen scrutiny."

Like an old itch, suppressed but once remembered, longs to be scratched, David could not stop himself from provoking his brother. With a bit of devilish humor he had not felt in a very long time, he raised his glass and with a sense of bravado began his toast,

"Then let me publicly and for any who wish to hear make it official, let the *ton* know the 'Graysons' are here. Now as always, may we be lords of fame and rakish lust for all fair maidens to behold! To my brother, the Duke of Summerville! May he reign long, have many sons, and may his pride never precipitate the fall of his grace!'

Once said, David's smirk became a genuine smile that without a doubt rendered him the most devilish rake in all of London. He could not let it be once he saw his brother's reaction. William was red with hellish ire, but not the manly sort expected of one of the peers of the realm. This realization made him even angrier. He had been baited by his younger brother, and he had reacted more like a young hellion than the Duke of Summerville.

Now in full humor, his green eyes filled with more mirth than they had felt in a long time, David continued.

"I am still quite good with puns. Don't you think? My grace the duke, very incorrect, of course, but then as your brother I can certainly call you the duke or simply Duke. A rare privilege, I think, but it is grace I struggle with."

His humor burst when he looked once again at his proud brother and saw that his dark green eyes reflected memories of the boys they once were: summers of fishing ponds, of falling in and being saved by an older brother, and of pretend battles all fought in earnest with wooden swords. The Grays, the five of them against the world. Even Jack at only four was part of the group. Granted, he was a tagalong and required supervision, but he was not left behind, not when they could manage.

William's left fist came forward. He was as quick as David had remembered. Of the five brothers', William's reaction was the fastest and the hardest. He always gave the first punch and often the last. Before David could block the blow, William's fist flattened, his palm opened, and struck him on the back. Choking spasmodically on his wine, David started to laugh with such abandonment of decorum that his brother for the moment forgot propriety. Their right hands still clutching their glasses of wine, they managed a partial embrace. The sentiment was quick, but the recovery of affection signified that their boyhood allegiance, "All for one and one for all," had not been forgotten.

Simultaneously, they regained their sense of place, and they expected to be the center of attention. Their estrangement had been no secret, and neither had the displeasure the Duke of Summerville felt concerning his brother. For the *ton* had enjoyed the gossip concerning David's gambling and involvement with women of sundry reputations. Yet, to their amazement, the *ton* had been totally captivated by someone else.

The hush began to fill the air as it became known that Lady Ariella MacClaig, granddaughter of the Duke of Rothbur, would be announced. By the time she stepped to the center of the ballroom entrance on the arm of Hamish MacClaig, the most powerful Highlander to ever be a peer of the United Kingdom, the hush had spontaneously become a moment of expectation for the gathering of the *ton*. All had either read of her beauty in the *Times* or heard a description from an acquaintance and now were among the first to judge for themselves. Was Ariella the enchantress, the Aphrodite she had been likened to?

Ariella paused, accepting the attention that her presence brought forth. She gave herself the time to prepare, to accept what she must do.

I am no longer a child waiting in darkness, waiting for time to turn round to bring me this hour. I must be ready. Please, my soul, my heart, and for my mama and my strong knight, Papa, let me keep the promise made in Broceliande.

Just as Laura had predicted long ago, Ariella, no longer hidden in the tunnels of Broceliande or in the Highlands of Scotland, was without equal, a beauty to be envied in the patrician world of the *haut monde*. Her grandpapa's first wish had been to keep her hidden to keep her safe, but that, he learned, would never suit. Her passion burned with fire, consuming her with one purpose: to cut the heart from the man she hated, Faucher. She wished for nothing less than his life.

Only when her grandpapa knew he could not dissuade her did he agree to teach her the many ways to kill a man.

His intent was to break her, to show her the difficulties a woman would face in an arena filled with men trained as soldiers. She should marry and have grandchildren for him to spoil, but when he realized Ariella would not, only then did he relent. Her childhood had been stolen, and her dreams of elusive knights who rescue virginal maidens were illusions. Her knight who had promised protection from the world's evil died when she was a child.

Tonight, she wished to prove that she had learned a great deal about the world of subterfuge, where favors were bought and sold. Tonight she would show her grandpapa she had advantages a man did not.

She was prepared to reveal her powers of persuasion and the effect her exquisite beauty might have in a political stage governed totally by men. Women could not serve in the House of Lords, but their influence should never be underestimated.

She had measured each step, imagined every gesture, rehearsed a thousand times.

> *If I smile, wet my lips with the bare tip of my tongue, and think of Sagath by my side, my hand resting on his soft fur, then my eyes will fill with love. The* ton *longs to be loved, and so my grandpapa says, "It is easy to deceive such as them for they believe they rest on a pinnacle far above all others and by name alone deserve unconditional adoration."*

Candles glowed in crystal candelabras; silk wallpaper woven with silver threads reflected light; all was beautifully fashioned to fill the gilded mirrors with an aura of enchantment. Ariella saw the beauty at once, but it was not the *ton*'s wealth of exquisite possessions: gowns by the finest modistes, diamonds, or lush velvets that brought such a lovely smile to her heart-shaped lips. What she saw reflected in the mirrors were the gardens. They too were captured in the room's meticulous design. Centered, captured in symmetry, Ariella could see reflection in the mirrors of the evening moonlight where lush plants, marble fountains and stone paths led into what appeared to be a wooded wonderland. It made her think of Broceliande.

She wet her ruby lips, making them appear supple, more inviting. Her eyes, their color a gift from her mamma, were incomparable. Their purple hue was the color of dark wine, filled with fire and passion and a promise of deep and lasting pleasures. Her long black lashes enhanced their incredible color, and her brows, arched high and finely shaped, were in perfect symmetry. Ariella's beauty could have been sculpted by the same hand that created Aphrodite.

She filled the room with more loveliness than it had ever known as she stepped from the portico onto the marble floor of the ballroom.

The moment her eyes lifted to view the room he was there, standing in the far corner of the ballroom, the most handsome man she had ever seen. She did not look away. Heat began to build inside her core. An awareness of her own inability to retreat from this moment flamed through her. She knew she blushed and that he had affected her reaction. A quiver never experienced before sunk into her, and she closed her eyes to stop what magic he had perpetrated. Being innocent of such feelings, she had no idea of what the man she stared at was capable of. His eyes had not once left her, and for one breathtaking moment as she was drawn into her own fantasy, she was home in the green forests of Brittany. She wished this man held a key to help her find her lost memories of happiness, but as she looked deep into his shining emerald beauty she thought,

His eyes are empty and so cold. Why do they command my attention?

She did not move forward, nor did she look away until her grandpapa touched her arm. Even through her satin gloves she felt his intention to move her forward and direct her back to the purpose of tonight. Smiling, the Duke of Rothbur guided her steps and by his own discretion moved closer so only she could hear him. His voice had a bit of a Scottish burr, like that of her mama, and as always, there was purpose in what he said and power in his words, but his words were never tender.

"There is no room for tenderness in the path you choose, Ariella, and it goes against the very nature of a woman's being." He had told her this a thousand times. She shivered knowing the cold reminder that he would deliver before releasing her from his protection.

"Ariella, expect pain and betrayal and know you will only survive by sheer will. Once you enter this circle of the *beau monde* trust no one. Misplaced trust is the ultimate sin for a courier carrying treasonous messages. Your death would be immediate and without any sign of political intention." His cold words may have ended, but the message burned. She knew he would do anything to dissuade her.

Ariella gave her grandpapa a warm smile, but both knew it was a pretense, for there was no warmth in this thing between them. The stubbornness of their blood was equal in refusal to yield. Both were blood of the Clan MacClaig, and neither would ever leave behind a debt to be paid or give those they loved into the hands of their enemies.

> *All I once loved died because of political bargains, trust, and manipulation. I invite such deceit to find me, for I am ready. Never again will I turn from taking the blood of my enemy, for I can, without hesitation, sink a knife into the heart of any man who threatens me or those I care for.*

Breaking her moment of self-absorption, of relentless determination was the voice of her grandpapa, and his own discourse seemed born of the same desire for revenge as hers.

"Know the task assigned you and stay the course. It is the only way to survive: stay whole and do not back down when you find the means for victory. Those are the words I gave to your mama before she left her home in the Highlands. Tonight, I release you into an extremely dangerous world of lies and subterfuge, where no one will watch your back. In the underworld where you fight, your enemies will wear masks of deceit, never showing their true faces."

She listened as he spoke, maintaining her sweet smile of compliance, but she had already memorized those who would attend tonight, studied them in depth. He had acquainted her with his own spies and paid informants long before this night, and she had learned all she needed to begin the game that only spies know how to play.

Hamish MacClaig's mouth gave an embittered twist before he continued with instructions for his granddaughter.

"Ariella, tonight you will dance with three men, and one, not of the three but the one you meet at midnight, he is the one you must persuade to your purpose. I will introduce you to the three. The first is Lord Lieutenant Wolfe, the second, Earl Gower, son of the recent Ambassador to France, and the third is the Duke of Marchester, an undisclosed Jacobite."

Hamish would sooner entrust his granddaughter to a rabid dog than to one of Pitt's covert agents, for that was indeed the man she would meet at midnight, but he left his concerns unspoken. Sentiment would not suffice, not now. Both had deep wounds, and reopening them, bleeding once more for those lost, that would never work.

Now they were surrounded by the first crush of the *ton*'s finest who wished introductions, and so the game began.

"Aaaah." Clearing his throat rather loudly to bring back his brother's attention, the Duke of Summerville said, "I see you have found the current sensation of the season. I am surprised; it seems you have not yet been introduced."

The duke immediately saw the look in his brother's eyes. The infamous rake of London had been thunderstruck. His attempt to deny his own response was unfortunately being very closely scrutinized by one who knew him exceptionally well. As he watched David's discomfort, the duke smiled with a devilry he had not felt since the two were boys. He literally puffed up his chest and strengthened his posture at what he saw as a perfect opportunity to enjoy a bit of brotherly discomfort, and what better than a game of pursuit for a beautiful woman?

David brushed back his hair, a nervous habit and one that, to his own consternation, brought him more attention.

He was very aware he had captured the eye of several young ladies. Such attention he had accepted like second nature, and it had served him well when he wished, but his brother was a different matter. His attention was more of a myopic nature that knew him well, so he paused without appearing the least thrown back by the beautiful goddess who was even now surrounded by the *crème de la crème* of the British nobility. He was well practiced in hiding his emotions, but now he would see how well this ability served him when he was put to a test by his own brother.

An exceptionally well-appointed servant stood close. *Only the most striking serve the house,* David thought. *After all, it is part of the ambience to be beautiful.* He wondered even as he considered this tiny bit of hubris that delighted the wealthy, when he began to notice such things.

With a slight hand motion, he beckoned the servant, exchanging his empty glass for a full one. His action was tactical, giving him time to consider what he wished to say to his brother.

David pulled his gaze away from the beautiful enchantress and forced himself to think of his perimeters, just as he might if he were still a captain responsible for the lives of new recruits depending on him.

Never forget where you are. Never imagine there is safety because of those who surround you. Even in your own regiment, in the company of friends, there is always much to consider. Becoming complacent, thinking danger takes a holiday – that is the day you draw close to your own death. Breathe and know the air, listen and hear silent footsteps, think and always know what lies in front and behind you.

David sipped his champagne, letting his lips linger on the crystal rim of his glass, taking another moment to relax even as his own remembered words brought his attention back to his surroundings. Now, more in control, he allowed himself to feel the soft vibrations captivating the dancers who followed its magic, pulling close, then back again. The waltz, what a lovely way to seduce a woman. Ahhh, seduction, he smiled as a distant memory claimed him. Once his brother's reputation would have rivaled his own and with deceptive charm thought to bait his brother, unaware that the duke was thinking of doing the exact same thing.

"My dear brother, I think you forget who of the five Grays was the first to earn the scandalous title of libertine, and I think the reputation in question was earned by way of an enchanting lady!"

David could not resist smiling as his brother's jaw tightened and his eyes dilated. He almost laughed as he saw old memories surface.

"If you ever make reference to my wife, my duchess, in regard to any past events, brother or no, I will take your head!"

"My head!" And then the rake that he had always been surfaced as he said, "I would think it was another body part you would take but, please, not now. Let us remember where we are and let me strive to be a better brother and friend."

The teasing, for David, helped to turn his thoughts away from the beauty that had charmed him. Maybe his brother's presence had been a godsend. William had proven himself by accepting the title, Duke of Summerville, and regardless of their bantering, David respected him more than he would ever let him know.

So far, the unexpected encounter with his brother had not affected his plan to blend in, to observe, and to listen as he judged the loyalties of those in attendance or, more precisely, the loyalties of men who mattered, the men of power.

Attempting to regain his demeanor and once again assess the political interests represented tonight, he managed a light smile, his way of showing the *ton* that all was well between himself and the duke.

As though on cue, William knew. Something was not right. Whatever brotherly instinct had prompted him to bait his brother was still very much intact. Something was going on with David, and, by God, if he could find a vulnerable nerve, if he could find any way to break down the barriers between the two of them, he would do so!

William was every inch the duke, a man of stature and dignity, a man whose very words, by the force of his own entitlement, carried weight. He relied on this power when he spoke to his brother, and it was obvious he planned entrapment of some kind. Exactly what was impossible to determine.

"The lady who caught your eye, the one who led you to remember indiscretions of my own? I would like a little payback for your own part in those indiscretions. I think I will achieve a bit of recompense by offering a wager you *cannot* refuse."

David's next sip of wine caught. He choked, only a little but enough to make his brother's smirk grow into a bold smile.

Continuing, William obviously felt smug in his own cleverness.

"A simple wager. I will keep it between us and forgo registering the bet at White's. Just between brothers, so to say. You win a dance with Lady Ariella MacClaig, and I will pay all your debts accrued over the past year," he paused for emphasis, "for you, my brother, have considerable debt!" Again William stopped talking in order to weigh his brother's reaction. His brother's eyes betrayed him.

David looked once again at Lady Ariella MacClaig. He was drawn to her and, in an unguarded moment, had neglected to exercise restraint. He looked at the lady in question with a pensive vulnerability, and regardless of his own obvious desires, his eyes were still filled with pain. He did not know why he felt such longing, but his brother knew. William knew, for he had once felt the same, and a Grayson, specifically one of the five brothers, was not one who could ever leave one of his own brothers to suffer, not if he knew the antidote for fixing something broken. William continued his wager, his own manner of torment for this very reason.

"You win a kiss from the lovely lady, and I will assign you the money earned for one year's time from the profits of the Abbey in Summerville. Last is one I cannot resist because I know you do not have the slightest chance in hell of achieving such a challenge. If you are ever received by her grandfather, the Duke of Rothbur, as a respectable suitor, then I will deed you the Summerville Abbey!"

With all said, the Duke of Summerville's chest filled with more mirth than he had known since he had watched his younger brother step between their father and Jack, the youngest son.

Their father was a self-serving, manipulative bastard, and yet his sons wished to earn his approval and be recognized for their own manhood. Ironically, they achieved this only after they realized their desire to please him would always be met with disillusion. Their mother gave him five sons, dying in childbirth with the fifth, and only pleased him five times in their marriage for nine months every other year, when she bore him another heir. She was a beautiful lady, kind and gentle. Once married, their father had little use for her endearing kindness. Such a quality was no longer important to his ambitions as Duke of Summerville.

The memory that prompted William to engage in such a wager had reminded him of two things: his love for his brother and his own unpaid debt. What he remembered had initiated a turning point in his life. It happened when he was twenty and David only eighteen. It happened when Jack, the youngest, came home for Christmas with an academic report from his boarding school not to the duke's liking. It happened on Christmas Day.

Their father was overcome by the intoxication of his own anger and self-righteousness. He released a lashing of unrestrained anger at Jack, a child of eight. He did this publicly, in front of servants and his four older sons, daring anyone to challenge his rights to abuse the child, calling him lazy, stupid, and unfit to be the son of a duke. He had always commanded and succeeded in receiving unquestioned compliance. None of his four other sons had ever challenged their father. No matter how wrong he was or how false his own bigotry, no one would challenge him.

David stepped between them, told the duke what a self-righteous prick he was, and then announced without the slightest show of emotion that he would be joining the King's army.

Jack was not yet practiced enough to know love could not be won from their father and had strived with undiminished desire to please. Now, as his brother David turned away from this man who had seemed a mountain of immeasurable force, Jack abandoned his desire to emulate his father and chose a new hero, his brother. The three remaining brothers were now without such obligation, one son given to the King's army was sufficient. David had been sacrificed, to stand alone without money or support.

As these memories had broken free from his own guilt, he knew why he had uttered such a foolhardy bet. The answer was twofold. First, he knew the Duke of Rothbur personally and by reputation. There was not a more fearsome adversary in the House of Lords. Whatever power he held over the wealthy lords of London was formidably persuasive and indisputable. They voted for his interests, they paved the way for him to start the Highlander Society of London, and they were organizing support for him against the Duke of Sutherland and his Highland Clearances. The suggestion had been made that Ariella's grandfather would do anything necessary to support his interests, not short of blackmail or possibly worse. Whether he had scruples was a matter of debate. What was not a matter of debate was that anyone who took an interest in his granddaughter walked a razor's edge: one slip and their life was not worth a farthing.

This knowledge inspired the first reason for William to place his wager. He really thought David's chance of success was inconsequential, but such a challenge as the Duke of Rothbur would present, that would be for David the *pièce de résistance*. A challenge, to be told he could not do a thing – that was the rub! William wanted to see his brother strive for a lady who had clearly made his heart race, one who might even bring other emotions back to his torn and ragged soul. The second reason: he had noticed the moment when David was transfixed by the look of Lady Ariella MacClaig. David had never been affected so, not so much as William had ever been aware. It had made the duke wonder if there was such a thing as redemption for his younger brother, if it was possible for him to care, really care, for a woman. He had studied David as he pulled back and took a second glass of champagne, and he had thought,

He will avoid her. He is afraid of something he does not understand, and he will walk away. What I would not give to make him face a true threat to his heart.

David's eyes were angry. A storm raged inside him and could not be concealed. There was nothing of the softer green, the teasing color filled by the shimmer of laughter when he had enjoyed teasing his brother. He did not want to play this game.

"A fool's wager. Your game could cost me my freedom. To get close to such a lady could mean the end of my independence. She would be compromised, and I, as a Grayson heir and a gentleman, would be honor-bound to marry her. No! that I will never do. Marry, I have no desire to and as a second son no responsibility to."

He had him. The duke knew immediately his brother had stepped into his trap. Nothing was pretense or joviality now. Now it was a contest of male bravado, and once engaged by Grayson brothers, they did not step away until dead, ground into the dirt, or victorious.

The Duke of Summerville simply pulled the line tight.

"Look again! Look at how many of the *ton*'s wealthiest circle her. The Duke of Manchester appears to be making quite the jackass of himself. And Lord Lieutenant Wolfe? I think he just ranked himself as a hero defending Pitt in Linconville against the Jacobites. I presume you admit you are outdone and have not even a chance for a simple dance. What's wrong, little brother? No longer interested in games concerning your male prowess?"

David should have walked away, even as his mind willed it so, but his body had betrayed him, and he walked directly toward Lady Ariella MacClaig.

She knew the minute he turned toward her and began his approach. The emotions this elicited were like to a hailstorm of shattered glass, the pricks and impact impossible to deny. She reacted instantly, smiling as though she welcomed him but only by sheer will.

Why is he pursuing me? He is a danger, his presence a distraction. Grandpapa will see and extinguish him as though he were no more than the flame of a candle. Quickly, instantly, he will be gone.

She motioned to Laura, Laura Soveneau. She was standing just to her right, watching for any indication that she was needed.

Leaving France had been necessary to save her own life and necessary in order to help Ariella. They had grown apart over the years and this was understandable, for the path each had taken was very different. Their relationship now was based on one mutual connection. They both cared deeply for Laura's brother, Philippe Souveneau, but for very different reasons. Tonight was important to both for the outcome would affect the life of Philippe.

Laura was presently engaged in conversation with Lord Tamerlane, a young aristocrat of no consequence but tall, handsome, and evidently smitten by her warmth and beauty. With her sky-blue eyes, golden cornsilk hair, and a smile like the first breath of summer, of course he would find her wonderful, and her attention to him was sincere but not complete, for she noticed immediately when Ariella, with practiced feminine poise, retrieved her fan from her reticule and touched her lips for one lingering pause. Laura responded, knowing she was needed. First, she sweetly, and with seductive intonations, dismissed her admirer, at least for the moment.

"My lord, nothing has pleased me more this evening than listening to a gentleman such as I judge you to be." Saying such, the imp that she was enjoyed the sensual gesture she employed as she ran her sweet, honeyed tongue casually over her lips before continuing.

"I find myself a bit warm, and I credit it to the depth of my intercourse with you. My lord, you have left me with a dire need for refreshment. A small glass of Madeira would suit, but only if you would be so kind." As Lord Tamerlane's eyes visibly dilated and his fair complexion revealed a slight blush, Laura wondered if she had gone too far. She could not control, it seemed, her baser instincts. She knew, she had even giggled to herself, about the "new" connotation of "intercourse." *How silly,* she thought, *that the French are begging to make it a sexual word, and how interesting Lord Tamerlane is aware. I think even his fine, tight-fitting breeches bulge a bit in response.*

"Miss Souveneau, my pleasure is to serve you in any way possible. Please allow no one to take the next dance. I could not bear to see you so engaged with anyone as I leave you only for the barest moment." Hurriedly, he took a quick bow and then, as though he had been given a great boon in being asked to alleviate his lady's thirst, he all but skipped as he turned to find a servant.

Close enough now but still with the fan softening her words, Ariella could speak to Laura.

Ariella was entrapped, for David was within moments of an engagement, and she had not been able to pull her gaze from him, so she simply nodded in his direction and uttered three words to Laura: "See who approaches!"

The two were spirits locked in silent understanding, sisters of the soul, rarely needing to explain their emotions.

"Ahhh," she said and then smiled at Ariella with the most infuriating devilry she had ever dared to impose.

"I see, my little sister. He is the most handsome man you have ever imagined, and now he comes directly for you and scares the fine lady sensibilities your *grandpère* has endowed within you. Did I not tell you such a man as this would show you some things you perhaps have not considered?"

This said, Laura could not help herself as she added, "Ohh my! His eyes are unbelievably beautiful and only for you. Prepare, my sister, he will spar with you."

"Hush, consider yourself. Grandpapa will take care of him! Just do what you are so good at and distract him until then."

Laura, with the ease of a practiced flirt, thoroughly regarded David Grayson, for he was perfection of masculine form, so much taller than any other men in attendance and every taut muscle well defined by his very tight-fitting breeches, but the breadth of his shoulders and the strength they suggested, they made her imagine just what an erotic experience his body could command. Her lips pursed into a sensual little incitement of its own, and with pleasurable impropriety she willed him to notice her.

"Oh, *Mon Dieu!*" Almost with humor, she thought, *He does not see me; his eyes can see only Ariella.* Ah, my *petite soeur,* you are in for it now. All your training, your devotion to your strict taskmasters is for nothing. You may be able to dance with your lovely sword when you fence with your *grandpère* or throw your silver knife better than your friend Liam or do all else a beautiful lady should not do, but can you defend yourself against what you know nothing about? Something your body will recognize, oh so quickly, and you, my *soeur*, you will be so very lost."

The backdrop of gilded mirrors paired with walls of brocade silk, all in a wash of candlelight, created a golden light of infused enchantment. Yet this was of no significance to Ariella and David. For them the world had turned to vanishing mists, and all awareness was focused on only the attraction that drew them toward each other.

For one blink of awareness, one burning moment of recognition, their souls spiraled beyond the gilded cage where the *ton* watched to a place where love was the essence of existence. Here their moment lingered and then, like melting snow, ended as if it never happened. For David and Ariella were not free to partake of their own desires, not free to know what promises were held by love's attraction. Both were tied to their promises, and such promises were unforgiving. They were brought back to the world around them, back to point and purpose. That moment was gone. Both accepted the lie: nothing had happened. Such a thing was not to be, not in the here and now on such an earthly plane.

David had felt her presence as an amazing sexual pull, but that had not been what unsettled him. Something else was here in their meeting. *Something he could not explain,* whatever it was, made him for the first time in his life feel vulnerable, very vulnerable. His thoughts made him very uncomfortable and forced him to touch sensitive places inside his memories he did not wish to examine.

The mood of gaiety continued to grow, becoming more vociferous, more expectant, enveloping the elegant couples who danced in swirling radiance as well as those who flirted in quiet corners of the ballroom, trying as they might to steal a few moments of unchaperoned conversation. Even as the *ton* responded, complied to a certain rhythm of such an event, to see everyone, be seen by the select few, even so, even when all in attendance seemed engaged in their own conversations, it happened. An underlying electric current of awareness seized the moment, and those close enough watched what would later be reported in the *Times* as the event of the evening.

The eyes of the *ton* watched as the Duke of Summerville and his brother David Grayson stood waiting, giving their complete compliance to the rules of etiquette – waiting for the Duke of Rothbur to grant his permission for an introduction.

Gloria J. Prunty

Ariella looked directly into the eyes of a man who would give no quarter, surrender nothing of himself, and who looked at her with complete understanding of the sexual power he possessed. She, through no little effort, thought of the reason for her presence at this ball tonight, and she reminded herself of those whose lives depended on her.

Her silken dark hair, perfected into an exquisite coiffure with tiny glittering diamonds, surrendered an ebony tendril to touch her cheek, to show in contrast the most beautiful complexion of sweet perfection, more cream than ivory with a dusting of pale rose for her cheeks and ruby red for her lips. Even as she moistened her lips and smiled, her thoughts were far away,

Tonight, in Paris a lord of Brittany, his wife, and his daughter will face the guillotine. Citizens will cheer and wait for their heads to fall. Some will even wait to hold the basket, for they are delighted by such murders. The beautiful golden hair of an aristocrat has value to these monsters who rule the city. This is what I must remember.

Assuredly, Grandfather will not permit an introduction. Lord David Grayson cannot be anyone of importance or I would know his name. Laura can see he is rude in the directness of his intentions. He stares at me as though I am a morsel of sweetmeat or a confectionery to be tasted. I will not speak with him, nor will I acknowledge such a blatant discourtesy!

Think what she might, still her body grew warmer, and she felt faint shivers unlike any she had known. A place within, only a woman could know, spoke clearly to her of what unrequited sexual arousal could be. This feeling scared her because it made her feel something she had not felt since long ago in the tunnels of Broceliande: vulnerable. Lord David Grayson was dangerous, very, very dangerous.

Her thoughts were of such intensity that her lovely breasts and slender neck reacted against her will. The noticeable blush made her wish even more to force her eyes downward, away from his, but she could not. Her anger, if that is what the emotion could be called, would not release her. She remained caught in the depth of his regard for her.

As for David, even though he felt he did not have a chance in hell of being introduced to Hamish MacClaig's granddaughter, he still pursued this game with his brother. Hell, he knew more about Hamish Mac-Claig, the Duke of Rothbur, than his brother ever would. Hamish was skilled beyond anyone of his caliber in terms of how to fight a war from the inside out. David was one of Pitt's secret agents, and subterfuge was a murky undertaking where allegiances changed in the blink of an eye, but he knew about Hamish MacClaig. MacClaig was deeply involved with the French émigrés.

What David did not know was his motivation; it was either personal or it was money and the French aristos now fleeing Paris had a great deal of money in London banks. As far as most knew, Britain and France were at war, but that was the obvious. Yes, this was the part David had learned so well in Yorktown: the soldiers are called to duty and lives are lost but where comes the victory? Death and sacrifice are rewarded; this is thought the greatest end to winning wars, but there is so much more that determines victories.

Here was the rub. There were ways to weaken the current political state of Paris, and there were ways to strengthen it. Both could be brought about by money, and Hamish owned more ships, more mercenaries, and more political favors than Pitt or possibly even King George. David's thoughts were heavy as he considered the Duke of Rothbur, but his eyes had never left Ariella.

I may rethink this wager. She is far above me in every way, a princess of wealth and position. My aspirations fall far short of such a beauty, and I find I am most comfortable where no one employs high expectations for me.

Knowing this, he still waited to see what the Duke of Rothbur would do and, interestingly enough, his recriminations of himself had no sway on his stature or his suave affectation. His emerald eyes became sensual, leaving nothing back as he enjoyed every inch of Ariella's beauty.

David's brother had indicated to Ariella's grandfather by slight eye contact that he desired an introduction. The Grayson brothers waited, and still the pause of the *ton* was evident. Only Laura smiled with devilish delight for she felt the inevitable. Her French blood told her never could sensual attraction such as David and Ariella felt be denied. Laura's silk fan swayed softly to the waltz in the background. Her sky-blue eyes laughed, and she knew, *This will happen! If not now, then at another time, but, my sweet sister, it seems the gods of Broceliande still watch you.*

When the Duke of Rothbur nodded, indicating he would allow this, possibly the more sensitive ear would have heard an accumulative gasp from the *ton*. Even David, arrogant as he was claimed to be, felt his own neck grow warm and hoped he did not appear taken back by the unexpected turn of events.

Ariella felt her entire body grow stiff with disbelief, and she had to bring the silk fan once more to cover her lips and the stilled words of protest she almost uttered. Why was her grandfather doing this? It made no sense. In just an hour it would be midnight, and all her efforts must be focused on the meeting that would take place. She was angry at her grandfather and at Laura and her silly teasing, and most of all she was angry with this man who so obviously distracted her.

With perfect decorum William Grayson, Duke of Summerville, began,

"Your Grace, may I present my brother, Lord David Grayson. He has returned recently from the Highlands and expressed his love for its beauty and has also confided his respect for Your Grace. He understands your efforts alone slowed the Clearings and improved the productivity of the farmlands. It goes without saying that he would also enjoy the pleasure of an introduction to your granddaughter, the Lady Ariella MacClaig."

William, was almost as broad through his shoulders as David and almost as strikingly masculine and fit, but not quite. Even so, there was no doubt the Grayson men had earned their reputations as fortunate in their physical endowments. They were all over six feet, all athletic and trim through the waist and thighs but broad through the shoulders. It was evident both the Duke of Summerville and his brother had needed to have their tailcoats fitted to accommodate their exceptional size.

Confident in his own political rank, in his assurance that he would be acknowledged by Hamish Rothbur, he smiled with a bit of the devilish playfulness the Grayson brothers were known for.

He had done well, very well with his cock-and-bull story about the Highlands and his brother's interest. What a brilliant fabrication that was. At least these were William's thoughts as he watched his brother give an appropriate bow to his Grace of Rothbur and with reserved expectations, deliver his response,

"My pleasure, your Grace."

"Ahh, indeed, yes, my Lord David. I too know you by reputation and, that being said, even so I will introduce you for reasons of my own to my granddaughter and her lovely companion, but let this be known. Although I am sure it is not a secret, one slight to her person or reputation and I will not challenge you to a duel as seems to be the solution for English lords for I am of the clan MacClaig and we are much more direct and our rage much less controlled. So, let us just say, your demise would be painful and permanent." Then with deep laughter that gave even more prominence to the slight lines of age, feathered touches accentuating the wisdom and dignity within his gaze, the Duke of Rothbur, with an exaggerated Scottish burr he used only when it pleased him, introduced his granddaughter and her companion, Laura.

Ariella did not curtsey, nor did she offer her hand, but it did not matter in the least to David, for he expected as much. In truth, her intention to slight him provided more amusement to his smile as he greeted her than anything else, for he knew the attraction between them was impossible to deny.

Still entrapped by the beautiful color of his eyes, their depth, and yet the impenetrable coldness that lay within, she did not even notice when he had taken her hand, even though unoffered, and brought it to his lips. She only became aware when warmth, unlike any she had known before began to awaken every thread of sensation that was part of the hand he held.

She stared, lost to words, and heard only the last of what he said. She vaguely realized she had neither blinked back the heat of her reaction, nor had she withdrawn her hand. Now she did both with as much indignation as she could pretend. His voice held a masculine timbre, strength she wished to dismiss when he spoke.

"My lady, the next dance I believe to be a minuet, and though I do not claim to be a master of such an elegant dance, I would be honored if you would accompany me." He waited, wondering how she would choose to refuse his request, for he had no expectations to the contrary. Before Ariella could utter a word, both he and his brother were taken back when the Duke of Rothbur took the hand David had so recently held and presented his granddaughter once again to the one man of the *ton* least expected to win a dance with, the Lady Ariella MacClaig. Rakes and second sons did not achieve such heights in the lofty strata of dukes and royalty.

Ariella had never felt so vulnerable, so exposed. Raw emotions inside flamed, intensifying, challenging her to taste the mystery of her own sexuality. Such a thing was beyond her, for she had neither felt nor believed such feelings existed. She was in full view of the *ton* who watched her every move. Her hand, the hand Lord David Grayson held, trembled, and she fought with every fiber of her being to regain power over this thing, this unwanted, powerful thing that held her at its mercy. Anger was her only recourse, and she burst forward with it.

"My lord…"

Her violet eyes pretended nothing as she looked at him very directly. Composure and pretense did not exist, for the exchange was theirs alone. The moment was protected.

Only her eyes met his, and only he saw the darkness and the fire she possessed. Her eyes took him, purple-colored, flames, emotions burning in her she could not extinguish. He looked inside, felt what she could not conceal, and never had he felt more alive than he did in this moment. What social decorum had imposed upon her did not for the moment exist. She looked into him as no one had ever dared before, with the intensity, the certainty of who she was and what she was capable of taking from him. She burned hotter than any fire he could conceive. No wonder he wanted this woman with total and unequivocal lust, more than life itself. When she spoke, her voice was soft, for him alone, her smile beautiful, formed for the *ton* that watched, but her words were meant to turn him to cinders, and it seemed she simply wished he would disappear.

"I have evidently been presented to you by my grandfather. I am uninformed as to his reasons, but please, my lord, I would ask that once this dance is over, you let it be the end to any intercourse."

His smile, incredibly sexual, incredibly knowing, was his only response and his thoughts – they were more than obvious.

I will do as I desire, my lady, wager or none. I will take this dance with you, and I will take another and a kiss from you. That is far too innocent a word to describe the deeper touch I will feel within you. When I am deep within you, I will watch the fire of passion in your lovely eyes reach such heights of exquisite longing that you know not whether the height you desire brings freedom to your very soul or enslavement to my touch.

Her hand, freed from his hold, caressed with bare perceptibility the satin folds of her gown of deep purple, a color that defied the *ton*'s obsequious dictate of propriety. He had noted from the first moment he saw her, before he had taken her unoffered hand, that she wore no glove, not on her right hand.

Such observations seemed trivial, unusable information cluttering his memories, yet he knew it was simply the way his mind worked. Details from the past and the present accumulated like leaves of autumn scattered to await winter's snow and their demise, but his memories never died. He recalled words of his youth, faces, times, dates. Terrible and wonderful, all were filed away but never beyond an instant's recovery. He most often hated his accursed memory, but then there were times when he wondered if this was the reason he still lived while many of Pitt's covert agents had been found out long ago. *Many*, he thought, *who lived in the shadows of espionage did not have the fortune of a long life.*

"My lady, allow me to hold your glove so it ceases to be a burdensome distraction."

"You test me, and I will not play your silly game." She had already removed her hand from the satin folds and was without blush or care putting on her glove. He could not resist teasing, testing the extent of her obeisance to the rules of British society. His thoughts held no respect for such rules, for it made him see ladies as no more than obedient sheep who regarded every nuance of their behavior as a reflection of moral character. These thoughts, as libertine as they might be, gave him such a devilish twitch he could not restrain his next words or his rakish tone, masculine sexuality slowing his words, warming his breath as he leaned close to her.

"Test you? I have had you freely given to me by His Grace. To touch your bare hand or your slender arm would be beyond the pale for even me, at least in view of everyone, and they do watch!" She was not like anyone he had met before, nor was she the lady she pretended.

The dance began. She was relieved, for she believed the time for conversation was at an end.

He led her out for the opening minuet, and she realized this was not the reprieve from his scrutiny she had imagined. He would not touch her as he would have in a waltz, but she would be within his gaze, eyes locked in an embrace far more intimate than even the touch of a waltz would command. She breathed and faltered. He had her. She was watched by a thousand eyes, and he would see everything. She hated the minuet. She hated the dancing instructor who had spoken the words.

> *Be careful, Ariella, the minuet à deux, it is a deadly trap if you do not wish to be explored, questioned by a man who wishes to entrap, for the minuet does exactly so. You are entrapped within his eyes, and societal decorum dictates that you never look away. He sees all you try to hide. The eyes, they will betray you.*

"You, my lord, are arrogant and presumptuous. These qualities seem second nature to British gentlemen such as you."

"Aaah, yes, I am arrogant, as well as presumptuous, and alas for hopeful young maidens, I am a second son and have no wealth, but, my lady, why do you count my British nobility against me? Clearly your voice reveals this, and I cannot help but wonder if your disapproval comes from a part of you that I think might be French. I detect a slight intonation, definitely not of the Highlands."

Ariella was taken aback by his perception. She stiffened, drew back, and tried with immense deliberation to slow her breath, to hide her thoughts. *I must excuse myself and quit this man.* Even at the thought, her hand sought again to touch the secret pocket within her satin gown, but she drew back and tried to beg out of the dance convincingly.

"I cannot..."

Ariella's words were lost to the beginning melody, the music already claiming the dancers, demanding their obeisance. It would have been unthinkable to leave now. Each couple in turn performed in a singular fashion so all eyes could watch their every move. She was now standing at the apex of a social display, and she was expected at this moment to acknowledge Lord and Lady Chandler, the hosts of this grand ball. The dance dictated that participants first acknowledge the couple of highest regard and then wait for their own turn to dance *à deux*, as a couple, alone for everyone to watch. She simmered and wished she could show Lord David Grayson what a truly arrogant ass she thought him. She could not speak, not now, not at this point in the dance. Etiquette dictated such, and she could not look away from him. Etiquette dictated this also, but she could think hideous thoughts of all the many ways she wished to strangle him. She watched with hidden anger as she smiled. Her beauty was not lost to the gentlemen and ladies who watched, the men with desire and the women with true awe, for she really was more unique than even "a diamond of the first water."

> *This dance I could perform with my eyes closed and so I did. Grandpapa insisted on perfect form, on impeccable precision, and always, always on ascertaining the thoughts of the one you danced with.*

She smiled with a bit of devilish humor, thinking of her fencing master, for he was almost as skilled as her grandpapa. Thomas Fagan. She loved him. For him all dancing was about strategy and timing. Sublimation and execution; yield but only to gain advantage; know the moment when victory can be claimed and never retreat, not in the final step. She stepped forward with perfect three/four timing and pointed her dainty toe, but in her imagination, she held a rapier pointed at the heart of David Grayson and she spoke her imagined words, "*En garde.*"

"*En garde?*" Grayson's amused response embarrassed her and at the same time angered her.

She tightened her lips, transforming the top lip with its perfectly formed cupid's bow into a tightened but seductive little pout, refusing to explain her *faux pas*.

"My lovely lady. All eyes are now watching us in our single performance, and instead of your sweet fingertips touching mine, I think you would prefer a rapier in your hand." He stared at her with complete amusement as he continued.

"Smile, my lady. Curtsey, and then I think we will retrieve our moment, for no one could hear your, ah, passion in response to my touch. I will keep your sweet thoughts a secret." His smugness was contemptible, even more so as he executed a perfect bow, every part of his masculine form paying homage to this difficult movement, and still he managed to turn every female head within view, for his physique was exquisitely male.

She hated him. She hated the British and their superiority, but she could not deny the echelon of power that moved within their rigid system of entailed wealth and the political control such dictates wielded. She knew the danger she invited, but she also knew what was at stake. This was her whole reason for being here. To contact one of the few who felt for the French. Someone with compassion who, like herself, would risk his own life to save the innocents who were even now imprisoned, some in lunatic asylums, others at Conciergerie or La Force. Where they were kept, how they suffered was not important to the so-called Patriots nor to their monstrous leaders Robespierre and Danton.

She looked into his eyes. Beautiful, the color of green reminded her of the forest, of Broceliande, but despite his obvious interest in her, they were still cold, lacking in any compassionate warmth.

The dance ended, and she immediately sought her escape.

Lord Grayson, with a gentle touch, his hand caressing her arm, brought her eyes back to his, and his subtle words persuaded her to stay for at least a moment longer in his company.

"My sweet, look around you. The *ton* has now seen your beauty fully displayed, and I think they prepare to take you into their embrace, one morsel at a time. If we walk in the direction of your grandfather, I see at least a dozen very distinguished gentlemen who wait for an introduction. Most I know well, and I assure you they will not step aside without considerable effort on my part.

"Unfortunately, the opposite direction is not a better option. It seems I have been remiss in my familial obligations, and now my siblings have gathered *en masse* to defy my exit without a brotherly confrontation." As he spoke, Ariella noticed a touch of loneliness in his eyes. She actually felt her heart soften slightly, very slightly, for family was an inherent reminder of her own loss.

David saw his brother William give a devil's look directly at him and smile. 'Aah, he wondered, *maybe William did not make the wager with the Grayson brothers' knowledge, but they sure as hell know now!* They were there, all four of his brothers and all together, they would be impossible to ignore if he chose to escort Ariella in their direction. He could see every last one of them, even Jack, smirking.

Without a pause, he very securely fastened his own arm under the lovely, gloved arm of his Lady Ariella MacClaig, and before she had the slightest idea of his intent, she found herself exiting the ballroom and entering the baroque loveliness of the Chandlers' famous gardens. Fountains were everywhere, some flowing with champagne, others filled with clear crystal water where beautiful lilies gently floated and filled the air with sweet scent. Soft candlelight bordered the footpaths made of pink shell, crushed and flattened to ensure comfort even for the most delicate foot. The rest was a thing of enchantment with birds in gilded cages, flowering trees from the Orient, and at every turn a clandestine retreat, precisely architected, designed to give the appearance of natural beauty, a bower with simple seating framed by tree boughs intertwined to grow in perfect symmetry. Even now they stood by a path that led, she was sure, to an intimate alcove designed for secrecy.

He stared at her, enchanted but surprised by how compliant she had been as he escorted her from the ballroom. Surely, she knew that being alone in his company was not a good thing for a lady's reputation. He studied her, taking full advantage of her quiet acquiescence, looking into her unguarded moment, into the depth of her eyes, more consuming than the darkest midnight but filled with longing, certain innocence, and deep, deep sadness. Who was she? How could she affect him like this and what had happened in her life to instill her soul with such pain and such passion?

He gently touched her lovely cheek with his fingertips, flesh to flesh.

"My lady? Are you undone, my sweet? I apologize. I think even I have gone too far with my rakish behavior."

She stared at him almost lovingly. Her enchanted state had redefined him from rake to prince, at least in this unexplainable moment. David, completely transfixed by the same enchantment responded. His skin became so warm, his lips so desirous, and so hungry for her, that his body, without the least interaction with his thoughts on the indiscretion of this moment, enclosed her in arms exceedingly strong and trembling with need for more of her touch, more of her scent. When he bent his lips to kiss her, he was a man on fire, burning with passion. In her embrace he was free of the past and the unbearable pain he had known. She was nectar to his soul, and he wished for all of her. He thought of only how close he could pull her, how he could touch her warm willing lips with his own, how deep he could press the need of his tongue into the sweet honey of her mouth. He trembled desperately, hard and aching to find release from his many demons through the intensity of pleasure he knew she could give him. The attraction between the two had undone the iron of intentions, the clandestine purpose that had guided them through the evening. All encounters and conversations, controlled by their own designs, marking them as servants to political espionage now faded. Now the two, in all their nakedness of feminine and masculine desire, wanted only to embrace each other and make the world disappear. Indeed, this longing would have been consummated if they had been given one moment longer, but instead the sounds resonating within the garden invaded the only true awareness of another's soul that either had ever known.

She heard voices arguing, a man's and a woman's, shattering the melody that had bewitched her. For one precious moment she had heard the winds of Broceliande softly rustling pine needles, brushing the leaves of ancient oaks, and whispering to her the song of the harvest thrush. Time had melted, and she for that moment stood embraced in the arms of Broceliande. Love looked into her eyes, touched her lips, filled her with passion, and she longed to succumb to this magic that made her body disappear, giving new life to her soul and teaching her the meaning of desire, the meaning of joy. She felt a tear fall, and it was all there would be of regret for the moment was gone.

Before she pulled from his arms, she saw he had been there too for that moment. He had been with her in that unexplainable moment, but now he too returned to reality. His eyes began to turn from the passion of desire to the coldness she recognized as that of David Grayson, be he a demon molded from the hand of Satan or merely a mortal man overcome with lust. She would not allow this strange power he commanded to draw her any further into the passions he could arouse within her. Now she could see clearly. She was not in the enchanted forest of Broceliande but in a garden of pretentious wealth where all was shaped for the sake of beauty, but nothing was here by nature's hand. The song was so beautiful, but was it from the harvest thrush her papa loved or from one of the birds here, imprisoned in a gilded cage? It did not matter now. She must leave this man and very, very quickly.

"I have no excuse for my behavior, and I will make none, but I would ask as a lady and as the granddaughter of His Grace, the Duke of Rothbur, that you release me and allow me to make my way back to the protection of His Grace, my grandfather." Expecting no resistance, she began to pull from his arms, only to find them tightened. As she looked up at him with surprise, he saw sweet fields of heather, lavender beauty all within her innocent eyes, and he saw the remains of the tear that had left a soft wetness on her cheek.

"No."

"No," she repeated, first with disbelief and then with growing anger. Whether it was this man or simply his own arrogance with his simple and commanding "No," she reacted the minute he pulled her closer into his embrace. With an instinctive reaction faster than he could ever have imagined, Ariella's right hand went to the side of her satin gown, but now there was no pause. She drew from the secret and well-crafted pocket a dagger so small and so delicate that it could not have been made for any hand but her own. She turned in the blink of an eye and, as though second nature, brought a blade to his throat. His first thought was to confirm what he already knew the moment his eyes first touched hers.

She was unlike anyone he had ever imagined. His second thought was startling even to himself. *She was deadlier than a dozen men of his acquaintance who had thought they knew how to wield a blade.*

She gave him no quarter. He had no doubt in this moment that she was a soldier through and through and that she had seen death aplenty and knew how to take a life. Even as a slight drop of blood seeped slowly from beneath her blade, he did not move and waited to see if the berserker inside her would come to rest. Her eyes softened faster than he expected, and he felt the blade's slight release, so he knew he could trust a few gentle words.

"My sweet, I would ask, I hope not as a last request, but as one you might consider, that you pay heed to the couple who is walking in our direction. I did not desire at this moment to take your virtue, for I would never choose such an open encounter. Even I, rake that I may be, would have sauntered down the path a little further. If you agree that we should perhaps move back to the alcove a few steps behind, then I think we could prepare for a more acceptable return to His Grace's protection." He almost laughed. If her blade were not still at his throat he would have. This was one incredibly beautiful woman who certainly did not need the protection of a man, at least of most men.

Once he returned to the ballroom, he could not avoid his brothers. They waited, not far from the location where they had been when he left.

As one of the servants walked by with a silver tray carrying several flutes of champagne, David paused, considered whether to take a glass, and decided there was no point. Wine was not to his taste, and it did little to soften his mood. If the circumstances had been different, he would have proposed his brothers join him in one of the smoking rooms for a brandy, but that thought had little wisdom. His time was running out, and he had much to consider, especially in regard to Lady Ariella MacClaig, but first he must deal with his brothers. They would never allow him to leave without first taking their pound of flesh, and even David knew this confrontation was well overdue.

He could not avoid his four brothers or the effect of their combined presence. The four of them, all more handsome than sin, more arrogant in stance than their wealth and titles could merit, seemed perfectly relaxed in this inner sanctum of the *haut monde*. David mused as he approached, *I know all the family secrets. I wonder if I am a threat.* He felt no sibling warmth as he continued to appraise the changes the last five years had brought to his brothers, and he wondered if he was even more callused by the war than he had considered.

Change was most apparent in Jack, the youngest. He had been a boy, probably only fifteen, when David left the tyranny of his father behind him and went to find a new kind of hell in the war with the colonies. Jack had not yet gained his considerable height and herculean stature at the time David had joined the King's army. It amazed him to find his shadow, the small and somewhat anemic boy who had followed and imitated him, the boy he had defended against their father was now the largest of the Graysons, and he thought, *I should also throw in the most handsome.* David had always thought Charles, only two years older, would turn out to be the handsome one, but no. He had taken on a very serious, very arrogant look. He held himself slightly to the right, a step away, outside the circle of the others. William, the Duke of Summerville, was center circle as he would expect, and the last he noticed was his middle brother, the quiet one, Edward. *He is inebriated. Now why does that not surprise me?* The *question remains: is he a very unpleasant drunk like our father?* As though in reply to the unspoken question, Edward raised his flute of champagne to David, smiled as though he was ready for the entertainment to begin, and drained the final bit of liquid before replacing it on a silver tray and retrieving a new, full glass of the sparkling liquid.

Jack could not wait another minute to address his brother. His grin had deepened into a genuine smile of undisguised affection, but he knew decorum dictated he should wait for the duke's permission.

A nod from the duke determined it was acceptable for him to approach first.

He could not help smiling with warmth as he put an arm around his brother and pulled him into a close embrace. It was apparent that Jack was the least damaged from their father's abuse. His smile confirmed a solitary exuberance that he, alone of all the brothers, enjoyed.

David felt himself filled with pride and gratitude. One of the five Graysons had escaped the dark shadow of Soames Grayson, their father.

"I am taller now and stronger if I can judge by how easily my arm rests across those Grayson shoulders. I think I would win now. I do not have the same boy's arm you took down so easily when we arm-wrestled!" He laughed, and all that saved him from looking like a pompous ass was his handsome face and his very enviable charm.

David was so finely tuned for physical confrontation he barely stopped himself from taking his brother's wrist in a hold that would have twisted his arm into a painful break. Thankfully, something lingered in him of a familial nature and a memory spoke: *This is your brother, Jack.*

It also mattered that they were within view of gentlemen who harbored political secrets and who hungered for morsels of leverage, always assessing relationships, weighing their import, judging the possibility of coercion. His brothers would never be involved in this world of political betrayals where death hung on every misspoken word or every unguarded moment. Never, as long as he breathed, would he let them know what his life was truly about.

I'll be damned! he thought. I must still have a bit of care within me for I do not wish to bring my sins into their world.

David grabbed Jack's wrist but not with his true strength, just enough to turn the shoulder hug into a handshake, then stepped back and assessed this handsome brother of his, whose emerald eyes were an exact match to his own. He spoke to Jack for the first time in over five years.

"Yes, I see the Grayson arrogance has finally caught up with you!" Then he smiled with forced levity and tried to handle this very ill-timed reunion. "I think maybe I would truly enjoy such a match, but for now tell me, why are all four of you here tonight?"

"A great deal can happen in five years, David, so I will say only that we have a half-sister, and the Grayson brothers are here to give her the opportunity our father did not. Anything more you need to know should come from whatever acquaintance you wish to establish with her. Lady Claire Grayson. Sorry, not my place to say more, but now I wish to get down to the evening entertainment, and of course by that I mean the *wager!*"

There was not even time to breathe in the information Jack had just dropped at his feet, let alone prepare for the brotherly onslaught that had been barely contained by His Grace of Summerville. They were waiting for him, and they had heard the word "wager," so now David expected all hell to break loose and it did.

Just how much had William told them concerning the wager and how quickly could he put all questions to rest? Midnight was only minutes away, and so was the arranged meeting, introducing him to the covert agent of the French émigrés.

His Grace, the Duke of Summerville had decided it was time to see what would happen once he backed out of the center and threw David to the siblings. He had little doubt that David could hold his own, but he still harbored considerable anger at David's long avoidance of his filial responsibilities, so he stepped back to watch the tortures his brothers would inflict on him.

Inebriation seemed, as always, the winning element in social contention, so Edward wasted no time, not so solemn or cocky as he had appeared earlier. He had already drained his most recent flute of champagne and acquired a new one. With animosity in his eyes David did not understand, Edward turned the conversation to directly insult him.

"Quite the event this is becoming! So many Grays for the *ton*'s amusement. Your timing is perfect, and so is your open and rakish behavior in regard to the Lady Ariella MacClaig. The most beautiful lady of the season, the granddaughter of Hamish MacClaig, and you have, within minutes of your arrival, already thrown doubt as to the virtue of her character. Well done!" That said, Edward again pretended to toast to his brother and drained the rest of his champagne. David's retort was quick and very heated.

"Five years since I have seen you, and now I find you a drunk and an unpleasant reminder of our father who, as I remember, was also a drunk."

Edward's eyes and the fierce contraction of his hands into fists said it all. He had more hate in him, more angst than even his brother David could claim. At this moment the two would have enjoyed nothing more than a fist fight, a bloody and very bone-crunching engagement.

One question remained, and it was Charles who saw it, and his own thoughts supplied the answer. *Why is there so much hostility between the two of them? They barely had had time to know each other before David enlisted.*

Then he looked again, for this was what Charles had always done: he observed and remembered, especially the pain all the brothers had endured at the hand of the duke, their father. *They are perfect mirrors of each other, both refusing the recognition of their own bloodline. They see a part of our father within their own natures, and that they can ignore until they look into the mirror of their own heritage. What they hate is the reflection, their own recognizable similarities.*

Charles was the only Grayson who did not speak to his brother David. There was no point, and time was running out. All five Graysons knew they must end this family reunion very quickly. They knew the eyes of the *ton* watched every move, and one thing the Grayson brothers had been taught well was how to put on the proper demeanor and extinguish, within an instant's necessity, improprieties.

David was beyond any tolerable acceptance of the night's events; his nerves were raw. What still awaited him was of far more import than any family reconciliation that could be attempted here, so he did what he had to. He took his leave as inconspicuously as possible but not without deliberately passing by his brother, the Duke of Summerville.

"William, you were always a prick when it came to your own damn arrogance. Don't for one minute think of me as the boy you once knew, for I am not, and if you push me, be careful. The only games I care to play always end in deadly circumstances, so leave me be!"

As he turned his back on the other three brothers, who, he had to admit, were beyond the pale of an ordinary reckoning. He thought all conversation ended until he heard the amused voice of the duke.

"So I take that to mean you don't have the balls to pursue a true lady, someone who would prove you lacking in everything but your own conceit!"

With those heady words, the duke smirked, his own emerald eyes filled with Grayson iron. He knew, all the Graysons knew what David's response would be. They were all damned with the same devil, one beaten into them by their father. *A Grayson defeated is spit. Damn your name and you damn your soul!*

David, without a pause, matched his brother's smirk with a deep, knowing smile. No matter how handsome he appeared as he smiled with imposed charm, underneath an unquenchable ire burned.

"My warning seems unheeded, so let the game begin!"

CHAPTER 5

THE MEETING

She arrived in the library early, not more than ten minutes or so but deliberately early. She wished to ascertain the surroundings, make sure she knew the room well, find all exits and the possibility of hidden spaces where one might listen to uninvited conversations. The library was on the second floor. Plush carpets of Persian design had softened her footsteps as she walked past closed doors, quickly turning right at the end of a long and elegantly appointed vestibule. She had noted the French paintings by Boucher and the walls covered in the fine fabrics made in Lyon.

Once she entered the library she was taken aback by a distinct change. The room was the antithesis of the rest of the estate in being very masculine and very British. Cabinets, bookshelves, and even the massive desk that was set in the center of the room were cut from heavy block mahogany. *Obviously this was one room where a man dominated.* Her thought, she immediately realized, was a bit biased for she had reacted to the bold pungent odor of cigars and lingering trace of strong, rich malt whiskey, but this was not all the room held. The thousand books or more smelled of musk and old leather. The fireplace, though not lit, held lingering odors of pine and apple wood. The room smelled like home, like Broceliande and her papa. The earthy warmth was a reminder of all she had lost, her innocent belief that a mountain would stand forever, that little girls are kept safe by warriors and knights on white horses. Her papa had been her mountain and her knight, and now that little girl she had been was gone. Her grandfather had given her all she asked for – because she refused to live if he did not – and she had asked to be a warrior. She had asked him to take away her fears by making her strong. He had done all he could, and now she was no longer naive. She would never believe, ever again, that men were mountains, and the strong ones were indestructible. Even those as strong as her papa were made of flesh, and they all could bleed and die.

> *The man I meet here is no stronger than others I have known. He walks, as I do, through a world of deceit and treachery, a world where death watches and waits to take those who stumble. I will not stumble, and I will play this game with all the bastards who lie and swear they serve their God, their king, and their country. Lies, so many ways to lie, and secrets – there is only one way for secrets. Tell no one all your secrets for if you do, your life is theirs unless, as my grandfather says, "you test them and are prepared to take their life if you are betrayed. This is the way, Ariella. Decide now if you have the mettle, if your heart has turned this cold, for nothing else will ever suffice if you are to play the game of war the same as men do."*

Her thoughts made her hand tremble slightly as she softly brushed her satin gown, reassuring herself of the placement of her dagger. Unavoidable emotions surfaced, and with the effort of a soldier preparing for battle, she tried to subdue them. Her mind was trained and focused, but her body betrayed her, and she was too innocent of men to understand why her lips still remembered his kiss, why a place low within her stomach fluttered with unexplored desire.

This is not the time or the place to think of Lord David Grayson.
I hate the man! For whatever witchery he forces on me I hate him. Soon I will know why my grandfather practically threw me into his arms.

So many thoughts had broken into the few moments she had allowed for preparation, in order to tighten her control of the moment, she stepped back just a few steps into the shadows of the dark velvet curtains. Here, through the room's only window, a bit of moonlight glimmered and, to her eyes, now adjusted to the darkness, gave just enough light to watch the door.

Even before the door opened both Ariella and David knew who they would meet at midnight. Each had pushed their certainty into a quiet, subconscious corner of their mind and cloaked it in denial, but they knew.

The Duke of Rothbur would have never let Ariella dance with David Grayson if he did not know. He loved Ariella more than his own life, just as he had loved her mother, his only child. Now, allowing his last heir, the last of his blood, to test her life's worth as a spy, aiding the French émigrés and helping the royalists in Brittany, was against all his wishes, yet he had found no way to save her from the demons that pursued her other than show her how to fight them. If she had been a son, it would have been the same, without question. Such a great wrong to the clan of Rothbur and to his son-in-law's name and in turn to all descendants of both could never be forgotten. For both families, there was only one heir who remained. He wondered if it had been the moon goddess Eluna who had whispered the name Ariella, Lioness of God. Was that why her papa had given her the name? If the Duke of Rothbur had been a man who could be brought to tears, this would have been the moment: the moment when he knew the bloodline and the path his granddaughter had inherited. The Duke of Rothbur was his own legend, and he knew the way of power and how to make men bend to his will. Tears would never suffice, only strength, and so he accepted fate's decree when he took Ariella's hand and placed it into the hand of David Grayson.

The moment before either spoke was a gift enjoyed and then a breath forgotten, for that was the way star-crossed lovers escaped the fate of love. Neither knew how to surrender to another nor wished to. They did know how to fight every feeling that turned them from their demons. As they stared at each other in the midnight, each guarded their heart and their thoughts.

David Grayson stared at the beautiful woman, and he knew the most gifted of poets could not describe how the moonlight caressed her raven silk hair or touched her cheek.

> *I am cursed beyond endurance and truly fucked! Damned like the unrepentant bastard I am between the bloody Grayson brothers and this fucking assignment straight from his holiness and the master of deceit, Pitt himself. If I had a chance in hell of being heard, I would pray to God to take the Lady Ariella MacClaig and put her somewhere safe from my touch and this world of lies and political corruption.*

His confident poise and casual perusal of the room denied his agitated thoughts as he closed the door and turned the key in the lock. With a stern gaze that blocked all his sexual desires in regard to Ariella MacClaig, he spoke with a voice deliberately perfected to intimidate her.

"This must be a contrived joke and I feel the brunt, without the least humor. For whatever reason you are here, my lady, I suggest you gather your lovely skirts and run back to the protection of your grandfather."

Then she stepped from the shadows, and the light seemed to follow at her behest, for it revealed, first, eyes of a devilish purple filled with more passion than most would know in a lifetime and enough iron to send him to the devil. Then she spoke, in language that immediately adjusted David's thoughts of her ladyship's heritage.

"I do not cling to any man, especially my grandfather! And if you think for one minute I will step back from this assignation, then you are the bloody rake and sorry excuse for a supposed war hero I thought you the minute my eyes touched your worthless hide! If anyone should require a different emissary to guard their back, it would be me. I doubt your memory of what it takes to fight in this world of filth and deceit has kept you fine-tuned enough to be of any use to me."

Now those were not the words of a lady. For a full moment all David Grayson could do was stare. He did not know whether to take her in his arms or turn her over his knee and teach her that she was indeed a woman.

His disbelief settled quickly into a condescending smile as he boldly assessed her stunning beauty, fully visible now that she had stepped into the light. His inspection was meant to be an insult, just as his words that followed were.

"Sweetling, you obviously stir my passion, as evidenced by my rakish behavior, but please know that a woman, and certainly one who lacks any intimate experience, is of little use to me for what I intend. Give my regards to your grandfather and advise him that I do not play spy games with little girls."

He started to turn toward the door, knowing that this woman with her incredible beauty and his own sexual desire, was deadlier to him than the French emissaries planted in sundry places with one game: to find the identity of and to kill the British agent known as the Rake of Hearts. *What a joke that affront had become, but in the world of counterintelligence, names were not always acquired by admirable deeds.*

His hand reached for the key in the door. As it touched the key, as soft as a whisper, Ariella's blade flew through the semi-darkness to pin the white lace that hung from his wrist to the door.

David Grayson held his breath and, by God's mercy, his anger. Woman or none, soldier or none, she should have known his left hand was free. Within an instant he had released a blade of his own, previously concealed in his right cuff. Even before freeing his right hand, he had turned at such an angle that he was able to return the favor of her throw before Ariella had taken a second breath. His blade skimmed the side of her head and took with it a small lock of her hair. The feathery strand fell to the floor, easily seen as the soft moonlight touched it, the ebony hue distinct, lying on the beautiful Devon carpet of cream and rose. The opposites of color suited the nature of the moment and of the two agents of Pitt: the beauty of one, the arrogance of the other.

Now they both stared at each other like the wild and untamed beings they were. Her eyes were on fire, like flames consuming every bit of his pretension. She spoke first. She did not speak with a woman's voice that would bend to his will but with a voice not unlike the bravest of the soldiers David had led into his last battle, the battle of Yorktown. He knew when she spoke that she would never be turned from her intent. *God help her and whoever it was in this world she wished to kill, and God help him for now she was his to protect or to watch die.*

Ariella did not need to judge her words for they had been formed long before and merely waited for the moment they were needed. She knew this was such a moment, and she knew the instant David threw the knife that he carried a demon in him to match her own.

"I see we match better than either of us might have imagined. At least it is clear my blade, like your own, was never meant in jest. I think you must know that I am bound to what I choose to do as surely as I would have planted my blade in your heart if it had suited my purpose."

As she spoke, David watched her intently, memorizing every gesture, judging her sincerity. He had lived this long by trusting no one, and he knew as he watched the slight tremble in her hand and the quickened rise and fall of her breasts, her passion was very real. Oh, he remembered every soft angle of her body from their kiss, and he had known her passion then, but this burned in her with heat unlike any he had known.

Her voice was soft as a whisper, but it cut into his heart, for he knew the words to follow were from personal experience. The terrors of evil once seen are never forgotten and what she remembered forged her words, words of steel forged by fire came from her beautiful crimson lips.

"It is best for the two of us to be clear from the start. In my eyes you are an *anglais* bastard who serves Pitt, and the game he plays is to supply means and support to the French émigrés. He cares only to gain his own advantage in the war between England and France. I will help with his plan, but my reasons are my own. Never think that I am like any woman you have ever known. You know nothing of me, so make no assumptions."

He stepped closer, and she moved back, a dance as familiar as the one that began with Adam and Eve, for they both knew the sexual tension between them was undeniable. She had retrieved his blade and held it in her very lovely and seemingly delicate hand. He paused, held up her own smaller blade, crafted to fit her hand perfectly, and smiled his most handsome and rakish smile before he responded.

"Honesty? Is that your desire? If honesty is our game, then I doubt I will ever look into the beauty of your eyes and see the passion they hold without desiring to feel you against me, my hands around your slender waist."

"And you, I am sure, think you know all women, conceited buffoon that you are, but why would you make such an assumption about one you have only met?" Now she waited, feeling like a silly girl, which she had never been, waiting to hear a rake ascertain the state of her passion.

Oh, how he loved this moment, to give back to her the angst he felt at being in this intolerable situation. He was a British agent; he prided himself in knowing his value. He had never before depended on the discretion of another emissary, but now, being forced into this relationship filled him with anger, and his response was unkind.

She knew he was filled with anger, and she knew why. He would gladly bed her, but respect her or trust her, those things he would not do. Even knowing this, she could not still her heart, and she hated herself and David Grayson for the desires she felt. His deep green eyes smiled at her, and he moistened his lips as an invitation to her before he spoke.

"The kiss, my dear. It is always the kiss that unmasks a virgin. I have no desire for virginal maidens who have no knowledge of how to please a man. Most confuse sexual arousal with a deep romantic love, and that, sweetling, is a damnable lie. One is not the other. Ah, but then I lose the point. Your kiss was unmistakably your first, I would guess. A woman who knows passion yields her lips to a man, softens them and desires a deep and engaging consummation with his tongue."

At first, his very sensuous lips smiled, for he took pride in his ability to crush her. Then her eyes revealed something he had not expected.

Ariella had never been sheltered by her grandfather. He did not believe the world to be a kind place, and he did not believe one survives without strength and knowledge of the evils that can readily destroy the weak and even the best of warriors. When Ariella refused to accept the finer training required of a lady, refused to hide away in the safety of his protection, she and her grandfather struck a deal. The only thing that allowed her to match Lord David's anger and cruelty was the wisdom of her grandfather, for he had said, even as he forced his own heart to remain cold,

"Ariella, if you will not be a lady, for that is what a girl of noble stock is destined to be, then I think you will need to know what it really means to choose the life of a soldier, and, my darlin', regardless of what your heart may tell you, you are a rare and lovely lassie as was your mum. This is something that will require great effort to alter, and there are dire consequences to changing all that is natural to a woman's gentle nature. You must be prepared to take another's life, to learn the power of a blade. Such a task as this turns my very soul. I see your mum within your smile, within your eyes. You give back to me memories of my beautiful Katherine. Ne'er a kinder heart was born, soft as a kitten, my sweet. and she was loved by every lad, young and old, that lived in the Highlands of Scotland.

"I know your mum would not wish this life for you. If we begin this path, you will be fostered by someone I trust, and you will be trained, in most ways, the same as I would a youth I wished to prepare as a soldier. Each year will be more difficult, for, my darlin', I do not wish for you to succeed. What I wish is for you to return to my protection and to be an heiress and a lady of Scotland."

Her grandfather was the most unyielding man she knew. He had taken her to the Isle of Man and delivered her into the hands of Taggart McClure, who had taken one look at her, then, with eyes hard as flint and the weathered face and sturdy form of a man who had spent his life at sea, he said to her grandfather,

"What is the name of this small and worthless-looking whelp you bring me?"

Ariella looked at this monstrous man with skin more akin to leather than flesh and with an air about him that said he would as soon kick her overboard as give her even a minute of his time, and her eyes began to well with tears of fear.

She had balled her hands into fists and pressed her nails deep, deeper, until she remembered Broceliande, remembered pain, and remembered its ability to numb her heart. Only when she knew her hands bled did she repeat her sustaining prayer, "Blood for blood." She repeated the words over and over in her mind until the fear began to subside. She looked at her grandfather, and his eyes offered nothing. It was words he had spoken earlier that raised her stubborn spine: "You do have the limitations of a girl." She had sworn then and she did now. "No matter, man or woman, I will not forget my name and I will not forget my papa!'"

Yes, there was that lady part of her. But nothing her grandfather said would ever take away the loving memory of her papa, who had said,

'Ariella, I named you, my sweet. You come from a lineage of legendary warriors, so you are my lioness, Ariella, Lioness of God and a beautiful little lioness."

David Grayson saw the tears begin, and then he saw them disappear. Lady Ariella MacClaig had shown a vulnerable part of herself. Her eyes affirmed how cruel his words had been, for he had seen the tears gather, but her violet eyes did not shed one tear. Unless someday she told him the truth of her childhood, he would never know how she maintained such control.

Taggart McClure had taught her how to act as the warrior and not the girl. He had never put her to the lash, for that would have been kindness compared to other ways of turning a lass into a soldier. Her past, though more at the time than she thought she could endure, made David Grayson only a minor difficulty.

Now it is time to show David Grayson who I am. He thinks I have lived in a grand castle, properly taught needlework and deportment in order to appear the model of elegance and moral rectitude. He sees me like all the other virginal debutantes, perfecting the evanescent social skills necessary to enter the beau monde. I can show him the lessons I was really taught when I served my apprenticeship aboard the corsair Elegance. My teaching masters were not dancing instructors, but men who knew the skill of the sword and the value of a well-weighted blade. Instead of perfecting the touch of the brush to accomplish the delicate art of watercolor, I was given a sword, and what I learned was how to draw blood. Polite conversation was not the language of the crew of the Elegance, and the words I know could surprise even Lord David Grayson. While maidens were counting the 3/4 time of the minuet, I was counting the thirty-two points of a compass and forcing myself to place my footing tenderly as I climbed the "stairway to heaven," the upper gallant of the highest mast. What I must remember is that Lord David Grayson cannot break my heart, for it has already been shattered, and the scars that hold it together are made of my own tears.

Ariella moved very close. Her dark lashes fluttered as though she flirted with him. She did not speak but wet her lips with her tongue. The angle she had chosen, as she drew even closer, was with obvious design. Her breasts were fully exposed to his view as she caressed his arm with the tips of her fingers, then brought them to his cheek, and looked up at him with passionate eyes he knew belied her true intention. A lock of her black-silk hair had fallen from her coiffure and begged for his touch. His fingers did touch her cheek, and she leaned into them, encouraging him to pull her closer.

Ariella, with the sultry voice of an enchantress, cut through his rakish façade. His manhood reacted immediately to her feminine wiles, but in his mind's eye he could see the truth. Her affected flirtation was an obvious ruse, for despite her wanton pretentions, David saw the truth. Her bearing and gentle features were qualities of nobility, and she had an unmistakable dignity that could not be disguised even by the fine performance she gave. His desire to know the truth about Ariella MacClaig was stronger than his certainty that she would be an inordinate distraction in his sworn duty to the Crown.

"It would be so easy to hate you now, my lord. Is that what you wish for? I think that would earn me nothing, and I do want something from you, Lord David. Your own words have given you up. I think words as cruel as yours are exquisitely chosen by a man only when he is threatened."

Now she stepped back and looked to see if her thrust had taken him by surprise.

Who was this woman? David Grayson did not even try to hide what he felt; he simply looked at a woman unlike any he had ever met. He felt admiration as his eyes lingered on her loveliness, and he felt loathing for the man he had become. At this moment he did not wish to spar with her ever again. He just wanted to take her in his arms and bathe in her innocence. David took her fingertips from his cheek and kissed them gently. His voice was kinder, less guarded as he stepped back from the kiss he desired and surprised her with his response.

"I will call on you tomorrow, my lady, and ask permission from His Grace to pay my addresses."

Seeing first surprise in her lovely lavender eyes and then an unmistakable brightness of understanding, he smiled with a gentleman's respect, bowed and departed.

Chapter 6

THE FAMILY

It was past noon, still, for Lord David Grayson's purpose, an inappropriate time to call. He knew this as he did all the vanities of the *ton*, the rules upon rules that set the nobility above the working class. David Grayson did not care, and he doubted very much if the Duke of Rothbur gave a damn. There was no question in his mind that His Grace knew everything that concerned his granddaughter, and whatever the blazes the man was condoning by allowing her to act as an emissary for the émigrés was beyond any rationalization he could fathom. In his opinion, the man's disregard for Ariella was despicable. David knew every lowlife, every treasonable bastard associated with these supposed political assignations, and to place a beauty like Ariella in such company was beyond insanity.

He tried to calm himself as he approached the front door. He breathed deep, not inhaling the same fresh sweetness as the Highlands he imagined, but this less-than-clean air of the town, which suited him. He stared at the lion's head, impressively centered, dominating the entrance by its placement. The damn door knocker, a brass lion – everything relied on impression and power. Before he took the metal ring and hit the back plate, he allowed himself one ironical smirk as he thought,

> *I swore to myself after Yorktown I would never play the gentleman caller, following the way of all lords and ladies of the haut monde. Yet here I am paying my addresses to the wealthiest, most beautiful heiress of the season, and what a fucking mess this is. My brothers be damned and their bloody wager and now Pitt and his promises to the Nantes sympathizers. Well, my lovely Lady Ariella MacClaig, let us see where all of this will lead.*

Then with an unquestionable force of agitation, he hit the metal door plate and waited, expecting a dignified butler of refined qualities to open the door.

Darin McCord ripped the door open and glared at him with the disinterest of a hired assassin who considered David at best an irritation. He smirked as he saw the calling card extended in David's right hand. Darin McCord was obviously not a butler, and he sure as bloody hell wasn't the kind of man who carried a silver salver collecting calling cards from the nobility. He and the nobility were not even close to the same social pecking order. He was larger than David Grayson and taller, which made him a giant of a man. David assessed him to be about the same age and then wondered if, despite the Scottish kilt he wore, he was either a bootlegger or a mercenary. David was still trying to decide whether he should prepare to fight the man or request to see the duke. Before he could do either, Darin McCord, in an unmistakable Scottish brogue, settled the point.

"Get yer bahookie o' th' front step so I can shut the blasted door! Th' MacClaig of the Clan MacClaig is waitin' fur ye sorry self, and that is something ya dae nae want. Third door tae th' left. Dae nae knock!"

David did not say a word. He had not completely decided he did not want to fight this Scottish Goliath, but even his male pride doubted he could win. The Goliath was a handsome man, and this rubbed Lord David's nose in a bit of jealousy, which made his anger more obvious and his desire for a "pissin'" contest with Goliath even stronger.

What the hell! he thought as he made his way down the very large entry hall toward a third set of massive double doors.

The room beyond was filled with light from high Venetian windows facing the east wall. It was long and spacious, obviously a study from the mahogany-paneled walls, the high, beamed ceiling, and the endless rows of leather manuscripts filling the bookcases. The room spoke of the Highlands with oil paintings of hunting dogs and horses undeniably Scottish and vibrant deerhounds in pursuit of their quarry. Even David, Englishman that he was, knew no one other than nobility, no less than that of an earl could own such magnificent dogs. The paintings of horses would have truly pleased his brother Jack, who knew the breeding and worth of stallions better than he knew how to be a proper gentleman. Magnificent ebony stallions captured in oil he knew were the best Friesians a man of wealth and power could own. This room belonged to the Duke of Rothbur, the MacClaig of the Clan MacClaig, and if any doubt was left about that, there was the undeniable collection of whiskey on display, totally illegal in London but of great value on the bootleggers' market.

When the Duke of Rothbur spoke, there was no Scottish brogue. David knew this intimidating man could choose his words as well as his articulation to suit his purpose.

The purpose of this meeting had nothing to do with Highland Clearances or the Highlanders Club recently established, in part by MacClaig. This meeting was about France and England and the war between the two. It was also about the devil's game all the politically powerful play under the table to turn the tides of war for their own personal interests. The demeanor of the duke's powerful shoulders, the way he held his jaw, square, rock-hard in manner – it was all his way of saying, "I do not trifle nor do I pretend. I take. There are no rules other than my own." His physical presence was proof of what he was capable of in battle. He was of the oldest lineage of ancient warlords who gave no quarter, no mercy. Rothbur spoke in the direct and indubitable fashion David had anticipated, and he did so without one hint of any emotions that would suggest his own vulnerability for the one person in this world he truly loved, his granddaughter.

"Lord David, we will not insult each other by playing by the rules of the *ton*. I know all there is to know of you, more than your four brothers, more than my granddaughter, and, I would venture to guess, more than even you know of the underlying ramifications of the service you engage in with the Right Honorable William Pitt. You know from my actions at the Chandlers' and from the fact I have allowed you into my home that I accept your relationship with Ariella, but what that means I would like to clarify." Rothbur shifted his weight slightly, gripping the glass goblet he seemed to have forgotten, oblivious to how close he was to shattering the crystal into a hundred pieces. The amber liquid swirled as he increased his grip. Golden fingers of the rich liqueur touched the inner rim of the goblet, and the hair on the back of David's neck stood on end, reacting to the man's bare control, lest he thrust a sword at him or any interloper who dared to insult his granddaughter.

Without asking but with the presence of a man who would not have accepted a refusal, His Grace handed David a glass of the finest whiskey he would ever have the pleasure of tasting, at least not for a very long time.

The grey eyes that bored through him were Highlander through and through, a hundred years and then a hundred more of clan breeding. They were filled with cold, barren earth and the blue grey of the Celtic Sea, a fierce savagery veiled by controlled propriety. Rothbur was not like other men David knew. His blood was bred from a fierce and unforgiving land. Scotsmen such as Rothbur lived beyond the ephemeral light of tranquility that seduced most men. Rothbur knew just as David knew that strength is hard earned. It is surviving while others die, refusing to put down the sword others can no longer hold. It is that stubborn will that keeps a clan, a family, or a country from disappearing into a legacy of forgotten time.

"David, when it is the two of us, it will be David. No Lord this or Your Grace that. Now I will tell you the reason we are meeting. My granddaughter's life from this moment forward is in your trust, and if she dies, you die. If you hurt her in any way, I will hurt you tenfold. If you take her virginity, you will marry her, and if you ever ask me why I have made these decisions, I will take your balls in my fist and crush them. I share my reasons with no man or woman. My life is the Highlands and the clan, but Ariella has demons she fights, and this I cannot change, so I leave it with you and with her."

Grayson remained silent. For the first time since Yorktown he actually considered life with his four brothers a viable alternative to dealing with the man he now faced. Grayson did not lack courage, nor did he feel physically intimidated by this Scottish leviathan. It was the simple awareness that his fate was now irreconcilably fused to that of Ariella MacClaig. This fact had more ramifications than he ever wanted to consider. Her beauty and her passionate spirit drew him. After he left her at the Chandlers' he found he could not sleep without dreaming of her. He was unable to dismiss his desire to caress her luscious breasts, to kiss every inch of her soft, skin, and to teach her the heights of passion. He had never before wished to teach a woman anything. To take what was willingly offered had been his way, but to give back? That had never defined David Grayson.

Now, at this moment when the door opened and Lady Ariella entered, he wished he could be anywhere but here. At least that was his wish before his eyes met hers.

Ariella MacClaig needed him. Nothing was said and denial would have been immediate, but something had happened, something very dire and something she could not accomplish without him. David Grayson felt himself pale. A physical jolt unnerved him, and his thoughts were even more disturbing.

Someone she loves is in danger, and those beautiful violet eyes of hers are filled with determined will. She thinks I am the warrior who can right wrongs in this hellish world. That thing is dead in me – faith that I can find the demons that feast on war and that I can slay them. I am no fucking Crusader! He thought for an instant he had shouted out his profane musings and that the devil was there to challenge him. Before he had moved a muscle, something larger than any man could be and strong enough to send him to the floor was looking directly into his eyes. What he saw was a frightening and unnatural creature. Its eyes were fire, its mouth open with fangs that could take his hand, and its growl was a.... wolf!

"Wolf! There is a bloody wolf trying to take my head off! What the hell!"

"*Arêtes! C'est suffisant!*" Ariella shouted in French. At the same time, she pushed her hands into his thick pelt of ebony fur and pulled the animal back. The massive beast turned toward her, stared into her eyes, and whimpered like a docile pup before lying down close to her feet.

David starred in stunned disbelief, not even hearing the voice of Hamish MacClaig as Hamish walked to the great mahogany door of the study, bowed with a silent understanding to his granddaughter, and then said with his own Scottish burr, "It is in yer blood. Broceliande, the home of your father, but mah princess."

Ariella exchanged no look of love with her grandfather, for the common blood that flowed between them could not be described in such a way. It was built from a thousand years of clan lineage that lived within them. It gave them no choice in what they did, for the blood marked them according to their calling and who they were.

Ariella could not resist giving way to the imp inside her as soon as she heard the sound of the heavy door closing. While still holding onto the fur of Sagath, she spoke to Lord David. She solicited her sultry feminine voice, just to rub in a bit of salt to his male pride as she teased,

"My lord, Sagath is but a pup grown big, fed by my own hand since birth. A gentler beast I have never known."

Whatever her concern had been when she first entered the study was momentarily subdued. The ways a woman could torture a man when she had the upper hand were too delicious to dismiss, and she had the upper hand. Sagath was now playing into her hands. With a sweet whimper he rolled over, twisting and turning on the plush Axminster rug, his paws hanging playfully in the air, inviting her to rub his belly and to run her fingers through his fur, black and soft, softer than the finest furs worn by those of the Blood Royal.

"See how submissive my pup can be? I thought you, my lord, would be a man who enjoyed sensual pleasures. Surely you cannot resist such an invitation to stroke a beautiful animal? For I have heard you have a great deal of practice in taming even the most wanton creatures. Will you not indulge Sagath, just a small stroking pleasure for him?"

If ever a woman could delight in a devil's teasing, it was Ariella. Her eyes glowed with sensuous pride. With Sagath present she was utterly safe to say whatever she willed to this handsome rake, knowing that he would temper his remarks, for no one could deny that the wolf had a head the size of a lion's and fangs that could tear a man's arm from its socket in one biting jerk.

Lord David stared first at the most beautiful and *most self-confident* woman he had ever known, wanting nothing more than to turn her across his knee and then take her in his arms and make love to her. Instead, he drew himself to full height, gritted his teeth, pulled his lips tight into the semblance of a smile, and spoke with, he hoped, the tone of a man who had not known unbridled fear.

"You, my lady, are a minx, and your protector a more admirable foe than I have ever known. Since I can think of no reason to explain why you have a wolf in your home, I will leave it to you." Even as David spoke, his eyes did not leave those of this deadly but undeniably beautiful creature. He even felt a touch of envy, for there was no doubt this beast loved his mistress with an uncompromising loyalty. David felt caught in a romantic perplexity as he wondered if a mere mortal man were capable of loving with unconditional devotion. Whatever had happened to bring them together, it had resulted in a bond deeper than anything he had ever shared with any human being; that was obvious as he watched the wolf's great head push against his mistress, touching her hand with his cold wet nose, waiting to feel her fingers slide into his thick fur and push close to his skin. A knowing between the two rested here, waiting for unspoken words only the heart could hear, captured by this touch, each knowing the sense of the other.

David broke the moment with intentional sarcasm. Every fiber of his being jolted at such an unconditional surrender of love, especially one coming from a wild beast, one that had, he dreaded to think, a finer sense of devotion than he could claim.

"My lady, I feel you are not ready to break confidence. This beast... his presence might be explained by the powers of enchantment, but then you should know my nature at least this well. I do not believe in fantasies or in beasts tamed by love. More likely, he is a product of some nefarious breeder."

David's back was to the Venetian windows; the morning light cast his face in shadow but did little to conceal the strong definition of his features. The cut of him, his nobility was the mark of his own lineage. Bold and aggressive lines were set firmly within the slant of his jaw and the strength of his profile. *He was marked,* Ariella mused, *by his own breeding.* Nefarious, maybe, from what she knew of his father, but something about him defied the ordinary, made the other men she had known seem lacking. In what, she had not determined, but even now as the sunlight touched David Grayson's hair streaks of gold were visible, she had her own fanciful thought that a halo of fire surrounded him. This impression awakened a part of her that always clung to the memory of Broceliande. Try as she would, she could not dispel the image of Lord David Grayson standing before her, sword in hand, slaying the dark demons that haunted her dreams.

"Will you have him leave the room?" His question brought her back from her musings, and she laughed, mostly at herself for imagining such a noted rake as Grayson rescuing her. More likely it would be the other way around.

"No, he will not leave the room. I think it would behoove you, my lord, to make friends." Still Ariella stroked the fur of her Prometheus, and still her lips teased Grayson with words meant to test his patience and his manhood. She softly wet her lower lip and slowly lifted her long dark lashes to reveal lavender eyes. He remembered how deep the color, a dark purple, when she was consumed by ire. She perused him with a deliberate challenge.

David moved closer; within arm's reach of the wolf she had named Sagath.

"Do you have any suggestions for how such a friendship might take place?" Even as he asked the question, his reluctance for such a friendship was evident by the set of his handsome Grayson jaw. Ordinarily relaxed and confident, it was now set so tightly that even a lean muscle in his cheek showed a noticeable tic.

Ariella was enjoying his discomfort. David knew the risk he took by offering a hand of friendship to Sagath. Though cloaked in an ebony beauty, the beast, Grayson imagined, had more fury than Satan himself if challenged.

David knew he had no choice. The gauntlet had been thrown at his feet. He either stepped forward or returned to Pitt, mission unaccomplished. Ariella would never dismiss Sagath, not for the comfort of Lord David Grayson.

Every step David took was forced, and he wondered why this beast that seemed as docile as a kitten beneath the hand of Ariella intimidated him. He was a soldier who had survived battles so deplorable, so brutal that fear, he thought, had left him, had certainly made him numb to the prospect of death. Death! That he did not fear. At times he even welcomed it, for living after the wars where others died – that had been a far greater difficulty.

He drew close to the beast and extended his hand.

The head of the great beast did not move. It was as though Grayson was not worthy of the wolf's attention. The closeness of Sagath's mistress was far too pleasant for him to be disturbed for the likes of this mere mortal. Grayson persisted, and now he knelt to the beast and on one knee presented his hand, palm up, just beneath Sagath's powerful jaw.

Without the slightest move of his giant head, Sagath opened his eyes, and a cold predatory glare gripped Grayson with an undeniable warning. The wolf's top lip curled back to reveal fangs that could easily take David's hand.

Ariella watched, mesmerized by the exchange between the two. It was a palpable moment when both knew the measure of the other. Sagath's growl intensified, daring David to touch the fire that burned between them.

His hand did not go to Sagath but to Ariella, and his fingers intertwined with hers.

"By what magic I cannot conceive, but you hold the spirit of the wolf within your grasp. My only means of making peace with this massive beast is through your consent. I think if you allow me to rest my hand in yours, I may make a sort of truce with this bloody pet of yours!" His voice was tight with frustration, but his dark green eyes were calm. He let his fingers intertwine with hers. The softness of Ariella's flesh and the coal-black fur of the wolf filled him with a primordial pleasure he could not explain.

Ariella let the warmth of David Grayson's touch travel through her fingertips, and she allowed herself to intertwine her own with his, but she would not let herself look into his eyes. She was afraid. She feared he might be much more than a rake and heartless libertine. She was afraid of the attraction, and she was afraid he had awakened a sleeping maiden inside her. These feelings could distract her, possibly even cost her life, or worse, the lives of the Bretons she wished to save. The task at hand was a deadly game, one involving lies and deceit, but then this was what espionage was comprised of, and she felt assured that David Grayson would be very good at it, especially if he were given the opportunity to engage his male charm. There, she admitted with considerable vexation, he had no equal. A man's smile should never possess a sexual presence capable of weakening a woman's knees, forcing a blush so knowing that she could not pretend to be untouched. He was not going to be easy to work with, but she did believe she could trust him. If she confided just enough to secure his confidence and make him believe that what she wished him to do was in the interest of England and would indeed fulfill his commitment to Prime Minister William Pitt, then she could believe in the possibility of saving Broceliande and those she loved.

Having turned toward David, she was aware that he was watching her, and she needed to know if he was ready to accept her, to trust her.

David was certainly watching her, but then he was a trained spy, and he was very good at reading people. His life depended on such training. The tilt of her head, the slightly tightened bottom lip, the slight flutter of her long dark lashes – he wondered how much she would try to hide from him.

It was obvious in the unwavering and intelligent way she spoke to him, the knowing in her eyes, and the way her hand remained always close to the dagger hidden in the folds of her blue satin dress that she was not pretending to know the game she played, she was a master of the game. He likened her to the phantasmal beast that even now watched his every move and was prepared to kill him without hesitation. Ariella was very hardened, he thought, not unlike himself, and he wondered what she was capable of. Her eyes, at times, were void of light. Only memories, bled from innocence and passion could produce such guise, such desire for vindication. He knew, David Grayson knew, as well as any soldier, the demons that haunted survivors of war, and he knew how unremitting they became. Ariella, he decided, was very dangerous to anyone who stood between her and whatever damn mission she had sworn to. Her voice had a slight tremble. He should listen, he knew this, but he wished it were not so, that instead, just for once, his life was not always drawn to war and death.

"My Lord David, it is time we talked of sailing the English Channel and of weighing our dual purposes. We must decide now if we trust each other. If there will be enough mutual gain to be free of betrayal. We both know betrayal can come from anyone at any time, and now we must choose to trust, for neither of us can move alone."

Slowly he disengaged his fingers from hers and lifted his eyes from her lips. He denied the sexual desire he felt, he denied what their senses had embraced, he denied how his eyes had been lost in hers when his hand and hers were given one to the other, and he denied what had happened between the two: the rare desire that had breathed the truth of what love could be between the souls of men and women. He could not deny that this love had quivered before them like the soft light of a fading candle, and it now was lost.

She had begun the conversation with the intent of rejecting all she felt for the good of something much greater. Now she wondered if she had given up too much.

Ariella moved with grace, with perfected elegance. Her hand trembled slightly as she lifted it from the warmth of Sagath, from the touch she and Lord David had shared. She brushed back her hair and a dark curl loosened, fell across her cheek. David Grayson watched as she walked toward her grandfather's massive desk and began to pour honey-colored liquid into crystal glasses. She drank from one, deeply, without thought to the correct deportment of a lady, for certainly whiskey at noon was far beyond the pale.

"You have met Laura. She accompanied me to the Chandlers' ball. We are closer than blood sisters for what we have shared is far more than even those from the same womb could know. Those she loves I love, and her brother Philippe has sent a missive. It is time for us to go to Brittany."

David's hand froze mid-air. He was in the process of pouring himself a hefty portion of her grandfather's golden honeyed fire from its crystal decanter. He gauged the amount he had allotted and doubled it. Before speaking a word, he downed half the glass, expecting the burn to be significant. He was not disappointed. Ten seconds was all it would have taken to feel the liquid and adjust to its sweet taste, but that would not suffice. He drank deeply. He wanted to feel its fire, needed the burn to remind him that she had set him up, locked him into an unconscionable position, and nothing, no one, not the Prime Minister, not the Clan MacClaig, nor the wealth and weight of the émigrés, none of these would save her from certain death. She had only him, but she was too headstrong and bathed in her own ideas of righteous glory to even know this.

His fear for her and his understanding of the risks involved for the two of them in venturing into Brittany now, when men and women were being butchered, guillotined by the thousands, was insanity.

With significant effort his dark green eyes reflected a sense of amusement as he responded.

"So you have a letter. Of course, you know the Secret Office of Correspondence reads all foreign missives, and King George himself takes quite a delight in reading the ones that arrive from France. I think he must view himself as an expert on decoding potential messages of sedition, but I fear Pitt has him there. The Prime Minister has created a code for himself which is used between embassies. I am told only the Bishop of Bath has perfected its complexity.

"Yet I should give you proper credit and assume your letter has nothing that could incriminate you or your grandfather. If that is the case, then I must move to my next reason to question your sanity."

He was numbed by her suggestion of plunging headfirst into the gathering storms of what had begun to look like one of the bloodiest revolutions since the Holy Roman Empire had forcibly brought its own peasant uprising into a state of subjugation. One hundred thousand had been killed in battle, and the other 300,000 who survived found themselves in even greater servitude with more peasants than ever dying from starvation and brutality. His thoughts on the matter bordered on sedition, so he kept his secret, but he believed that with a united effort and better leadership the peasants would have been victorious. That thought alone would probably have seen him hanged by his own monarch who, like others throughout Europe, feared for his own safety. Even now Marie Antoinette and King Louis XVI were imprisoned at Versailles after being caught trying to flee France.

David continued, "You are a princess, a female, a pampered heiress who has ties to the French aristos! You think your beauty a weighty influence on the men you would persuade to align to your political efforts. You know nothing of war, of men drunk with bloodlust, animals who wish only to survive, driven beyond any thought of right or wrong, or even of whom they serve, for they serve no king, no God, only their own soulless purpose. You think to go to Brittany, but what or whom, might I ask, will see to your life or even save you from violation and capture?" David was beyond himself, his self-composure forgotten, his own honed and powerful body tensed, responding as if actually facing an adversary. His hand splayed, fingers grasping at his own memories of soldiers, his brothers in arms, dying, screaming in pain. His hand trembled from the remembered dirt and blood, handfuls he had grasped to pull himself out of the pit of hell.

David felt a tinge of the pain begin. Bits of fire awakened his nerves, and his sense of presence diminished. *God, no! No more! I will not succumb to this damnation, this pain that eats at my heart, feeds on the very marrow of my soul. It finds me and I cannot stop it. There is no one to stop it from dragging me back into the bloody pit! God, help me!*

Like every time before when the panic came, David waited for the cold, the dampness of the sweat that always seized him, rendering him frozen in darkness for long moments of time, time taken from his own awareness of the present.

The soft warmth he felt instead unnerved him, and his voice died in his throat, replaced by the tight restraint of unexplained emotion. Beneath his hand was the head of a giant wolf, his massive form leaning against him. The wolf had chosen his right side to stand in a flanking maneuver, the same as one of his own men would have chosen. The beast's nostrils flared as he waited next to David, waited for David to know he was not alone.

David trembled in a state of utter disbelief, and then he steadied and felt, for the first time since Yorktown, that he was not alone.

Ariella breathed and let herself accept his anger. Then she spoke the words that in all the world were all that would have turned him round.

"I see you, David Grayson. I see you in the pit you fear, and I know your hands are covered with blood, blood of those you loved and of those who were the enemy. I see the shattered pieces war leaves behind as it goes on and on, always feeding on more hearts and more lives. I see because I have been in that same pit. I have been in that same hell, and I now ask your leave to trust that I am none of the things you have said.

"A princess needs a castle, and mine was taken by the Devil, Papa killed in front of my eyes, and my mama violated before her throat was slit. My fairy kingdom of Broceliande was covered in the blood of innocents while I hid in the pits of hell and the horses of my enemies walked above me. Always I believed I waited inside a tomb, a place where I would die alone and forgotten. I know about your Yorktown, and I know about the redoubt, the great hole dug as a defense, the last barrier of defense for the British. It was made to hold one hundred men, but a thousand soldiers fought. The moonlight turned blue to red, and colors were indistinguishable. How many of your own men did you kill, David Grayson?"

David's hands, his arms, and the blood within his veins turned cold. He did not recognize his own voice. Someone else spoke, the man, the soldier who had been in that redoubt. It was his voice, but from another time. Anger would have been better, more protective of his true pain, but what he heard in his voice, the voice that echoed between them, was sadness, a true, unremitting sadness that lingered in the soul for it had nowhere else to go.

She saw his pain but refused it, just as she had refused to yield to her own pain turned inward that was her strength, and he must know this or he could not be here, a spy, risking his life and for what? Only such memories as these explained the reasons.

The air was thick between them. What had consumed their anger was a dance of words not unlike a duel, McKinney blades, McKinney words, both like razors testing the thickness of one's skin or possibly even one's soul. But now there was nothing but silence, not even the sounds of passing carriages from the busy London streets were audible. All were awake and stirring within the House of Rothbur. Laura in her dressing room, the duke outside waiting in the garden, and Darin McCord standing as guard just outside the great mahogany door, but still there was only silence. Ariella felt the vibration within the stillness between them. She counted as she felt the sound shatter the stillness. She listened as the brass arm of the wall clock struck every hour and silently, she counted. Twelve times it sounded, echoed, and filled the thickness between them. Both knew this would not end, this thing between them. The clock ceased to count the hours, and Ariella's reprieve was over. She had awakened the beast inside him, and she ceased to fight the inevitable. She watched and waited to see if he were capable of facing his past and finding the control to move forward. His voice was more controlled, but his anger had no mercy. It was in the cold darkness of his stare. It was in the tightness of his hardened muscles, and she wondered if he would strike her.

David felt hatred coiling inside him. He tasted the bitterness of it as he spoke.

"You could not know this! Only those who have survived know this. I can name those who served under my command, and I can tell you who lives and where they are now, who they married, how many children they now have, and I can tell you which are without an arm or leg, which are blind or damaged in other ways. They are my men. They will always be my men! Who are you to know this?"

Sudden silence filled the air like a reprieve, a hushed prayer evoked by David's pain. It was such a palpable entity that the silence dispelled itself as though of a purloined but sacred nature. A massive head of pure black fur pushed against the body of David Grayson, and then the beast stood abreast of him in a posture that dared anyone to approach, silent and filled with raw primitive purpose. Whatever his purpose, he was tied in some inexplicable way to David Grayson.

Ariella watched the silken head of the gentle giant she loved. As she saw him move closer to David, she understood. Sagath, a gift she dreamed, a gift promised that led her into the forest, saving her from certain death. There was purpose, but it was not wrought without pain, without loss. Always she thought there must be faith, and then she spoke, calmly but with purpose.

"You will find there are no secrets from the MacClaig of the Clan MacClaig."

Her face warmed, as she lifted her eyes, looking up at this man who could turn her stomach into tiny knots with a smile. Then, with her own Scottish stubbornness, she continued.

"Most English like yourself see my grandfather foremost as the prodigious Duke of Rothbur, a peer of eminent power. That image serves his purpose in London, but in Scotland he is a quiescent power, a man who embodies all the word 'clan' means when wrapped in the steel of a thousand years of family loyalty. I know what he knows, but earning the right to be called a MacClaig and gaining his confidence did not come without a price, for he is The MacClaig. Any who doubt this will know what it means to be brought to their knees.

"If you find me unrelenting, then know it is because my grandfather has made me so."

When she spoke, she might have been an imagined princess, stepping from an enchanted castle, for beauty shrouded her with compelling persuasion, but she was not a princess. She was a MacClaig, a Lantenac. Beauty was only a cloak. What was underneath David Grayson would soon learn.

"My grandfather has prepared me, but others, those you would call pirates, have gone beyond what he was willing to teach. I know the sea, David Grayson, and I know the Channel between Portsmouth and Brittany. I know the impassive Eddy stones that hide beneath the waves, those that have caused the deaths of a thousand seamen. I have stood at the helm and guided a hundred sailing ships into the bay and coves of Rotheneuf, and I have stood the watch and held the wheel of the fastest ships made, the *Arrows of the Sea*. I know my grandfather's secrets, and I know his men just as you say you know yours. I was ten when my grandfather gave me into the hands of the most infamous pirate of Rotheneuf and his brigands. Those men, God bless them all, were my family. I have not lived in a castle since my childhood, and my childhood – that is a dead thing I do not wish to remember. Soon we will cross the sea together, and you will see, Lord David. You will see who I really am."

He stared at her in wonder and actually believed she could do this, that she was capable of taking up a sword and fighting in a bloody revolution. He reached out and touched her cheek. Then part in jest, part in truth, he asked,

"So, this Philippe, what is he to you and why must you do as he asks?"

The surprise of his words and the feel of his fingers softly stroking the tiny pulse that now throbbed in the slender curve of her lovely neck left her utterly speechless. Mischief glittered in his very sultry eyes, and she could not fathom what had just happened between them. She had no understanding of why David Grayson had capitulated to her somewhat histrionic and, possibly for him, unbelievable account of her ability to command a corsair. What she was capable of doing was not something any man of the British nobility would easily believe, and yet he now stared at her as though he would truly follow her into battle.

Her fiery nature had left him in awe of the very spirit she possessed. For the first time in his life, he felt as though life could truly have a purpose, even if such a purpose forced him to fight in a bloody revolution.

As though on cue, the giant mahogany door was thrown open but not by the strong and very intimidating force of Darin McCord. In his stead stood Laura Soveneau. Quite a beauty she was, dressed in blue silk the color of a robin's egg, soft but captivating.

Without a second thought she had stormed into the room, not caring that it would be quite obvious she had been listening at the door. As soon as she knew her brother had become part of the mission, she chose not to wait. She had literally propelled herself into the room, looked first at David Grayson, saw his fingertips stroking Ariella's cheek, and then, without the slightest hesitancy, broken their lovers' spell.

"Enough! You are no longer discussing what needs to be done. Both of you forget Nantes, and you forget what is at stake for Philippe." Laura paused to make sure she had both David's and Ariella's full attention. Moistening her lips, she allowed a deep breath for what she planned to say because the persuasion she wished to convey touched close to her own heart.

"My brother, he could be found out at any moment, and the two of you have lost sight of your purpose. This is not about this thing between the two of you. It is not about personal desire, nor about what you try to prove with this heat and anger you throw at each other. This is about a monster who is murdering the priests and children of our homeland, Brittany. This is about the murder of a thousand Bretons, and it is about a devil who forced them onto wooden rafts, rafts so small children could only cling to their mothers and wives to their husbands as their weight began to draw them beneath the currents. Unmarried virgins were stripped naked, tied to the naked bodies of men of their own village and then, together in their shame, they were drowned.

"Philippe could do nothing. He saw Faucher, commanding the rebels. He heard their laughter and heard Faucher's own voice as he declared this act of base depravity a 'republican marriage.' This was his order, his savage cruelty of viciously murdering any who were found to be Royalist sympathizers."

Again she paused, now because her voice had begun to shake, and her throat tightened with tears. She waited to see if the truth of what was happening in Brittany had awakened the need for urgency, and she prayed her sister would not again refuse her help.

Ariella's turn from David was immediate, leaving both with a sense of loss. The thing between them had been real, a moment without their demons, a moment of freedom to love, and now Laura's presence took them back to the truth of what was happening in Brittany, a reminder that the world without was brutal and hopelessly flawed.

Ariella's full attention was now focused on Laura, studying her fear, looking deeply into her eyes. She knew what Laura wanted from her. She knew this the same way a mother knows or the same way a lover sees. The truth is always behind the iris, behind the colors that hide the lights of the soul, like a thousand mirrors, a prism of emotions was there. Laura and she were sisters, closer than blood, for both had been saved from dying only through the safety they had each found within the arms of the other. Laura's arms held Ariella when she had cried for her own mama. What she had seen that day destroyed something she had once known. Now the only truths she knew were but pain wrapped in fear and death. The pain and the fear of losing one you love tied her to Laura, and she remembered all that she owed to Laura. Most of all, she remembered her promise.

She had made a promise when she was only ten, hiding in the tunnels of Broceliande, hiding from Faucher. She clung to the hard earthen walls of the underground tomb where she hid as she heard the sound of horses treading above and the voices of the men who searched for her. She had held Sagath tightly to her breast and prayed for death, prayed that she could return to the arms of her mama and lie with her by the side of her papa.

Her prayers were heard. Whether it was real or imagined, she felt a presence, a serenity. In the darkness of the tunnel the long-dead warriors of Broceliande, those who knew both the warmth and the coldness of the earth, spirits that had once lived and fought against evil, were with her. They alone knew what she had seen: the naked body of her beautiful mama folded in the arms of her dying papa. These were things that could never leave her, but the voices of Broceliande gave her faith that she had survived for a reason. She promised then that she would never see another one she loved with her heart and soul die by the hands of the devil, Faucher. *I will do what must be done. I give my life and all the blood that flows through my veins for one promise. My mama and papa, for them I ask to be given a blade so fine that it cuts the finest line so bleeding comes slowly, so slowly that death lingers, waiting for the dying devil, for Faucher to die by my hand. He will know as his life and all its blackness pour from his soul that there is a price for evil. There is retribution.*

These were the thoughts that filled her soul, and when she looked at Laura, she took on a mask with eyes devoid of emotion. For Laura must never follow her into the dangers she had chosen.

Laura must never know why I cannot take her with me. I will never risk her life. It's better she thinks me cold.

"I know, Laura. They were drowned in the Loire, bound together without hope. Most were priests, their crime their belief in God. The others were children and men and women who refused to forsake their church. Who could be more innocent than those who die for their faith? Your brother, Laura, is my responsibility, not yours! Mine."

David Grayson stared at this vibrant young woman who had forced her entrance. He could not help but be taken aback, for Laura was intoxicating. Still, what impressed him most was that when she turned from her sister to face him, her movements were appreciably calculated. She leaned toward him, offering a view of her perfectly rounded breasts. She did so with such an impressive nonchalance that the effect was sweetly commendable. He thought, *What a little vixen. She knows how to keep a man off balance and vulnerable to her whims.* David smiled. *She would be quite the match for the youngest of the Grayson brothers. If Jack were here, he would be drawn to her like a moth to a flame, for her sensuality leaves no doubt that she would love nothing more than a game of wanton deliberations, something Jack excels at.* David's smile deepened as did his musing. *I would love to place a wager concerning who would conquer whom.*

Turning his attention to Ariella, he was surprised to see her frowning. Her lovely brow tightened, and her eyes showed unmistakable jealousy. His heart skipped a beat.

She is jealous. David observed her bewitching lips, the very ones he remembered kissing, fixed in an unyielding pout. Nervously she brushed back a lost strand of her silken hair, an innocent gesture. Yet as David watched, he imagined his own hand on hers, and he wished, "If only their souls were free of demons, free of what they know of wars and revolutions."

He remembered once being told "if" is not a word meant for soldiers. He remembered, and all he remembered became his own nightmare, the battle of Yorktown where men killed their own comrades. In the moonlight, all colors, all uniforms looked the same, and whom he had killed he would never know. Blood was indistinguishable, whether British or French. It covered them all. Only a hundred men crawled out of the ninth redoubt at the battle of Yorktown.

Ariella was not for him. He was nothing, he was damaged beyond repair, but yet as impossible as it seemed he could not dismiss her, his eyes were glued to this spirited woman, one he knew would never forsake the obligations she had sworn to uphold.

David was like a moth caught by a flame of hypnotic beauty. He indulged his senses, watching as her. With long slender fingers she pulled back the silken veil, transfixing him with violet eyes so deeply colored with her own passions that he was lost in a moment of wonder. Then, like quicksilver, they flashed a fiery warning, refusing to release their own secrets: intensely subdued by familial memories. She was now staring at her sister, and whatever she felt was at the heart of their discord. David saw it, recognizing it at once. He knew something of siblings, of jealousies that simmer unspoken, unheeded, and then explode. He saw an anger that had materialized between them.

Laura's eyes filled with unease for she had struck a tender nerve. She wanted a confrontation. Something between the two needed to be vented, and the teasing and the jealousy she had evoked had worked, but could they resolve the pain that separated them? Sagath had been watching both Laura and Ariella, but now his attention moved to the warmth of the hearth, where logs were bursting into new flame. He was drawn by an earthy smell of oak.

David Grayson stared at the giant beast, reluctant to believe such a creature existed as a pet in the home of one of the wealthiest and most powerful men of the ton in the heart of London's west end.

As though in answer to David's own judgment of what was acceptable to believe and what was not, the massive animal stretched its full length across the hearth, choosing a rug close to the warmth of the fire. He rested his great head on massive paws. His eyes, dark as coal, stared directly into the flames, ignoring everything except the dancing embers. David's own gaze followed. The colors were unearthly flames that transformed into a phantasmal prism of magic. For a moment he shared with the giant wolf another place and another time where mystery and reality blended. The flames he watched held him for a moment, and then he blinked and thought,

> *What a strange beast. He's an aberration that makes no sense here in this upper echelon of London's nobility, but then neither does his beautiful mistress nor her sister. Something between them is unre-*

solved, and I think it vexes them, like an open wound that neither will tend to.

Why do they play such games? They only hurt each other. He continued to study the two, surmising that Laura wished to break through her sister's protective barriers. She knew Ariella hid her feelings masterfully, cloaking her anger and possibly her pain.

Laura's eyes darkened with concern as she watched to see if her actions had taken a nick out of her sister's protective amour. She knew when Ariella's spine stiffened, and she and David noticed the slight tremble in Ariella's hands as she gathered her long satin dress closer, unconsciously gripping the soft fabric. A blush of fiery heat appeared on her cheeks as she tried to cool her temper.

David knew she was wavering on a line of impropriety, one that she tried desperately to master. She tried to be a lady, to follow the *ton's* genteel rules of behavior.

More than once Laura had wished to see the tables turn on her sister, to see her frozen heart melt just a little. She thought, *I would wager a hundred quid Ariella has never felt one prurient longing nor one ounce of jealousy until now, until David Grayson.*

She watched as Ariella failed to manage the emotions tightening inside her. Anger showed in her dark violet eyes, in the tightness of her brow. The sound of her voice was harsh, wrapped in anger. Laura listened, already knowing nothing would ever change between the two of them.

"Laura, you irascible hoyden! You know as well as I do this is not the time to tease and act like a flirting strumpet!'

Unbridled exasperation filled the air between the two. Laura refused to stand quietly by and be dictated to.

"Call me whatever you choose! We both know you will do anything you can to keep me here, to keep me from returning to Brittany. You are a coward, Ariella Lantenac, MacClaig, or whatever you choose to call yourself. I am more than a sister to you. I am the one who saved your life, remember?"

Ariella did not look at her. She pulled back toward the hearth, toward Sagath, and replied as though her sister's demand to go with her to Brittany had never been voiced.

"The plan is made and was made long before the missive arrived from Philippe. If it were not for Pitt and his manipulation of the émigrés, I would need no one, certainly not a rake such as David Grayson, and as for you, Laura, you have no training. Your place is here. What the two of you know is only what Pitt permits, what cannot stay hidden. The atrocities of the sans-culottes, the massive murders ordered by General Faucher, those have witnesses. Both you and David know what happened in Nantes.

"What I seek is hidden: the orders, the motivations of those who serve by coercion, and those who wait to turn the tide, to stop the storm. Only by knowing these things can I stop the murders of innocents. Everything I do is cloaked by secrets, and I do not share my secrets."

Ariella paused.

David, feeling he had been left out of this conversation far too long and attempting to change the course of the anger he heard in the voices of both Ariella and Laura, cocked his handsome brow, gave a knowing smile, and added, "Because the first rule of any spy worth his or her salt is 'trust no one'!"

Ariella glared at him, thinking, *He is too damn cocky, and I would like nothing better than to smack his cheeky face.*

Laura stared at both Grayson and this sister of her heart. She wished to reach inside Ariella's heart to remind her of all they shared. They were tied by the murders they had witnessed and the secrets they now kept. Even when separated by Ariella's grandfather, what they knew of Broceliande had stayed wrapped within them, smelted iron fused to their souls.

After they arrived in Scotland and they were physically healed from their wounds, everything changed. Ariella's anger and hate became the only emotions she could feel, and she welcomed them into every fiber of her being. Nothing would dissuade her from her desire to return to Brittany to kill Faucher. Neither her grandfather's love nor the comfort he offered would dissuade her. A battle of wills between Ariella and The McClaig began, and its destructive path was heartbreaking.

The McClaig's words to his granddaughter came from his own past and they were the same all McClaig's were baptized with.

"Live or die! If you die, you were never meant to be a McClaig of the Clan McClaig. If you take the blood oath, then it is the only oath you will ever follow. Know this, girl! If you falter one hair's breadth from the razor's edge you swear to walk, no one will pull you back because McClaigs never turn aside. You face it, the blood debt. It takes your life, or you take the life of Faucher. Girl or not, if you choose this way, a way that fills you with blood revenge, then do it as a McClaig. If you survive where I send you, then you will be a McClaig of blood iron, and you will know how to kill or lie or steal because, my very beautiful girl, there is no other way to survive when you decide to fight monsters like Faucher. You have the choice of being a lady, protected and cherished by men who love you, or of being a McClaig bent on revenge."

Laura had seen sadness in the face of Hamish McClaig. His hard-weathered features looked vulnerable, and his lips tightened from words he forced himself to say. Laura saw tears behind those silver grey eyes and knew he had found no recourse, no part of reason that could reach the princess.

When Hamish sent Ariella to Taggart McClure, Laura was not permitted to go with her sister. Left behind and without any way to return to Brittany, she remained at the request and generosity of the Duke of Rothbur, and he was a man who did nothing without purpose. She was tutored and indulged in refinements befitting a lady and made aware that for every comfort she received, her friend had none. It was all done to break Ariella; it was the way of Rothbur. Refuse him and pay the price.

> *She will never let me go with her. I stayed behind for eight years, and she believed I was safe from the dangers that our lives were due. For such as me, one who knows the same things as Ariella, there is no safeguard. A paragon of the ton's esteems, a lady by my own pretense. I now own it. I am what I am, but Ariella, she is steel, the same that lies in that stubborn spine of Hamish McClaig. Never have I known two more pig-headed and willful humans. Hamish bartered her to a damnable pirate, a gunrunner, and a deplorable Scotsman, a man I feel is close in kin to McClaig's own clan.*

Laura knew; she knew the truth of how much those eight years had separated them. She knew, and she closed her thoughts like a steel trap, refusing any more sadness to filter through. Incensed with her own failings, she responded with hurt and anger.

"Go! Find Philippe and Daniel and even Pierre. Find Faucher! Kill the guilty and free the innocents, and then, if you still live, find the graves you seek, but do not shed any tears for me, for I will shed none for you. I will do your bidding, my princess, but if you die there alone without me, you will never be free of the ghosts of Broceliande!"

Ariella's face lit up as she felt it, tasted it, Laura's own bittersweet form of loving endearment.

"Don't be such a child, Laura. You will stay! I will return, and Philippe will be fine. Maybe I will even bring Daniel back with me for you to torture with your flirting machinations. You have overlearned your *lady* etiquette and grown bored with it. I think your underhanded coquettishness serves us both best when you stay here. Attend the social events of the *ton* and take from all the men who have any political standing every bit of useful information they divulge.

"Enough!" David Grayson's composure snapped. Sagath sensed his mood change and knew he was now ready to end this fruitless discourse. The time had arrived for a final word, and Sagath raised his head from the other world the embers gained for him. Removing himself from the transcendence of a solitary serenity, his giant head lifted, his ears now raised, and an intelligent awareness in his dark eyes waited.

Something had changed, and it was time to go back to Broceliande. The game had ended, the game of sisters. Who suffered more, who loves more, and who will win the endgame? That was done. The verbal duel was over, and now was the time for a real plan, for the stuff that espionage really survives by was subterfuge, lies, and a strong backup of murdering bastards!

Chapter 7

DISCOVERY

The Duke of Summerville's home was as Ariella expected: a grand Romanesque mansion, framed by giant columns, pilasters, and accents of ornamentation. The stucco finish gave it a clean and modern veneer as opposed to the more traditional brick covering of most houses in Mayfair.

The three of them, Laura Soveneau, Ariella, and David Grayson, followed the butler, a long-term servant by the name of Bartholomew. At first, he did not recognize the young lord he had cared for at Summerville, but once he did, all guise of decorum broke. David watched his old friend as the heavy lines sunk deep within his face disappeared. His somber expression, chiseled by years of servitude, lifted like a curtain, as the truth of his feelings for David Grayson sparkled with warmth. The special kinship he had felt for this brave boy sparkled in his eyes, and a hint of tears floated free as he embraced David.

Bartholomew's arms tightened with emotion, then with an embarrassed smile, he pulled back from the embrace. His pride for David, "his own brave lad," who for so many years had endured abuse by a tyrannical father, swelled his chest and allowed one bit of the glistening moisture to dampen his cheek.

"My boy! You brighten my day! Once the war was over, I waited for you to return, and now, well, you will see. You will see what the Graysons together, what you and your brothers can make of Summerville! The three of us, my wife Mary, Lucy, my only daughter, and myself, are still here, my lad. If it is true that you plan to take a wife, then we are twice blessed with your return." He paused then, but showed no shyness as he gave a beaming smile to Ariella. His blue-grey eyes sparkled with pride, and he couldn't help but add, "She is a beauty, my lad, a true and rare beauty." If not for Liza, the maidservant to his right, waiting to help, the old gentleman might have gone a bit further with his memories. Liza's distinct "Aahem!" gave him pause, but not for a minute did her obvious rebuke shatter his happiness.

Even at sixty Bartholomew was still a stately man. Well over six feet, he squared his shoulders, lifted his large barrel chest, and regained a posture of dignity. Then, with his smile still evident, he went so far as to give Liza a slight rebuff, just a frown of his brow and his serious look, where he attempted to tighten the lips while jutting his chin slightly forward. If ever a man were ill-fitted for his size and stature, it was Bartholomew. His male height and girth were intimidating and even his stately composure, but when he tried to look threatening, something in his eyes gave way to an undeniable tenderness, and he fooled no one.

Liza loved him, as did all the serving staff, so in respect for his feelings, she bowed sweetly and replied, "Yes, of course. Please, sir, excuse my behavior," and then, with a swift and silent turn, she disappeared.

With complete composure, he directed the three guests to the drawing room where all the Graysons were waiting with grand curiosity.

Even though Ariella was within arm's-reach of David Grayson, she smoothed her dress. She needed to feel safe, to soothe her mind. She needed to know her small blade, razor McKinney, was there, in its own secret fold. Survival was an ingrained part of her education, survival she had learned from Taggart McClure:

Never leave yourself vulnerable. Forget everyone who is given for your protection; there is never need to count. The number is always one. You, my lovely child, will soon learn who protects whom on my ship and on my watch.

Taggart McClure, a bull of a man, stubborn and ferocious, had been her teacher, and she learned from him. So well, in fact, that she became a bit like him. The sea changed her, and Taggart McClure changed her. He was the one who saved her from turning inside herself and dying.

She had told herself give David the lead; play the lady and think only of the mission. Patience first, then the ruse. Subterfuge was the key to success, and they must convince the Graysons and the rest of the *ton* of their engagement. Once done, her plan could fall into place: the trip to free Philippe and the transportation of the guns: that Pitt had agreed to send to Saint-Malo. She knew David was right to establish a cover for them, but whatever devilry lurked inside her would not be quiet. She pulled close to his ear, her lips almost touching him. She wished to take a bite out of him, to make him feel as frustrated as she felt. Softening her voice, she let her femininity pull him as tight as she dared.

"So, my Gray prince, my Machiavellian rake, I will be your besotted naïveté. I will rub against you and purr like a kitten, and then do you believe the Graysons will believe the Duke of Rothbur has given permission for you, a disreputable second son without title or wealth, to become my husband?"

Ahhh, he mused as his eyes, now darkened by sexual promise, met and held hers. *She knows nothing of men who spy for the crown, who play games without the luxury of rules. I think, my sweet, I should teach you that virtue and chivalry do not exist in the back alleys of London nor in the rookeries that crawl with swindlers and thieves. My lovely lady, it will be my pleasure to play your game to show you there is nothing pure or noble in this job of espionage.*

With that thought, he pulled her into a heady embrace, tasting her lips before she realized his soft mouth had persuaded her to respond.

His timing was impeccable. The giant mahogany doors swung open, and she was there, standing in front of the Grayson brothers with her lips fully responding to those of the prodigal brother, David Grayson.

He pulled back from her responsive lips just to the tip of her earlobe where he whispered, "Yes, my sweet, I know I can. Your lips melt with desire that I think now is evident to all the Graysons."

Her hand went to the blade folded within her dress pocket so quickly it took the best of David's reflexive response to hold her close enough to steady her, close enough for her to feel the strength of his very male body. His eyes darkened with a wicked intention. Then he spoke, his voice that of a devilish rake resonating with sexual desire. "Not now, my love. Later we can play with whatever blades you choose."

The endearment surprised her. *"Love."* She was not his love, more like a thorn in his side. She preferred his displeasure, for when his hand touched her, when he pulled her close, she felt undone. The warmth, the strength of his very firm touch were so pleasurable, a feeling she could not handle unraveled her, causing her to tremble with a need to draw even closer. These were emotions she did not wish to feel, and her only weapon was to turn her desire for David Grayson into something she could control.

Anger was her refuge, and it filled her like quicksilver. Once again, she thanked Taggart McClure, a damnable freebooter, but the best profiteer of the Emerald Seas. His words came back to her like a jolt of lightning:

"Know, mah wilde beastie, mah wee lioness, when jesting is over and when a hard, unbending backbone is needed."

His words went through her, reminding her why she was here. David Grayson was a devil when he set his mind to play the charming rake, and she was a fool for responding to him, for playing his games.

Farmers and their wives and children in Nantes depended on her. A thousand had been drowned in the Loire, and it was only a matter of time before Faucher planned more executions. Ariella forced her thoughts back to the Duke and Duchess of Summerville and the Grayson brothers, all watching her and waiting for her to respond. David had purposely embarrassed her and insulted his family. Now the Graysons waited to see exactly what she would do.

She thought of wicked things she would like to do to David Grayson, short of his untimely death. A hard knee to his groin would have been immensely satisfying. With that thought, her eyes deepened, became more purple and less translucent. Her breathing steadied, and her hands relaxed, one now resting on David's arm and the other softly smoothing her velvet gown. She blinked away the room's distractions. David Grayson, duke and duchess, all disappeared. Gathering her self-control, she reminded herself control was her talisman. It separated her from the frightened child she had once been, the child she had been when first meeting Captain Taggart McClure, friend and *brathair* to her grandfather. He had called her a sad wee lion, as though he had immediately known her name. Ariella, her given name from her papa, meant "lioness of God," and she, when she walked aboard the *Red Dragon*, was an *enfant terrible*, a sad, angry little beast. She wondered if she had been partly mad then or just the sad little beastie he called her. Before the tutelage of Taggart McClure, her anger had taken her into a place void of light, void of trust and friendship, but this was not the time nor the place for memories. Now she must undo the damage that her despicable partner David Grayson had incurred.

She steadied her resolve, and from her repertoire of well-practiced manners, she fashioned a perfect response befitting the granddaughter of the Duke of Rothbur.

She looked now at the Grayson's, every lovely inch of her, the perfect lady. She paused, waiting for their full attention. Her commanding presence brought a silence to the room and her voice resonated with undeniable nobility. She introduced herself.

"Ariella MacClaig, granddaughter of Hamish McClaig, The McClaig of the Clan McClaig and Duke of Rothbur." She paused, looking directly into the eyes of the Duke of Summerville. Then she continued, "I offer an apology. It seems my betrothed endeavors to live up to a reputation as a rake and philanderer."

Pausing once more, she looked now at the three brothers: Edward, Charles, and, the most handsome of all, Jack Grayson. She knew David was just to the right of her. She could feel his devilish smile as she waited for her temper to dissipate. His thoughts had always been clear. He believed she was unfit for this game of pretense and espionage. He did not know the Ariella McClaig who had commanded the *Red Dragon*. David Grayson knew nothing. He thought he could intimidate her, and that was the rub she waited for. No one, ever again, would crush her soul as Faucher had done. She would never be that child again, a girl child worthless to avenge the evil of such men as Faucher. Her thoughts brought steel to her spine, and she thought of the honey-soaked words she knew, words to sway the Graysons, to ingratiate them to her charms. *Just you listen, Lord David Grayson, and you will learn how easily your three brothers can be persuaded to come to the rescue of a woman who asks for their male gallantry. Watch me and see how easily I can charm the Grayson men.*

With the smile of an angel, in all her beauty, she stepped one step toward David's brothers, leaving him to watch as the firelight touching her put him directly in her shadow. The three handsome brothers did not dare interject one word, for they eagerly waited to see what Ariella might say next about their scapegrace of a brother.

Even though Ariella bristled with desire to tell them what she really thought in words she had learned from her crewmates on board the *Red*

Dragon, she tempered her anger with her need to repair David's devilry.

"I hope to affect Lord David Grayson's reputation to his betterment. Although he keeps his best qualities hidden, so even I must strive to find them. Clearly, he has inherited a handsome bearing from his family. As to his behavior, I can see he is the one rare scoundrel of the Grayson family. I have no doubt that the dukedom of Summerville is entailed by gentlemen, all of the finest caliber."

Silence filled the huge paneled room accented by grand tapestry and exquisite wall hangings. Not one Grayson said a word to embarrass her. The smile she slowly and masterfully effected captured a perfect poise of innocence. Her ebony lashes fell slightly, and with the expertise of a gifted actress she became, at least by way of pretense, an innocent. Her compelling transformation persuaded the duke to believe the kiss had been forced upon her and she was as unblemished as a diamond of the first water. It was not the first time William Grayson chose to believe the worst of his brother.

With a glare that could freeze the devil, he remained ramrod-straight, his thunderous retort giving total absolution to Ariella and all the blame to his brother.

"My scapegrace of a brother does not show even a pretense of decency, while you, my lady, are an image of refinement. How David has managed to persuade such a rare jewel to accept his courtship I cannot imagine."

The duke did not offer his brother even a token glance. He knew all too well what he would see: a merry sparkle of mischief in those damned Grayson eyes that would always remind him he was sired by the same evil bastard. Repressing a scowl, aware the remainder of the Grayson brood watched him, he unclenched his teeth and turned to his duchess. He was embarrassed, feeling somehow responsible for his brother's behavior.

Elizabeth, with a flick of her wrist, opened her fan and, holding it close to her cheek for privacy, whispered softly to her husband, "Your

Grace, I think it is important that we let Rothbur's granddaughter choose what happens next."

The duke saw how quickly his wife's expression had changed from surprise to reserved curiosity. This girl had the face of a goddess, and he wondered if his wife was calculating her worth. A beautiful woman, in regard to the beau monde, could command, especially if she were the granddaughter of the Duke of Rothbur, a great deal of prestige for the Graysons.

Ariella wasted no time proving she was nothing like the ladies of the *ton*, those of molded expectations, tutored from the nursery to prove themselves the essence of splendid propriety.

The Grayson men, having attended Season after Season and watched the annual parade of debutantes, were caught completely off guard. They had never met the likes of Ariella MacClaig or Laura Soveneau. They knew fresh young debutantes and they knew lightskirts, but the heiress of Rothbur and her companion were from a different world, tutored in skills that had little similarity to the lessons taught in the finest English finishing schools. Both Ariella and Laura were from Broceliande. There was an unexplained enchantment bestowed on them by whatever magic had kept them alive. The two had clung to each other, babes in the heart of the forest. They had hidden within the ancient tunnels dug deep by those before them, other innocents who had also attempted to escape the tyranny of villains such as Faucher. The lives they might have had disappeared the moment they witnessed men maddened by evil murder and rape women they knew and loved. Neither Ariella nor Laura would ever again be free enough in spirit to claim the unburdened soul of gentle womanhood. They had survived by sheer will. The ideal of a woman's ultimate necessity – being born to express love – that ideal had died the same as they would have died, if indeed they had succumbed to the evil of Faucher.

Ariella looked first at Jack. He was youth personified and he was endowed with the devil's own charm. Handsome as sin, tall, golden, and immensely sure of himself. She thought, *He will be the easiest of all to deal with, for I have brought Laura, and she will have him on a plate before the evening concludes.*

Her first smil she gave to Jack and then watched as he sauntered forward. A bit of the wolf played in his manner: slow, teasing, but narcissistically confident. His wide shoulders and Herculean frame dwarfed her own slender form. Without pause and with an intoxicating charm, she, like a magical enchantress, exchanged positions with Laura. Before Jack had completed his gentleman's bow, the two lovely ladies had reversed places, and as he looked up expecting the lavender eyes of Ariella, he saw instead blue eyes of infinite sensual invitation, and for the first time in his life he stuttered in the presence of a lady.

"Myyu mh... lady, you take me by surprise!"

Jack Grayson found himself speechless. Never had any encounter left him, so incredibly undone, so lost in his own confidence; he just stared like a green schoolboy.

A strand of his hair, longer than the current fashion, fell across his sun-bronzed cheek, bringing even more attention to his blush. This, he felt, was the end of him. Every one of his damnable brothers had watched his rakish charm fail, had watched while he, like a bumbling schoolboy, failed miserably in his attempt to play the dashing cavalier.

Laura knew immediately what Ariella had thrown her into. " She wishes me to help her separate the brothers, keep their focus away from David." Then, with her lips poised to a pouting whisper and her fingers lingering close to his nether regions, she crafted a perfect response to his blundering greeting.

"My lord, it seems I am in need of your hand, for mine lingers in want of your guidance."

His bow, her hand, his immediate step toward her, and her devious timing had all undone him. All he could do now was move closer, speak softly, and pray the attention in the room left him to repair his awkward blunder in a more private corner of the room where he endeavored to move, trying to entice Laura to follow.

For a moment Laura's eyes met Ariella's, and they were true sisters, each knowing what must be done. Laura actually looked forward to playing a bit tonight with Lord Jack Grayson.

Ariella, her confidence fully unleashed, felt the Graysons yielding to her persuasions. *Charm the two remaining brothers. Convince them that you have accepted David's troth, and you will be free to make your way to Brittany.*

Taggart's voice, ingrained into her memory, held tight, directing her. *Always, moi wee lion, always walk forward, one hand close to a dagger, but dunna be a fool. Never turn your back to one you canna trust.*

She trembled slightly. Was David close to her now? Could she trust him, or did he wait for her to fail? He must wish her to do so, for he did nothing, said nothing to give credence to their betrothal. He had told her of the bet between his brothers and himself. Now, when it was of the utmost importance that he prove his worth, he refused to be anything other than the ass he seemed to pride himself on imitating.

If it is failure you are waiting for, Lord David Grayson, just you wait! You know nothing about me. I had no gentle mother's hand to teach me lessons of tenderness. Broceliande kept me safe; it kept me until I was no longer afraid of death. The spirits of the dead, the dead of Broceliande, walk with me, and they alone know my heart.

The room was warm, subdued. Shadows emerged and disappeared, cast by the flames of the burning logs from the large fireplace. Hardwood and oak turned to cinders, filling the air, reminding Ariella of Broceliande, the forest and those waiting for her to return. She breathed. Now her eyes focused on Charles Grayson and his brother Edward.

They were strong, muscular, with the Grayson stamp of rakish charm. Not as tall as David nor cursed with his indefinable hard veneer of masculine superiority that drew women like flies, all the same they were exceptionally handsome men. Smartly dressed in the latest fashion, close to Beau Brummel perfection, they appeared confident, proud of their gentle bearing.

Her smile deepened. She composed herself as elegantly as any lady of the *haut ton* might be expected to and paused as she took a glass of sherry from the salver of one of the attending servants. Before she brought the dark-rose sherry to her lips, she took one more look at David Grayson. He watched her, testing her with his insolent behavior and his devilish smile, waiting for her next move. She knew he played with her because he wished her to withdraw from the mission. He still thought of her as a woman, and women, as she had been told by more than one of Pitt's agents, should not be spies.

The world spins in chaos, she thought. Revolutions do not spare women nor grant them mercy. David Grayson, I am not your lady. I am not made from the stuff that most men imagine a woman to be. My eyes were opened in the dark tunnels under the earth, the tunnels of Broceliande, and there I learned from the spirits of the dead what happens when a woman does not fight back. So, you see, David Grayson, I have no intention of being a token of society's invention.

She turned her attention to the other Grayson brothers and to another who she had not been aware of before, a lovely young lady, dressed in blue satin, sitting at the grand piano. Her presence had been obstructed by the Graysons for they had gathered round her listening to her play before she and David had entered the room. The lovely young girl, the elegant duke and his duchess, and all the Graysons were an embodiment of the highest tier of London society. Most lived in a safe, insular place, one that little understanding of those outside their chosen circle. They knew nothing of the machinations of politics turning and twisting the fate of nations. What did any of it matter if all their battles were fought in the drawing room where none of their own blood was spilled?

Two handsome brothers waited with champagne in hand, looking dapper but unable to conceal a bit of impatient intensity. Charles wore a frilled white shirt and an impeccably knotted cravat beneath his fitted black waistcoat. Edward was attired in black velvet with long tails, tailored to complement his broad shoulders. Their smiles were a bit too complacent, she thought. *They think all is well and that the bet they made with David is in play for their amusement.* She smoothed her silken gown one more time, one of the few tells she permitted herself when she grew nervous.

> *"Watch the eyes, Ariella. Always watch the eyes! Find it: a flutter, a darkness, a thing so subtle it may seem unimportant, there in his eyes before his hand moves to do you harm. You will die, my wee lion, if you do not learn the smallest nuance of every man. Be he wicked or be he kind, it doesn't matter, my wee one, if dying is the price you pay."*

She thanked the old salty pirate Taggart as she used her powers of observation to study the Grayson brothers. Only one of the five gave her cause to worry: David Grayson.

The intent focus of his eyes, the slow dilation of his pupils turning his emerald eyes to a dark purpose, was evident, at least to her. He simply could not be in the same room with his brothers for more than two minutes without wishing to push every tender nerve or secret each possessed.

David, like a pugnacious hooligan looking for a fight, raised his wine glass in a mock salute, then looked directly at his brother, and with the devil's own guile, he said,

"Ah, Edward, it seems I have been too long from the *ton*. I discovered, while enjoying a brandy at White's, the Grays have become a source of amusement. At least his lordship, Oliver Blair, seemed to think so. He asked if I had placed a wager yet. Both your name and Edward's made the top of White's list. It is said that by proxy, of course, even Old Nobs has laid a wager."

Edward's smile disappeared instantly. His green eyes lost their mirth, and he might as well have been a boy of ten facing his older brother. Edward, though a well-built and handsome man, was the runt of the Grayson litter. What he remembered was always being beaten. In every contest of skill their bastard of a father had forced them to endure, he was the loser. David was the worst opponent. He gave no quarter and did not stop even for tears, tears that humiliated in ways a boy wishing to be a man could never forget.

His jaw dropped. His smile and the pleasure he had felt on first seeing David vanished, and he knew they would once again fight, no holds barred. What hurt the most was that they both knew the truth of the reason David Grayson would never let go of his anger and the reason they could not break from the sins of their father. David had once pushed his face so deep into the mire that he gasped for air. Edward had thought he would die, and he remembered wondering whether it would matter, for when they were boys, their mother dead and no one to give them even the slightest bit of kindness, it seemed that all the Grays were a bit dead already. All of them were stuck in their own mire, dying for lack of love. All he could do now was yell and try to fight back so neither he nor David would have to remember or forgive.

"What the hell are you talking about? How dare you imply either Charles or I have engaged in any questionable conduct!"

"Questionable? No, there is nothing questionable about your political choices. In fact, they seem crystal clear.

"To the contrary of what Lord Blair or any of the other *ton*'s gentlemen might say, I think you should count yourself in company with London's finest. I am told William Pitt himself loves sheep more than crofters and is proud to be among the progressive, meaning, of course, he is a Whig, and he sees the prospect of setting one thousand tenant farmers out of home as only a necessary part of inevitable progress, for, after all, grazing land for sheep is a better investment than providing a livelihood for poor farmers and their families."

David paused. Something about David defied anyone to call him a liar. His bearing commanded the room with an unarguable truth. It was there, an unbending sense of right and wrong, within his eyes. Beautiful Grayson green eyes, charming women when he desired, now they smoldered like embers that would never lose their fire, fueled by memory. David knew, had seen and held in his arms those who had lost all hope. He may have walked away from the pit of hell in Yorktown, but he would never again think himself immune to the suffering of others. His unbending sense of morality made him a formidable man to deal with, even if only words rather than swords were used. He timed the moment and waited until he knew the fire of his own convictions had gained the interest of all the Grays, then he continued.

"How do the sheep at Summerville fare, given their newfound freedom in inheriting a thousand acres for grazing?"

Edward's handsome face, with its patrician nose and high cheekbones, had lost its Grayson charm and was now marked with anger. He seemed more his father's son than the brother David had saved once from the duke's belt. His hand gripping the champagne flute far too tightly, he took a step forward. His intent was not clear, but it did seem evident that he was a man more likely to settle any dispute with his fists rather than discourse.

Charles watched and waited as usual, ready to intervene, always the peacemaker, or so he thought. He prided himself on his ability to abash any who might be arrogant enough to challenge his moral integrity. He was an Eton man, a Cambridge man, a man given the best sources possible to be sensitive to the world's current political state. David, he believed, only saw England's position from the viewpoint of a soldier, knowing nothing of the broad scope of war's necessity. He knew his brother had fallen from the ton's perspective, and he refused to follow suit. He took on David's challenge, convinced he, not David, served the moral high ground. His voice booming and his shoulders back, he felt confident in his posture of righteous indignation.

"How dare you pretend to care about Summerville! Ten years! You have not graced our threshold for ten years. When the hard winters took our crops, where were you, David Grayson? Hiding away, nursing your war wounds, and living by means of your inheritance, earning nothing by the bending of your own knee or the sweat of your brow. Is it the prideful arrogance in you that keeps you away from Summerville? You are a Grayson. That blood is far too thick to flow through any man's veins without him knowing the truth of who he is!"

David knew the implication. Always, always it referred to the man they all hated, their sire, and their bloodline. It only angered him more.

"Ah! But listen! First, dear brother, I did not say I cared for Summerville. Summerville is a place that I left behind when I defended your arse against our tyrant of a father. No, it is not Summerville that could be in imminent danger. It is you and all the pompous aristocrats who welcome so-called progress by evicting countless farmers from land their families have called home for over three generations.

"It is the peasants I speak of. The question is whether the peasants will grow weary of starvation and simply revolt. After all, France is an inspiration for them as were the American Colonies. My dear brother, it is your safety I question."

Everyone stared without uttering one word, for division was now the issue. The accusation of starving one thousand people – women, men and children – and forcing them from their homes was a heady charge and an explosive one. David had done exactly what he intended: forced his family, all of them, to look directly into their consciences to consider the suffering political choices inflicted on those who lived without the means to survive.

Edward's hands began to sweat, and every thought dissipated into thin air, except these words:

He is winning, Edward! David has you, and if he does not push your face into the dung, then one of the crofters' boys will! Get up, you piece of sorry shit!

His father, their father. Once again everything between him and David was a blur of abusive memories, distorted by one evil bastard.

"You are implying that we do not care for our crofters, for their families!"

"Nothing of the kind. I am confirming or disproving the bet. After all, isn't it the mark of a gentleman to make such bets, to prove himself more daring, more raffish than his fellow gamesters at White's? Didn't Lord Alvanley once bet three thousand pounds on which of two raindrops would first reach the bottom of the pane of the bow window? How could such bets be other than edifying, providing much needed amusement for the *crème de la crème* of society? So, dear brother, please confirm or deny."

"Deny! Confirm! What is this damnable, fabricated bet you speak of?"

Perfect. David smiled. *Perfect!* Now for the final thrust. His lips faintly whispered, "*Touché.*"

Only Ariella heard, and every nerve in her body tensed as she waited for the trap to spring.

"The bet, the bet! Aaah! Yes, the bet!" David's eyes grew cold. He paused, forcing the moment to intensify. He gave way to a half-hearted smile as he thought how their own ancestry would have damned them forever in the eyes of the *ton* if any knew their Scots-Irish roots, but his father had buried that bit of trivia long ago. The room grew quiet as David completed his barely veiled accusation:

"One thousand pounds now promised by the Duke of Raymond bets that both of the Grayson brothers, Edward Grayson and Charles Grayson, will be married in one year's time to the daughters of the Duke of Sutherland, and they will join the ranks of the most hated landlords to ever engage in the destruction of the clans of the Highlands."

"You are beyond the pale! No one, not one bloody member of White's, not one bloody member of the *beau monde* would ever suggest such actions in regard to the Sutherlands. They own the Highlands, one million acres. They own the House of Lords. No one throws such accusations at the Sutherlands!"

"Ah, and so my point rests, confirmed by you. Granted, I did embellish the wording in the bet a tad, but then the facts remain. Ill-gotten wealth, by way of replacing a thousand souls with sheep. That fact alone defines their morality, and now it seems our family names could be joined."

Everyone in the room was stunned, with the exception of the lovely wisp of a girl who had been partially hidden by the two Graysons, Edward and Charles. The silent and seemingly invisible, fae-like creature had been seated at the grand piano playing, with exceptional skill one of the softer, most captivating quartets of Beethoven. She was one of the Graysons' hidden secrets, a bastard daughter of their father. Her place in this family of combustible male virility was precarious at best, and she pulled into herself as she had always done when she found she was in a battle of such fire.

Ariella MacClaig tightened every muscle in her small but impressively strong hands as she now twisted rather than stroked her velvet skirts, obviously seeking a way to control her own emotions. Her voice belied the anger that her lovely hands had betrayed for she spoke with a voice of feminine charm.

"Gentlemen! Please, your enthusiasm has stolen my breath. I feel such strength in your words. Ladies cannot endure such heat. The implications made against the Sutherlands must be forgiven."

Ariella, as astutely as a soldier might place himself between warring forces, put herself between David and his brother Edward.

Edward could not help but notice how soft her hand felt as she touched his arm to pull him back from a heated confrontation. He, like the other men Ariella had chosen to entice with her lovely smile, responded to her touch, looked into her eyes, and reached for her hand gently placing it on his own arm. That, unknown to him and everyone in the room, was a grave mistake.

David did not like other men to touch Ariella. The touch, his brother's hand touching Ariella, was like fire to his own flesh. He lost control. Like a berserker maddened by blood fever, he reached for his brother, but quicker than his intended grasp, Ariella turned her lovely body toward him, trying once again to salvage the situation.

"My Lord David," her eyes begged him to back down, to calm his anger, "let us consider what your brother might say. Surely the Sutherlands are not so indifferent to the crofters."

Edward seized this opportunity and spoke with his own misguided and heady self-righteousness.

"Quite right, my lady! The duchess is giving them the seashore, six thousand acres of seashore, two acres for each family."

For a moment David met Ariella's silent plea, but then his brother had, with his own ignorance, undone it all. David's retort held back none of his contempt.

"Giving them? Bloody hell, she is giving them nothing! She is charging them rent, and they have nothing but sand and ocean. They eat fish if they are lucky, but for the most part they starve and die!"

Edward was lost for a response. Once more he was the brother on the losing end. His fists hardened, and he came at David like a bat out of hell!

Ariella saw it coming. Whatever Taggart might have said in way of taming her temper was insignificant, for all she could feel was the fierce anger inherent in her blood for she was half Gaelic. The granddaughter of the McClaig of the Clan McClaig would never allow such inhumanity to go unpunished, and by all that was holy, no one, surely no high-and-mighty Sassenach, could sanction such actions.

Edward's fist was only inches from David's hard-rock jaw. His blow never made contact. He felt a hard wrench on his forearm and his balance was thrown. He watched in slow motion as the slip of a woman, Ariella, sent him to the floor propelled by his own momentum.

What the hell had she done? In a split-second she had surely destroyed it all. Any Grayson who had thought her a proper lady, by God's breath, thought so no longer. With reflexes quicker than a cat's she had perfectly demonstrated every bit of martial arts she had learned on the *Red Dragon*, and now, how in Hades could she repair this disaster?

Before a word was spoken, she felt David encircle her with arms more comforting and more heartfelt than she had known could be possible.

He looked into her questioning but very lovely eyes and said with an unexpected sincerity, albeit with a rakish smile,

"My lady, you make me proud! Surely with such a display of support for your betrothed, no one could ever question that we are truly well suited."

CHAPTER 8

THE RED DRAGON

The ship rocked. David stood back from the gunwale and steadied his posture, grateful that he had nothing left in his stomach to empty. He could no longer see the stars; the twilight had deepened. He watched, appreciative of the breeze that touched his face, cooled his brow, and helped him to regain his sense of propriety. As the stars began to disappear, he watched the helmsman turn toward the large binnacle housing the ship's compass.

Jock McKinney carried a name the same as the sharpest blade in all the 'Seven Seas', and was proud to be related to the Master Cutler who deisgned such a weapon. Jock was not a man to trifle with. Nothing about this man suggested he was easy. He was as hard a man as the Highlands could make and as weathered as any seaman who sailed the Emerald Coast. He was a Scotsman through and through, and the name he had chosen for himself was done by pure malice. He had made sure David was aware.

"If any Englishman so much as calls my name, I am within my rights to bloody his ugly face. They know. We all know. *Jock!* It's what they call us Scots to our backs. Now let them insult me to my face. Be my turn to get in a few licks, make up for all their thieving of our land. Nothing but bloody bastards, the lot of them. Killed my poor Da, turned their bloody sheep loose on our land, and drove us to the sea," he had proclaimed all of this to David, the first time they met. It had been a warning, so even now, as David heard the footsteps of another man approaching, he kept his focus on the helmsman. It was the way of spies: Never turn into a man coming from behind. Wait until you judge the proper distance for him to make his presence known. If he does not, prepare for the worst.

Taggart McClure's dark grey eyes were boring holes in David Grayson's head.

"The only reason you are alive on my ship is the Lady Ariella, and the promise made before I took you aboard, that too has kept you from my blade. You abide by her wishes. Or I'll sink you so far down no one will ever see you again, David Grayson, no one but the bloody fish!"

Taggart, six feet of the fiercest-looking pirate imaginable, was solid mass, with arms that could squeeze the breath out of a man twice his size. He took two steps closer to David and stood, hands on his hips and feet braced. Without thought his stance fitted him to the roll of the ship. Taggart, unlike David, walked on a ship as though it were solid land. Nothing suited him more than to run his ship through the Channel. Now that England and France were at war, he was legal and fully sanctioned by King Louie to rob and destroy all British ships at will. He was no longer a pirate but a privateer of the French navy, and never had he been a happier man. To the British he was one invincible bastard; his reputation was one of genius. No one this side of the Channel could pull a victory out of the impossible except Taggart McClure. David's response was quick, he knew exactly what to say to pacify a man like Taggart.

"I reasoned as much. It's plain the *Red Dragon* is loved by Lady Ariella and the crew. I am sure any one of them would fall on his own knife

133

to save her, and I would venture to guess she is the heart and soul of the *Dragon*. So, what a fool I would be to harm her in any way." Taggart smiled, regarding the implied acquiescence, and also because he was a calculating bastard when he chose to be.

"Glad to see you know the first rule of the ship. Now, as for the second rule of the ship, that one is my favorite."

David weighed the grin on the face of Taggart. He had known men like Taggart, generals, men of rank who pushed one of lesser confidence to the ground with such a smile. Taggart was testing him. David hesitated, then responded with a smile of his own before he said,

"So, is it a fight you want, man to man? You want a test to see where I play when it comes to a battle? Or maybe it is a woman you have in mind."

The helmsman watched, fixed to the movements of the two men, both un-yielding, ready, eager to feel his fist full force in the face of the other. Jock smiled, gave his filthy forked beard a twist as he so often did when anticipating a change in the weather or, in this case, a bone-crushing fight. When it came to the swarthy bunch aboard the *Red Dragon*, Jock knew they would smell the fight, same as they would a storm that was coming. Just as he expected, his replacement for the helm had arrived. Now he could go below to let the rest of the men know. There was to be a settling, and it would be a fierce thing to watch.

David had watched Jock as he left the helm, and he knew it was only a matter of time before there was a crowd of men gathering, but he was surprised to see the first of the crew to make the upper deck was a lad. He was poorly fitted by his clothes, hand-me-downs possibly, but the lad was well weapponed. David had never before seen a boy, or a man for that matter, with four pistols strapped to his chest. Silk scarfs holstered them close to him, only a split-second from reach.

"A might dangerous," David said, eyes glued to the curious inconsistency of the boy's looks. He was a dirty boy. Tar and grease from the ship's hold covered his brow and smudged his cheeks, but the eyes, they could not be covered, were the deepest violet eyes ever created by God. Damn his hide! It was no lad he pinned. He was looking into the source of his own damnable bind, bound head to toe to this woman who unnerved him, enraged him, and made him wish to take her into his arms, hold her close and safe. She could pierce his heart with the beauty of those eyes, unrelenting eyes of soul-wrenching power.

"Ariella McClaig! So now it's a boy you are pretending to be! How the hell will that make a whit of difference when we face the same bloodthirsty lot that kills priests and old men? If the sans-culottes are commanded by Count Faucher, and you, in that damnable disguise, think it will be your sword that takes his bloody head, it will never happen. No matter what you imagine, the man is a mountain of evil, and whether a lad or a lass, you are not big enough to harm a hair on his head."

Her arm let fly a blade faster than a bolt of lightning. A flickering blur of shining steel cut between members of the crew who had gathered on the upper deck. The blade brushed the cheek of David Grayson before sinking deep into a wooden spar a foot or so away. The shock of her action and the damned accuracy of her throw were now burned into every man on deck, and not one crewman was surprised by what he saw. She was their cub when only ten, and they had all played a hand in raising her. Not one of them had expected any less of her.

The men were ill-mannered and lowborn. Men who had reasons to hate the English, so the fact that a highborn young lord of Britain was aboard, well, he was on their watch now, and not one man aboard the *Dragon* intended to make that an easy ride for Lord David Grayson.

Taggart swelled with pride, his own veins filled with more heat than he had felt in many a year, and he roared with spit and vigor,

"That's my lass! Deadlier than any cock-worthless male who thinks all right and wrong, all weaknesses and strength come by the right of his fucking bollocks. No man can out-throw the McClaig. Dragon blood flows through her, the same as my men. Ariella McClaig is the Lioness! The Lioness of the *Dragon*."

Taggart stared straight into the green eyes of the high and mighty David Grayson, son of the infamous Duke of Summerville. Taggart had known his father and hated the man as much as hatred allowed. Now he looked into the eyes of the handsome son. Taggart almost hoped he would be given cause to mop the floor with the blood of David Grayson.

Ariella anticipated this, knowing Taggart, for it was true she was his cub, but she was now a woman grown, and her feelings for David Grayson were struggling inside her. She might throw a blade at him but, damn her soul, she did not want anyone else to touch one single hair of his beautiful head.

David took a silk kerchief from his vest pocket. As he wiped the blood from his cheek, his eyes locked into those of Ariella's, and he thought of a thousand things to say. Before one word left his mouth, he felt the brush of the wolf. Like a sleeper awakening, touching, sensing, he slid his hand down the ebony fur. Stroking Sagath quieted him. Without any understanding of why, his anger dissipated with each touch, each silken movement, as his fingers ran through the warmth and softness of the fierce creature. Ariella's eyes still sparked with fire, but there was something else, and he imagined he heard her say, "The cut from the blade was fine, more like a lover's kiss. Lips are softer, but the blade is more to the point."

He stared at her, stared at her full lips, imagining the wetness and taste of her. His control came slowly as he continued to rub his fingers into the silky fur of the wolf, sensing the raw strength beneath. He stroked behind the ears of the magnificent beast. Sagath settled, lying quietly by his side. There was strength between this beast and him, and it found its way into the marrow, the subtle resonance of his voice. He spoke calmly, with renewed awareness of his sworn mission.

"If I believe your blade merely touched me as you intended, then I would have to contend that you have the best hand with a blade I have ever witnessed. So, we are tied together to this mission, and I will hold my own if you will do the same. Try not to kill me, and I will return the favor." He started to turn, heading back to his cabin to think how to deal with this hand Pitt had dealt him. He could no longer deny he cared for Ariella, and that, if nothing else, could destroy their chances of success. He killed men. This was the way of espionage. It did not suit him that it should also be the same for a woman.

"Where the hell do you think you are going?" Taggart boomed out. He still had that devil's grin on his face, and now at least thirty-odd crewmates had found their way to the upper deck. The lot of them sported with each other, gaining their own best view of whatever it was they knew was about to happen. As they continued to keep him in their sights, not one without a smirk, he began to hate them. As he looked at the rotten yellow teeth showing through their cocky smiles and listened to all manner of slurs against highborn English lords, he felt more and more the goat, without doubt about to be led to slaughter.

They all began to gather, closing him into a circle. He could feel their eyes on him, and here and there he heard muttered insults and snorts of laughter.

"Pay up if any be crazed enough! I am taking any man on who goes against the captain!"

The voice rang loud, coming from above the main deck. A golden-haired youth had gripped a line from the foremast and raised himself up to the higher deck. He was a handsome sort, more patrician than befitted an ordinary boatswain. David's spine stiffened, and a cold chill grabbed his gut. This was not good, and whatever was about to happen was on his head. Obviously, bets were in the wind, and if the words of the youth had any merit, he doubted he would find any backers looking to bet on him.

"I will offer ten Spanish pesos to be bet on David Grayson!"

David turned toward the very familiar voice, and staring him down was Ariella MacClaig. Her eyes were sparkling with light. Eyes that tried always to hide her feelings now hid nothing. Albeit he knew her reasons were her own, 'but by God, she was serious!' Ariella, like a small pit bull, positioned herself with iron grit, not one beautiful bit of her leaving any opening for doubt. Whatever she intended to do was hers alone. Legs positioned in a serious stance of stength and balance, in one hand she held a small leather bag, the other a new and fresh blade. Her position indicated unbending will, ready for whatever purpose she intended.

She emptied the leather pouch. Silver clattered as it landed on top of an oaken barrel lashed to the side of the upper rail. Raven black hair escaped from the bright red cap she wore; silken curls blew with the sea breeze across her cheek. She may have covered her porcelain skin with dirt, but her beauty was not hidden. The softness of her breasts could not be bound tight enough, nor her perfect round hips made less evident by the cut of a boy's trousers. She was a saucy bit of feminine perfection, and not a man on board would have denied the fact. When her voice rang out, crewmen seized the opportunity to gaze for a bit to take in her beauty and let their chests swell with pride. They might be freebooters and outcasts from proper society, but damn their hides, they had all in one way or another taught Ariella how to be a proper seaman, and she was now as good a sailor as the best of them. She knew the wheel, how to read the compass, set the sails, and climb the tallest mast if needed, and had more than once navigated through the worst of the Channel. So every man of them cheered her and listened to her proposal.

"Here you see five Spanish pesos, each to be broken into pieces of eight, making 40 pieces of silver, one for each man on board. Bet against me and one is yours if I lose. You lose and all bets are mine!

"Something the captain taught me is never swear to serve a man unless you also swear to stand by his side."

Ariella looked at the face of David Grayson, and something there, like a lost soul, spoke to her, something she had once known but lost in the tunnels of Broceliande. She blinked it away, he waited a breath, and then he let go of that true and serious moment and began to smile at her. Freed from silent looks of imagined love, she too could now finish, could come back to the safety of the devil's own game. With her feelings now in tow she took on one hell of a capricious smile and twisted her free hand around a halyard, just the measure to give her the agility required to hoist herself upward. As though by magic she positioned herself directly next to the brazen buccaneer Troy McDonovan, the handsome youth who had begun the betting round. She gave him the cat's own look, for she knew and he knew there was a trap, and someone was sure to be caught in this betting game. Ariella, now side by side with Troy McDonovan, finished what she needed to say.

"Even if David Grayson does not have a rat's ass chance of winning, he is my sworn mate, and by the power of my own word and the power of the damned British Crown, I am his sworn mate and I will be so, win or lose.

Grab the barrels, they will need a steady place to position their arms. Hand to hand, the captain against the lord of Summerville. The first man to lay down the other's arm takes the prize."

With a king's own confidence Taggart began to take off his clothes, first a dark woolen doublet, then a ruffled white silken shirt, very French in design. His attire was made of beautiful stolen goods, and he flaunted the law with style. Only nobility by law could dress so elegantly, a great boon for pirates who relished the freedom to break such laws and rub them in the face of the Crown, for they wore the brightest satins and silks they could steal. His upper torso naked, it was evident Taggart McClure had the neck and shoulders of a bull, and his upper arms were so thick with muscle they could easily squeeze a lesser man to death.

He bellowed at David as he filled his lungs with cold sea air, "What are you waiting for? No one ships with Taggart McClure without a test of his worth! And that, David Grayson, is rule two on the *Red Dragon*. Strip down to bare flesh, and let us see if you're muscled enough to take down the greatest arm-wrestler of the Seven Seas!"

David's skin had turned clammy, and his throat held acid bile. It was a gut reaction, but it was of no consequence, for he had learned to dismiss it. He had faced much worse than Taggart McClure. His own father had seen to that, but Yorktown, that was true hell, and those nightmares were larger than Taggart McClure could ever be.

Taggart watched as David drew his long sable coat free of his arms, readying himself for battle. He watched as the pallor of David's skin began to change, and as hidden emotions began to slowly release, a transformation happened in David Grayson that Taggart had not expected.

A smile began to form on Grayson's face, primal, dark, and without question filled with an understanding of what true evil was and how this match that now took place was nothing, nothing but a game that pirates play to feel their own version of savagery. He knew they had underestimated him, measuring brute strength by their own means – what it took to hoist a sail or bash a man's brains in with a single blow, how each stood in battle man to man, judging victory by size or by the strength of a man's arm – but David Grayson knew there was more. That was the reason he smiled with his own bit of cavalier smugness as he baited Taggart.

"I've played this game before with someone I think you have met. Least my father did mention a damned freebooter who ran the best of Scotland's whiskey all the way to France. It seems there were some things between the two: a woman and a great deal of hate. Whether you are the man or not, know that it was my father who taught me this game, and only the devil would fight such a bastard as him without being forced."

David's words hit a mark between the two, the air thickened, and both knew there was history somewhere in their pasts that made this much more than a game.

Ariella pulled her arms closer, hugging herself to thwart a chill, then released them as quickly. She could let no one know. She loved this roguish, foolhardy man, and the feelings sickened her, the feelings of caring, of wanting a man with such desire that nothing she did turned her round. The crew watched, jeering this English lord they felt justified in hating, and Ariella shook inside with the need to stand by him, to give him what she sensed no one in his life ever before had given him: support. Her eyes found those of Sagath; they were souls bound by something beyond human understanding. She watched and knew the wolf felt her intent.

The wolf stood, his teeth bared, the scent of battle pushing fire through his massive body. He moved toward David and stood to the side of him in a flanking position that without question made clear he was a shield for David Grayson.

David moved now with the strength of a man who had no doubt that he would beat Taggart McClure, and not only beat him but take him down before even one man aboard the *Red Dragon* could understand what had happened.

Elbows were placed in accordance with tradition, then forearms placed wrist to wrist.

The mates of the *Red Dragon* cheered!

"Give him a twist he'll ne'r forget!" Jock, the hater of all Englishmen, yelled out. Other voices joined in with barbs razor-sharp, all aimed to insult the high and mighty lord, David Grayson. David, hearing their jeers, smiled. His jawline turned to iron, and his shoulders broadened, strengthened. He shut his mind to the meaningless laughter of the men, men who knew nothing of what lay beneath his gentleman guise. Inside, he was darker than any aboard the *Dragon*. He knew this; his father and the wars had made it so. His smile grew cold, and his sea-green eyes became opaque, impossible to read. What was hidden memory was his strength. It was of a man whose insight and spirit had given him courage when he needed it most, Daniel Kerry.

"David, my lad. You've one bastard of a Da, and I think it time to teach you how to be your own man. Your Da, he will always hate ye. It is the way of soulless men like Duke Summerville, to hate their own, to dominate the sons and abuse their wives and daughters. Dying inside yourself, giving up on your own manhood, that I canna watch. You are almost full grown. He is a big man, your Da, and so proud he is of those giant arms of his. He'll break your arm if you try him wrist to wrist, but me, I am not the man who loses to bastards, and neither will ye be.

"Your forearms, lad, are twice the length of most men's. That is your leverage. Your Da is a large man, and he is a mean one. You dunna have his size, but I know a thing or two of winning when you have a man, arm to arm. The mean ones who win, you hear them, loud bastards, full of themselves and all their ways. The arms, yes, but true strength comes from inside, from the very thing that gives you reason to live. That is the only way: fill the body inside. My forge is fire, hotter than any man but a smith can stand, and the hammer is for fingers that curl round like steel, knuckles that are fisted hands of iron. You breathe from air that fills your lungs past what all other men can stand, and you build muscle on muscle. What I know will change you from a lad to a man, a man whose back can bear the weight ten ordinary men could not and whose stomach feels no man's fist, for iron on iron canna surrender. Strength comes first: the back, the stomach, the heart, and last, but the most important, your hands, my lad. Your hands. Your hand now grasps those of your Da, and he laughs at you. He will not laugh when I am through with you. He will never laugh at you again!"

No man had ever laughed once they felt the power of steel that gripped them, trapped them, every bone in their hand screaming in agony, pain that froze them to the point of surrender. Even before the match began it was over. David Grayson never pitted another's capable strength against his own. He took the hand with such an agonizing grip that there was no time for strategy, even for awareness. With his forearm stronger than any man's he had yet met, one twist, one turn, and his opponent, in this case Taggart McClure himself, was done, defeated, down for the count and looking into the cold sea eyes of Lord David Grayson.

No man was laughing now. Not a breath of any crewman aboard the *Red Dragon* could be heard, not for one full minute. All they could do was stare and try to fathom what had just happened in less than a three-second count.

"The gods of all seven seas be damned! I have just had my bollocks hand-delivered by a blueblood!" Taggart jerked his arm back so fast and hard the oaken barrel supporting their arms rattled like thunder. Taggart stood, all six feet of him so filled with rage and an equal amount of humiliation he could not form his next sentence. His broad shoulders shook, and his right hand trembled with pain.

The crew felt the insult of defeat with such anger that more than a few of the swarthy pirates reached for a pistol or saber, all with the intent of laying David Grayson down.

"You're a lime-livered, belly-festered cheat! You bloody bastard!" Jock yelled, grabbing his silver-clad saber, wishing only to drench his fine blade with the blood of a cock-sucking blue-blooded Englishman.

The words from his foul mouth and his vengeful anger were felt the same by every last mate on the *Dragon* except one.

Ariella could barely stand. Her knees were within a moment of buckling. What the hell was wrong with her? She had seen men cut down by swords, had been in the thick of blood-and-flesh battles where men she served with were taken down, and never had she felt any emotion such as this. Damn her hide, she did not want her mates to hurt David Grayson. No matter how she tried to hate him for the bloody Englishman he was, she could not.

Like the lioness of her naming, she was cursed with the fiercest of all curses, the female heart. Nothing, not anger or even hate could stop her. From somewhere inside her, raw emotion came forth, a raging wave of unforeseen dimensions. She drew her blade, dropped from the higher deck where she had watched this English blueblood take down the mighty Taggart McClure, and slammed the steel of her blade between the legs of the hotheaded boatswain, Jock McKinney. Her blade stuck firm, only inches from his intended direction and deep in the deck of the ship. Her voice was raised to the wind, and it blew over and beyond the heads of every buccaneer who raised a weapon to David Grayson.

"No one touches this man. He is mine. As the sun lights the day, as the moon lights the night, and every year brings another, I am with him, and by the right of a freewoman of the Seven Seas and a sworn mate of the *Dragon*, I take this man now to be my husband. For now and forever he lives in my protection. Touch him and you will die!"

She felt a fire of emotions she had never known. She felt a return of something lost long ago in the tunnels of Broceliande, and by God's hand, she once more knew what it was to love someone.

There were forty men aboard ship, and only a third or so could see what had just happened, but those close enough knew well that Ariella, their fierce and indomitable "wee lioness," had claimed the pirate's right, the right to any prize believed to be rightfully hers. Their creed, their freedom was open for every man. Any of them could lay claim to any prize they saw fit, and just the same, the others on board, should any wish to do so, could object. The first to yell out was the first to see the fire that burned in Ariella MacClaig, her eyes of deepest purple filled with thunderous light, willing to give all for this damnable Englishman.

"Our creed!

"Freedom, freedom to choose. Buccaneers, one and all, lowborn or highborn, every last man of us has our say. No bloody kings are on this ship, no black-hearted gentry are here wishing to hang the lot of us! I got me vote and I say, 'No one takes from me own mate.' If me own Ariella wants the man, then he is hers, ever' last fricking bit of him, and as for me, I'll not raise a blade ever against the most beautiful pirate of the Seven Seas. Aye! Aye! To me, sweet Lioness!"

It was Black Pete, the worst cook of the Seven Seas and the meanest man aboard, singing out at the top of his lungs, raising his blade and swinging it high in the air, challenging any freebooter to yell him down. Not a one stepped out to do so. No matter what David Grayson represented to each and every one of them, Black Pete had said it right. The reason for a pirate's life was freedom, freedom from the Crown, freedom from poverty, and freedom from always kissing the high-polished boots of them that claimed it all by right of gentle birth.

It was done. Some cussing and a lot of man-slapping and bravado all geared up to two things: finding the rum and celebrating the marriage of their beautiful Lioness to the damnable Englishman who was now by right of claim one of their own.

Chapter 9

THE MARRIAGE

There the two of them stood in the captain's quarters. This room, the largest on the ship, was exactly as she remembered: elegant, with furnishings fit for a king. For her, the large dining table and armchairs as well as the exquisitely carved bed were bitter reminders of her childhood, made in the same French Empire style with the same classical scrollwork and the same message: Wealth belongs only to those strong enough to hold it. A perfect sentiment for pirates, for everything aboard the ship, including the ship itself, had been commandeered from the British. The *Dragon* had once transported slaves and had been captured off the island of Martinique. The irony never escaped her, not since she had watched the murders at the Chateau de Venville, witnessed the atrocities and the deaths of her parents. Ariella could not forget the fine line that separates life and death, the rich from the poor, and men such as Faucher from the laws he should be answerable to. Everything depended on the ability and the strength to hold onto that which you love.

If for one night only, so be it. There he was, staring at her with the most damnable and most beautiful emerald eyes a rake such as he could ever need to seduce a woman. It all stood on her shoulders. As Captain Taggart McClure had said,

"You have just made your bed, my sweet, and you are no longer the wee lioness I helped to grow, so now, as the full-grown woman ye' be, I ask, will you go and lie in the bed you just claimed as your own?"

She would have given a thousand quid to know what was going on in that beautiful head of David Grayson, but that would never happen. All he was willing to reveal was how hard he was for her, and that protruding part of him she knew acted on its own accord with little need of guidance from his state of mind. His smirk of a smile made her want to slap his face and at the same time push her breasts tight to him and anticipate slowly as his hand inevitably reached around her body to grab her hips.

She weighed her choices. She could be honest, telling him that she loved him, or she could say nothing. Even if all were a pretense and he did not love her, what difference to the game of espionage? Chance had always ruled her life. She had chosen the sword, always in hand, always waiting for a final meeting. Either she or her enemy, one or the other, would die. She and Grayson were well matched at the game of pretending. *Best*, she thought, *to say nothing of love.*

He smiled, a different smile than she expected, softer, gentle, a waiting thing between them. When he spoke, she felt his words like a caress and breathed him into her. He was like nothing she had ever known before. Naked from his waist up, defined by hard muscles, he was more tempting to touch than she had ever imagined a man might be. To feel the quick burn of him beneath her fingers, to know from a touch that he desired her, wished to feel her naked breasts against him just as much as she desired him, that was what she wanted.

Strange, standing here in a room she had always thought of as the captain's, the most elaborate room on the ship, spanning the entire breadth of the stern, mullioned with dark mahogany, Teague's quarters.

They were beautiful, but she had never thought to see a man such as David Grayson here, waiting for her to smile at him, to let him know she did indeed want to feel his arms around her, his kisses on her lips, and the man of him, that part of him within her, joined.

The light became him. His muscled body glistened, still moist from the sweat, from the fight. His chest, his arms were taut, and his hair fairer, more golden than she had thought. She willed him to speak first, and as if on cue his lips formed the one word she had not expected. When he spoke, it was a question, and his purpose was to leave nothing to doubt, to let her choose.

"Wife?"

His voice came to her soft, a whisper. She knew he teased her, and she also knew he desired her. The heat between them had always been impossible, something both resisted yet could not escape, and now it was too late, far too late to walk away from him. She wished to say something witty or even flirtatious, but she knew David Grayson had her now in a place where such pretensions were pointless, transparent lies.

"I am your wife, David Grayson, on this ship and for tonight."

Before he could say anything, she stepped nearer, closer to him, until she could feel his bare chest. She was fully clothed, yet heat between them burned into her. The tips of her breasts ached for his touch. She lifted her face just enough for him to know her lips were willing, desiring him, his kiss.

David Grayson did not move. He had kissed a hundred women, made love to those he wished, and he had been satisfied. Never once in his life had he felt anything deeper. This was different, and it shook him, turned inside him like the twisting of a thousand pricks of fine-pointed needles, and that scared him. He knew he was damaged, had always known. Death, the dying of love inside, he had longed for that, prayed for love to die, never wanted to feel again, to awaken the soul that he had worked so hard to destroy.

When he spoke, his lips ached to taste her, and only by his own perfected Grayson control did he manage to slow his words, make them sound flirtatious and yet void of depth or tenderness. Tender things were but the hurt of memories, love ripped from his heart, pain that burned inward, promising to tear his very soul from him if he gave into it. The way he looked at her now, she knew before he spoke the truth of him. She was his split-apart kindred soul. The light of him and that of her blended. Pain hidden from all the world vanished in that instant of knowing.

"You are a perfect wife, my lady. One night to marry, to love, and then a war, a revolution to forget, but I think, first, to wash you. Forgive me, but you still have dirt and tar spread across those lovely white cheeks, and your clothes, well, I think to do better if you will permit me."

Touching her now, first her neck with a gentle stroke, then he slowly traced a curve, a barely visible vein, directing his fingers to the first button of her shirt. Two of his fingers, slightly rough, very male in their intent, slipped beneath the collared lace that covered the first and the second button. Her shirt opened, exposing the swell of her breasts.

By placing her own hand on his she stopped him from proceeding, guided by intentions she could easily guess, but ones she questioned. She knew it was her own inexperience, her own shyness that caused her to do so. She felt fear, a slight quiver inside, low in her stomach.

David looked down at her and smiled, but not with the rakish smile she knew. His smile was soft, warm and then he kissed her on the softest part of her neck, close to her ear and whispered,

"Let me wash the bit of dirt from your cheek. Your captain has left a basin just for such a task." His hand now free once again to do as he chose, took the cloth by the basin, wet it and begin to slowly wash her.

When he laid her down on soft white sheets, when he kissed her brow, her eyelids, her lips, and when his voice floated over her like sweet air of life, she knew more of love's promise than life had ever shown her before. His words made her feel that, somehow, she had found a reason to let love take her, to let herself accept the very being of her womanhood.

David had never before taken a virginal lover into his arms, never before desired to give such pleasure, such sweet love that all the world would vanish. That thought made him feel pure, free of his own pain and demons, and so he held her and spoke to her, knowing she was the only real thing he had ever held in his arms in his entire life.

"When I touch you, when I slowly and softly let my fingers stroke you, feel the softness between your legs, the most sensitive part of you, when my lips open yours and my tongue sinks into you, know it is you I desire, and there is no innocence, no virginal wall I would not penetrate to be within that woman part of you. I must feel you, your desire for me as it awakens you. The breath you hold, the arch within you, forcing your hips higher, that is for me."

Ariella gave herself to him as his name burned on her lips and filled the air for him to hear and to know she loved him.

She loved his breath and the scent of him, the warmth and strength of him. David Grayson wrapped her in a newness where she was nothing, and yet she prickled with every nerve, every point of her body, she trembled, tightened like steel, and together they transformed all the world into something more beautiful than either had ever known. For moments, for seconds, death and life were a nothingness for neither birth or death could ever claim knowledge of the "spirit transcendent," the awakening of physical and spiritual love between a man and a woman. It was a slow, beautiful dying of self-illusion and an awakening to the emerging brilliance of two souls transformed.

Chapter 10

PRISON OF QUIMPER

"Find the priest. Now! If he gets to the forest, I will have your fucking balls!"

The savagery of Faucher's voice was razor-sharp. It cut through the air like the sound of a hangman's rope, terrifying to those who waited, those answerable to him.

Both guards gripped their muskets. Their hands trembled as they tried to stand tall, but neither of the men had a chance of surviving the anger of Count Faucher. The two men, Joseph Chevenix and Pierre Grattan, had once been soldiers of the Royal Guard but deserted once the Terror began. Now they found themselves under the command of Monseigneur le Count, intendant of the Committee of Safety and head commander of the prison at Quimper. They knew Faucher was beyond rational composure. They had been under his command when he took the town of Nantes, where he had ordered children and priests to be impaled. These tortured souls were then drowned in the Loire along with 10,000 more condemned as insurgents.

Joseph and Pierre now felt the bitter irony of their own failed choices. Switching their allegiance from the King to support the Revolution was the way to save themselves from the guillotine, or so they had thought. It was now far too late to desert France as some soldiers had done or to return to the Royal Guard. The National Committee had ordered the arrest of all suspected enemies of the Revolution. This decree, *Law of Suspects*, gave unlimited power to the commanders, the officers of the Revolution. Count Faucher was now a Prince of Breton, and he was also a man who lacked even a miniscule spec of moral integrity. By all regard, he was a black-hearted madman who now, by right of law, was unstoppable in the atrocities he could render on the Bretons. Those who supported their King, loved their priests, and still believed in God were at his mercy.

"Scum-sucking bastards, not worth the price of piss!"

Faucher continued his tirade, turned his back to the men, and glanced from the high window of his office down into the courtyard where the remnants of a garden remained, a small reminder that Quimper had once been a Catholic convent, the home for two hundred nuns, *Sisters of the Sacred Heart*.

If hope had shown in either man's eyes, it was now dark or survived only by the thought their deaths might be quick. The two men, knew exactly what Faucher would do to them if they did not bring back the priest.

Count Faucher smiled, knowing the fear of the guards. His features, unflattering as they were, became even more so when anger gripped the muscles of his face, distorting his mouth by pulling it to a thin, tight line, giving dominance to an undeniably prominent nose. Its length as it merged with a back-sloped forehead marked him with repugnance. His eyes, blacker than coal, had a feline savagery, as he watched the men, delighted in their fear. He drew his blade and touched its razor edge.

"Wait one more second and I will gut you both! Take five men with you and bring him back! If you aren't back within the hour, the dogs will be set on you."

Two huge hounds raised themselves from sleeping positions to stand close to Faucher. The larger one's muzzle, where bits of meat remained between his front fangs, was damp with blood. The second dog, though smaller in size, was chained. Faucher watched as the guards' attention focused on the second dog.

"Give him the run of the prison walls, and it is only a matter of time before he kills someone. I keep him chained until I need him, and it seems I may need him soon. The priest has information. Very important information!

"Find him!"

Faucher was screaming now. The dogs advanced toward the guards. Driven by wild instinct, teeth bared, their desire to rip into the flesh of the two men was evident.

The guards knew their lives on this earth were measured in minutes unless luck might play in their finding the priest. Pierre, the younger of the guards, a bit more agile than his friend Joseph, was in the doorway, musket in hand before he heard a scream of pain from his comrade.

"Fucking hell, the damn beast has torn my arm from me!"

Blood dripped down Joseph's arm where the unchained hound had shredded the wool of his sleeve and the flesh beneath. Faucher's voice, as he responded to the attack, chilled the air.

"My pet, he needs a taste, a blood taste to find you again. Now leave my sight, you two worthless pieces of scum!"

Faucher returned to the window, giving him a view of the courtyard. Standing here in a palatial room he had chosen for his own, commanding those of lesser rank suited his own self-conceit. The other rooms of the Abbey, those which had once belonged to the Sisters, were all property of the Republic, confiscated by Faucher. Its reputation as one of the most heinous places of imprisonment was due to the efforts of Faucher. After casting out the nuns, those he did not have guillotined for refusing the oath to the new regime, he filled their empty rooms with prisoners: émigrés, nobles, priests, and resistance fighters captured after the uprising in Vendee. One of these men was of special importance to Faucher.

Leaving the hounds snarling over the blood-smeared piece of flesh ripped from the guard's arm, he turned from the window toward the closed door that led from his room down the main corridor. There was always a sentry stationed next to any room Faucher occupied. He had only to shout out, and his voice was easily heard through the closed door.

"Flaubert! Get your lazy fat arse in here. Now!"

The guard, within seconds, had flung open the heavy oak door and stood at attention facing Faucher.

"Bring the prisoner! The one called Philippe Soveneau!"

Philippe paced in the small cell room. He had been isolated from the other resistance fighters, and he knew it was only a matter of time before he learned the reason. He heard enough, knew enough from the conversation among the guards. None fared well in the Prison of Quimper, and he had expected to be found out, to be given up to Faucher. He heard the musket shots daily, and the dogs' bloodthirsty growls were more terrifying than the swaggers of drunken soldiers throwing dice to determine the next man or woman they might torture before execution. Not all were fortunate to find a quick death. Faucher's orders made sure of that. "Keep the dogs fresh. No food! It is human blood, only human blood I want them to taste!"

Philippe knew Faucher well, hated him and dreamed of ways to kill the man. The question was how well did Faucher know Philippe Soveneau?

The two men stood face to face, Philippe dirty, covered in filth with blood dripping from his forehead, yet he stood, even in his wretched state, with unhiden defiance

Faucher enjoyed looking at the man, taking a long moment to appreciate that he now had in his hand a key to the capture of Ariella Lantenac.

"No question then! Your eyes say it all. You are the brother of Laura Soveneau, and you are a spy for the émigrés!"

Faucher began to smile as he continued speaking to his prisoner, Philippe Soveneau.

"Did you ever question why I did not order your death? You did not escape Broceliande. I allowed you to believe that you were free. I allowed you to fight in the Vendean army. I allowed you such freedom until the time I needed you. And now I need you, Philippe Soveneau, for you are the bait, the bait for a trap I planned long ago! Ariella Lantenac is coming home, back to Brittany, and I hold here at Quimper, under my guard, the means to trap her, to finish what I should have finished more than ten years ago."

Chapter 11

THE TUNNELS

David Grayson was not permitted the stern or the bow of the boat. He was only fit to assist as an oarsman. He measured the job as part insult for his lack of knowledge and part his due as a Sassenach. He was not a shipman, even though he knew the workings of a small sailing craft. The punitive task, from his own perspective, had been sorely lost. He was not in position to view his lady, his wife, but her voice and her presence filled him with memory. The night before, their wedding night, had been for him an awakening. His soul, before forever broken, split asunder, now breathed with her nearness.

"Aahh!" he murmured in sweet remembrance of holding her willing body beneath him, inviting him to love her, to know pleasure enough to die for.

"Sagath! Down!" Ariella motioned with a slight raise of her hand, lowering her voice to no more than a whisper.

The wolf, black as midnight and large enough to snap a man's neck, vanished into the shadows. His form was lost in darkness, and yet in less than a heartbeat, Sagath no longer stood at the bow but lay silently next to David Grayson, his jaw touching the front toe of David's boot.

Where had Ariella found such a creature? Even as he asked the question, stroking the dark fur of the beast beside him, David knew: Broceliande. Every mystery, every impossible part of her, the secrets she carried, and the passions that drove her were tied to Brittany, to Broceliande, and soon, within a few hours' time, he would be sunk within the secrets she guarded. None of this was even slightly under his control. Once he had set foot on board the *Red Dragon*, all had gone to hell, at least for him. For Ariella, he wondered, *Just how far is she willing to take her revenge?*

Their mission, directed by Pitt himself, was to find Jean Chouan, leader of a group of Royalists, who fought the Republic. With his help they would safeguard a shipment of guns as well as a dozen cannons to be given to the émigrés. This was what David knew, but what Ariella knew, that was undisclosed, even to him. As to whether she would follow the mission as sanctioned by Pitt, David already knew the answer. His time on the *Red Dragon* had shown him Ariella would never submit to anyone, not even the Prime Minister, not if Pitt steered her away from Faucher, away from her blood debt for the death of her parents. That would never be. She was a princess of Brittany. Whether by her own will or by something more akin to the will of the gods, Ariella would never forsake the promise she made in the tunnels of Broceliande.

He loved her. The thought caught in his heart, tightened, and he knew he was now captive to her mission. *So be it.* Come what may, he would never step away from Ariella, even if it meant turning his back on the Crown.

David brushed a bit of his hair back and secured it under the cap he wore. He certainly did not look like a Sassenach but more like a pirate than a sailor of any worth. He had been given whatever the men wished to get rid of: a gray broadcloth coat, a blue silk shirt, a pair of knee breeches, and a silk sash. At least the sash was tight enough to secure a pistol, and his boots easily concealed a small dagger.

"Faster! Row faster, you crow-headed bastard! The tide is behind us but coming fast, fast enough to pull us far off the narrows. Row like your life depends on it!" The command sliced at him, dared him to speak, to utter even the slightest protest.

Jock's words concealed nothing, pretended nothing. The sea had them, turned them, and they pushed back from jutting stones, giant dragon teeth, jagged and pulling them straight to their death.

"Prepare!" Jock's voice, loud, angry, challenged the roar of the sea! "The tide rises! Bear it, men! Bear it! Beat the wind! Hold her, hold the bow toward the 'Six'!"

They saw. They all saw. Six giant reefs showed protrusions of what lay beneath the sea, a giant fortress, the plateau of the Minquiers. If they did not hold, if they did not find the strait between its granite fangs, they would die, crushed within the vortex of its pull.

David turned, just a slight movement enough to see her, to take in her beauty. Her raven-black hair had come undone, wrapping her in its silken strands, then blowing free with every angry gust of wind. Her beauty took his breath, and he saw her violet eyes, like stars of light within the mist of raging ocean. She had no fear but stood as though riding the tumult of swells, the crests breaching and then slamming down toward the buried rock beneath the sea's rage, was a simple game that she had played before.

Her smile was proof. She welcomed the sea; its rage was nothing she had not known before. She brushed her silken hair back, wrapped it, and knotted it securely. On the bow she stood high above the lashing of the waves, and with each jolt she balanced, maintaining an uncanny measure with the ebb of its force. Her violet eyes looked to him, into him, and there he heard unspoken words, as though the light of her eyes had thoughts to speak:

"Don't worry, my love. What happens now, all of it is on me. For you to trust is all I need to know your love, the truth of it, the truth of you, David Grayson."

David took her meaning and knew.

She is home here, more than she ever was in England. She knows these waters, the sand shifts, the hidden reefs, the ways that lead to safety and those to death. She is not the British lady she pretended to be and never could be!

He pulled the salt air into his lungs and braced himself. Every muscle was rock-steady, every nerve ready for whatever the sea demanded. Jock knew, and David had seen it in his eyes. A man who has seen death – his eyes don't lie, not when it once more draws close.

The three of them – David Grayson, Peter Cavanaugh at the stern, and Jock McKinney, the second man at the oars – would all see shore together or die right here and now if they didn't right the boat, for the sea had turned them one hundred and eighty degrees, and the next wave would slam them into the closest reef.

David had hands and upper arms of rock-hard muscle, but it was the upper body of Jock McKinney that pulled them round. The man was built of iron, and David guessed it was one of the reasons he was chosen as oarsman.

"Now! Push her! Four more, just four more pulls! We have it!" It was Jock's voice, and it was he who now waved them toward open sea, where the water began to mix and where they would find their way to the Odet.

The Odet was a tidal river, only filled when the tide was high. All this Ariella had told him, and now that the worst of the tides were behind them, they could measure their way by the hours left. Only three hours remained for the river to be navigable.

"The Odet, she's got us now, Sassenach. My fine Lord David Grayson, a man such as yourself, a man of chance, who plays the gentleman with his hand on the cards, know this well: what we bet on now is the river and the shadows of the summer sun. The shadows will play us. If we drift too slow on the tide as she rises, we will die, Lord David. Too fast, the same, we die."

Jock's mouth tightened and disclosed a wicked smile, but his intent was clear. David knew Jock spoke with a bit of the devil in his tongue, but the truth, that was in David's voice.

"Nothing will be left to chance, not in this game." David threw him a hard look before he continued. "This is naught to do with luck or fate, nor the gods! When and where we arrive, the path that leads to Quimper prison, that place and that time, is on my lady. She does not play the dice nor gamble with men's lives, so you, my *friend*, will not die by mark of the tide's fall. If this is your day to die, then it will be your own game."

Ariella was not standing now but kneeling low, close to the bow's end, watching the water's flow, judging the changing color. She waited for the shifting sand to tell her the water's depth. She was fourteen when she had been sent to ship with Durand Gargantua of the clan Rotheneuf. Taggart McClure had told her *The Red Dragon* was not the fastest ship of the ocean, it was the corsair and of those the fastest was built by the Rotheneufs. She had thought McClure the hardest man to sail the ocean, but she had not yet met the Rotheneufs. She remembered the words of Durand Rotheneuf for they were imbeded in her soul. They had been formed on the blood of survival.

"You have chosen the blade, the razor's edge, a path that takes blood for blood, that will open your own scars to bleed, for the blood of famille. You are a child born of wealth and privilege, and if you survive the lessons I will teach you, then you will never again be such a child nor grow to be the woman your grandfather wished, a lady of tender sensibilities. If you survive such lessons, then you do by defeating everything, every man or woman, every storm from the Sea, everything that would take your life. The Bay of Biscay is where you begin. For over four hundred years the Rotheneufs have learned

its hidden dangers, and soon you will know the first lesson. Why she is known by this name you will understand soon: "The Valley of Death."

Then, in a moment written into a memory that never left, he bound her waist with a line, a rope that seemed to have no end, picked her up with arms of steel, and slowly, deliberately dropped her over the side of the small skiff he had sailed into the mouth of the Odet. Ocean and sea, rivers and land met here, and here began to take and give, as changing winds, rising tides, earth, and sand follow a pattern of their own. The moment he left her to swim or drown, she began to understand the meaning of his words.

She was seized by frigid water. The cold was sudden and without mercy. Her arms began flailing for strength to swim, something to hold. She knew the shore was not so far, yet each stroke took her further toward the sea. For a moment she felt sand beneath her feet, and then the earth collapsed as though she had fallen into quicksand.

She knew and had always known since the tunnels. Inside her, within her, the dead of Broceliande had laid their loss with that of her own, and death for her was not now, not ever as long as blood rage tore her open. Fire burned within her lungs, the flailing stopped, and she gained the tide that took her inward, away from the sea, carried her. Even as she reached closer to the banks of the Odet, she stayed clear of the ship wreckage almost within her reach, for there was danger from the whirling cross-current it caused. Only when she saw the saplings that reached deep into the earth did she take hold and know she was safe. This earth would not sink beneath her feet.

After he reclaimed her, pulling her onto the skiff, he wrapped her in a cloak of fox fur, then forced a bit of bitter-tasting rum down her throat.

He turned to her, and his eyes were the color of obsidian, dark, impenetrable. She was caught in their energy, their power, and knew no one would ever challenge this man and live to do as they willed, for he would never step back from any who did so. His words were imbedded into her as no other would ever be.

"From this moment, till that which seems a thousand years, you are tied to me. You will hear what I say, and you will stay by my side. If I cut a man, you will watch him bleed and you will learn the blades, so if ever you step away from my side, you will have no fears. When I am done, there will not be one landmark, one measured tide, nor one storm from the North Sea that you cannot read, nor one man you cannot cut if he threatens you!"

She blinked, and time returned to the present, with the same river and the tides she knew better than any man save a Rotheneuf. Her words were clear, sure, and without any doubt or fear.

"Now! McKinney, pull to the right. Straighten the stern. In here. The sandy bottom will beach us, and the trees hide us till the light fades!"

David's response was lightning. Once a man had known the dying of battle, the time of seconds and choices, there was no pause. As he jumped from the skiff into the waist-deep current and headed for the shore, the painter was thrown to him by Jock, wet to the bone and surprised to see David Grayson drawing the line out and pulling them in. Jock saw the Sassenach was muscle and body with an instinct sharper than any Englishman's he had known, a man to watch.

David looked behind him, surprised at the light feel of the line, then smiled with more than a bit of pride mixed in, showing his pleasure at seeing that Sagath, dark beast that he was, carried part of the line in his massive jaws.

"Here! Pull her over! Now!"

Neither Jock nor David hesitated. The moment Ariella spoke, both reacted as men of the same mind and the same strength of body, pulling the skiff high up the bank close to a tall river oak that appeared at the least ninety feet in height and old. Close to a hundred years was an easy guess. The limbs were low, with some broken, but much of the grey-colored bark remained and cut into the side were the letters DR, rough but clearly carved for a purpose. Grayson knew this place was not chosen by accident.

David felt a slight movement, a whisper of air and soft fur. His hand reached out, expecting to find Sagath beneath his fingers, but nothing was there. The beast was gone, disappearing into the forest shadows, a phantasm blending into darkness.

Jock McKinney, standing near enough to have seen the wolf and to have seen him simply disappear, stared into David's eyes, gave him a weighty smile, and then a word of his own.

"You think too much, Grayson. You think the way of truth is only a thing that can be touched and can be seen. You are not in England now, me weighty lord, and neither is the Lioness or Sagath. The wolf is back to his own, and this forest is his. You, Sassenach know nothing.

"Whatever saved them in the tunnels of Broceliande lives here in this land, in this forest. It is stronger than you, Sassenach. Its power does not come from the living, it comes from the innocent, the unavenged, the dead. It was made from tears of blood, tears of sorrow, and tears of them, the likes of the princess. The Lioness, she lived within this forest. All she loved were murdered before her eyes. So long as a blood tie is owed to those within this earth, Ariella will never be free of its hold, and now, well, now there is no one, man, woman, or being of hell or heaven, that will ever step between her and that tie, not without dire consequence."

That said, Jock turned his back, his way of ending what could not be conveyed, especially to a Sassenach. He brushed back the thick mop of his heavy braids, retied them, securly, to stay back from his face, to give him clear focus. Jock's dark Scottish heritage marked him with hair the color of coal and a fair complexion, weathered and freckled by the sun. He was a handsome man, with strong, broad shoulders, sinewy muscles, hands that could easily snap a man's neck and yet arms that could gentle and love a woman with enough warmth to make her long to stay.

As Jock turned his back, David judged the weight of his words, words giving credence to unfathomable mysteries, to the ability of the dead to weigh power over the living. The thought that any such beliefs merited judgement made his blood freeze.

Phantasms who engage in earthly battles, blood feuds fought from the grave.

Any truth in power such as this he refused to believe in. To do so would render him helpless to protect Ariella.

David continued to watch the giant of a man as he began to gather brush and pine to cover the skiff. He compared Jock to the soldiers he had known, battle-tested men who kept their fears closed inside.

The truth of evil, of demons that feed on men, was something imperceptible to soldiers in the throes of battle, when life was measured by split-seconds of action, of killing or being killed. Yet, now as then, David knew the coldness in the air and the unexplained prickles beneath his skin were true, and it would be only a matter of time before both he and Jock came head to head with the ghosts of Ariella's past.

Without conscious direction, his hand brushed the pistol, secured within a belt and tied to his waist. His gaze returned to a copse of pines. Something there was not natural, but he could not explain why. If only he could reach just beyond the surface, step into forest, into whatever inscrutable magic surrounded this place, but he did not move forward. Instead he turned toward Ariella.

Ariella's eyes deepened to black with a bare hint of lavender, softening whatever memories were rising within her. She could touch him with a depth of love he had never imagined could exist between a man and a woman yet cover truths within herself to shut him out, to keep her past, her Broceliande far from his touch.

The moment their eyes touched, she walked toward him slowly, deliberately letting him see only what she wished. In her own eyes was desire, her own carnal knowledge of him, locked deeply within every nerve ending, every physical trace of her that he had touched.

When she was close enough, his hand reached for her, as natural for him now as to breathe air into his lungs. She allowed the moment to feel his hand, his warm fingertips stroking her arm. He willed her to speak, to give him the secrets of her past, the truth of her, why she had pretended to be William Pitt's correspondent. She smiled at him, his face so close she could see tiny bits of blue and gold in his sea-green eyes.

She let his fingers slip the length of her arm, just a breath away from touching her as she led him toward a tangled mat of coarse weeds, interspersed with briar and thistle.

She seemed different in this woodland. Her voice was soft, transcendent, as if she had drifted into a fairy spell. No pretense and nothing of the highborn granddaughter of Hamish MacClaig clung to her. The underneath part of her, the child sworn and born to serve the spirits of Broceliande, that child grown to womanhood took each step with certainty, and the forest responded. Lavender flowers appeared, winding through the briars, creating a path where the dark green leaves of thistle did not grow. Their tiny needles of poison that stick into flesh softened as she walked by. Clearly, Broceliande welcomed its princess home.

As he followed her one step at a time, most of the forest bramble seemed behind them, and now, standing near the pines, he saw that they were singular in a forest primarily of oak and beech.

They stood now in a patch of ground elder. Above them was a canopy of spreading leaves and branches high enough to catch the dimming light of a setting sun. Neither chose to rush the moment, despite knowing the urgency of the dangers they faced, but took a moment for unanswered questions.

David spoke first. His eyes darkened, narrowed, hiding the concern he felt.

"Do you really think you can defeat the bloody bastard?"

Ariella brushed back a strand of dark silky hair, breathing deeply of pure forest air. David wondered if his eyes betrayed him for it seemed as if an aura of tranquility enveloped her. Whatever truths she knew were the making of her, a Lioness formed of pain suffered and a will of iron. Her lips were moist, desirable, those of a beautiful woman, yet her voice was iron, a sword pulled from stone with knowledge of all that was needed to defeat evil. Her lovely lavender eyes burned with passion and conviction as she replied with a will that came from within her yet also from something much deeper, beyond the human realm.

"I know I will defeat him!"

God help him! was David's immediate reaction. He believed her, but belief? What did that matter without plans, without action?

"How so, Ariella? What do you know of this place, of the Quimper prison? What do you know of the émigrés and the war that is waging?" His questions came quickly, demanding, revealing his concern as well his passion for the woman he loved. "What are we doing here? Standing God-knows-where in a thicket in a forest that, if my sense of direction does not lie, is in the exact opposite of the prison."

"Trust me. I promise to answer whatever you ask if only you will allow my lead. Only for a bit, David. I will explain, but not until you have seen the secret heart of Broceliande, a place where spirits abide, a sanctuary for lost souls."

David's gaze bored into her. His striking features could have been carved in granite. His eyes held her as though judging the sanity of what she had just asked of him. Then, with barest hint of a smile, he answered, "Lead on, my lovely Lioness, but tell me what has happened to your mates, Peter and Jock McKinney."

"Those two are fierce Highlanders of sturdy stock and the best corsairs that sail the Emerald Coast. They will free Philippe Soveneau easily and without me. By now Sagath has already found the priest, and as for Faucher, this is not the time. I am sure he has already set a trap. One he thinks I am walking straight into."

Ariella's concentration remained on her own secret plans. She walked quickly, but each step was precise. The ground flora of tiny white blossoms remained undisturbed as did the river thistle and wood vines that covered most of the soil, a mixture of sand, dirt, and a hardened substance of fermented algae. She stopped at the root base of the largest pine, a tree with massive layers of bark.

"Soon it will be dusk, and where we are going there is no moon or stars to help guide our steps. How to make a torch from pine knot is a practical thing to know. But a wise teacher also teaches how to survive in a world of darkness filled with evil at every turn. You have met my grandfather and you have met McClure, but one you have yet to meet is Durand Aka Gargantua of the clan Rotheneuf."

Even as she talked, Ariella began to push pine bark back from the base of the tree, uncovering a long branch about six inches in diameter. She pulled a short blade from the double belt that wrapped her waist and began to clear the sturdy limb of stubs.

She glanced up, looking at him for a moment to confirm what she was already sure of. "You know the name. I see it in your eyes."

David was not ready to reveal this bit of information. Of course he knew the name Rotheneuf. The privateer was infamous. He was the scourge of the English Channel. His ships were faster and better built than any others that sailed the Emerald Coast.

Ariella paused. Her grip tightened, and for a few seconds she stopped clearing the branch. She had not yet decided how much she would reveal. She did not look up, but her body and her grip relaxed as her decision was made. She continued the task of trimming her makeshift torch, and her words formed slowly at first but then with passion as they took on her memories, her story of survival.

"There are many stories of the Rotheneufs. Maybe it is true that the first of the clan, those who lived on the Brittany shore over four hundred years ago, those Rotheneufs were fishermen and sailors, and the piracy came only when the channel was no longer theirs. What they did was what they knew best. They built ships faster than the king's or those of the British or the Spanish. They built the *Arrors of the Sea,* eighty-ton cutters that outgunned and outsailed whatever was pitted against them.

"It is true that for a hundred years the Rotheneufs created a coastal dynasty built on piracy and smuggling. They became a family of wealth, a family often feared. They ruled this coast by dominance and fear, but never did they take power through sheer torture or butchery. Never did they declare themselves the righteous citizens of their own holy order and begin the massacre of 17,000 men, women, and children. That they left to Robespierre, Danton, the sans-culottes, and the guillotine.

"The revolution has broken the Rotheneufs. They were a clan bred to survive, seamen who knew Brittany like no clan before them, but now that clan has been divided, swept into chaos.

"Durand despises the sans-culottes and men such as Robespierre, men who believe justice is only achieved by terror, by the guillotine, wielding the power of death. Seventeen thousand men and women, children, the failing, the elderly, and of course priests, in one year murdered."

Ariella stopped. She wedged the shaft of pinewood between two rocks for leverage and began to cut. First she cut the end, leaving it smooth, then she stood it upright and split the base four ways, placing twigs within the splits to keep them open to provide a holder of some sort at the end of the staff.

A chill passed over her warm skin, and she knew it was not from the cool sea air. Memories of the tunnels, memories of Broceliande, touched her like razors of ice drawn down the flesh, pulling blood from the pain frozen within her heart.

The years away from her home vanished, becoming nothing but a waiting moment. She felt through every fiber of her being, through every sinew of muscle and measure of a warrior's skill, the magic of Broceliande and the spirits of those she had loved and loved still.

It is time for a reckoning, time to melt the frozen abyss of ice and of darkness that stretches throughout the land of those I love, to give recompense to the souls of the true and valiant, and to bring the steel of my sword to the heart of evil, Faucher.

Her silent prayer was heard through every tree, leaf, stone, stream, and brook, through cave and mountain in all of Broceliande and filled the souls of the unavenged, who whispered their own undying lament and gave her welcome. For no one entered the tunnels without the blessing of the long-dead whose spirits still filled the myriad of cavernous passageways.

Not one of the thousand tunnels that riddled the hidden underworld of Broceliande was the same as any other. Each had its own smell, one of something old and musty, another of spice. One tunnel was warm and felt like sand, but strangely the next was wet and cold. Some ended in a dark abyss, another stepped into a maze of endless intertwining circles. Once she and David entered the tunnels, their fate was given to Broceliande and the souls of the unavenged.

David's emerald eyes watched her. He spared her his rakish smile, a teasing sort of smile he used when he wished to play a bit. Instead he smiled with the truth of what he felt.

Yet she could not give back, could not touch him, not now, not in this moment. Instead she proceeded to talk about the manner of torches.

"With a bit of tinder, the resin within this pine limb will burn for hours, allowing us to disappear and escape the trap that Faucher has devised.

"He will search for me! That is what he does, and that is his mistake. Jock and Peter will separate. Jock is the decoy. He will manage the west wall of the prison and create a planned diversion. Sagath will take care of Faucher's war dogs, and Philippe – he has all the friends he needs on the inside to do the rest."

Ariella lifted her face to meet his eyes, to judge his reaction. She knew how much she risked keeping secrets from David. Such secrets were more than an informant employed by William Pitt was likely to accept.

He smiled at her. "I am not surprised that you have planned the escape long in advance. How good is a spy, my lady, without secrets? Proceed as you will, and whether you choose to tell me your secrets, let that be your choice."

Holding the torch in her left hand, she guided him past the copse of pine trees, then the forest undergrowth. To his surprise, a meadow only a few hundred feet in diameter lay beyond the canopy of the forest, with sun enough for broom and heather to grow but no trees. The terrain was uneven with sloping mounds of different sizes and stone barrows. Two or more had stones, familiar stones. David knew of such stones at the Craigh na Dun.

"I did not expect to see a meadow," he said. "Such a glade is not uncommon in the Highlands, even close like this to the sea, but I did not envision anything other than more woods."

The feel of the place was puzzling. There was something here, something of importance. He could feel its presence. This hidden thing was primal, not at all like the meadows he remembered as bright and airy with a spicy scent of flowers. Here the forest ended. This was a place of deep silence that smelled of moist earth and decay.

As he waited for Ariella to explain the reason they were here, the night air shifted, and through the corner of his eye he saw movement, pale shapes materializing like lost ash separating from an extinguished flame. Phantasms, real or imaginary, rising from the ground, disappeared into the dusk, and he felt the night grow cold like a shroud of ice. He refused to acknowledge what he had seen, willing Ariella to explain, to tell him if what he saw was real.

Ariella pulled back the ebony hair falling across her face, secured it within the dark red bandanna she wore, and waited. The setting sun had turned blood-red, the sky was painted with crimson light, and where they stood became a suspended moment between darkness and light, heaven and hell.

Ariella's voice hung in the air, there was so much that she could not explain, what she possessed, a spiritual connection that shook her, awakened her. When she spoke, her voice was filled with emotions, more like a child who had just newly rediscovered the secrets of Broceliande.

"Look, David! Let your eyes guide you. The slope of land, the stones, just there to the right of the largest of cairns… do any of the mounds strike you as unusual?"

David felt numb. His voice was raw as he forced his words and his breath to calm.

"The stones were not stacked by chance. Three of the mounds are strategic! The shrubs which are just beginning to open, the sea lavender, as well as thistle and heather, draw attention away from the mounds. The earth is raised, designed, too symmetrical!

"The mounds are more like those dug in a cemetery, by hand, not built by time or by nature."

David felt her distance herself, as though she were listening to the spirits of those who had died here. She spoke with compassion, with understanding.

"The desperate dig into the earth to cover themselves, to hide from villains. I was that desperate. The earth was my salvation. Only the desperate like me understand. Only they can find their way in the tunnels. The unavenged souls of the dead are there, and they speak a language only a few can hear."

David's unease and his reluctance to speak of what he had seen were tempered by what Ariella had just said. His interest quickened when she spoke of her past. If he could only discover what had happened in these woods, in Broceliande…

Ah, he thought, my fate seems to be walking a fragile line. England and France, rebels, émigrés, and counter-revolutionaries. If I step too far to one side, I die. Too far to the other, my fate is the same. The good from the bad, knowing that, is a game more difficult than rolling the dice, but at least this game is with my lady.

"You prick my pride, Ariella. Maybe I have talents I wish to hide, and maybe you will tell me of the man you know as Rotheneuf. It is time to let your secrets go!"

She did not acknowledge his question, but instead turned away from him before she said,

"No more talking! The light is fading. Soon there will be no light to guide us."

Ariella walked to the third planted mound, which was the smallest and the only mound without the large monolithic stones. A full thicket of flowering shrubs blocked a sloping elevation of the mound. A small embankment had been raised and the higher ground was fortified by large rocks, and leveled against an outer protrusion.

Ariella carefully placed her pine torch on the ground away from the cairn of stone and began to move certain rocks back from the embankment. As David watched he surmised, *there is a method to what she selects.* Within moments her purpose was evident and she began to explain.

"Do you believe in Druids, David? Have you heard of the legends of Merlin? Broceliande myths say it was here that Merlin came and hid in a cave made of crystal. Brittany shores are the only place on earth where such a myth might be true. Mica, feldspar, and quartz crushed from the sea are transformed into pink granite that, with light, sparkles like glass."

He had been watching her, calculating why she moved certain rocks and others carefully remained in place. He ventured his guess as he pulled back one of the stones, placing it just as she had, only an arm's length away.

"The stones cover an entrance to a tunnel below. Behind the stones is an arch, methodically balanced by one central keystone."

Ariella looked back and nearly smiled. *Like a boy,* she thought. *Unraveling the secret to a hidden treasure.*

"The entrance is only wide enough for one. I will go first, and once I am inside, you will hand me the torch."

Once the crawl space was uncovered, David watched as Ariella began to wiggle inch by inch into a pitch-black hole like the entrance to a well made of stone and quicklime and glued by someone who knew the art of masonry.

"David, hand me the torch! When you see light, crawl in backwards, move the stones back in place, and keep moving!"

He felt as though he were burying himself in a dark pit as he replaced the stones and backed into a subterranean world of darkness.

The crawl space began to change, becoming larger, less narrow, until he could turn toward the torch, toward light that revealed an underground cavern of shocking size, large enough to hold a hundred men or more.

"How is such a thing possible?" He kept his voice low, but Ariella could hear the shock in his tone and then a quiet, and she knew he was watching the shadows that moved, weaving in and out of the catacomb. Multiple passages were now revealed in the flickering light.

The torchlight effected a kind of beauty. The stone walls were made of quartz and mica with a subtle rose hue. Such a color as this was known only to the coasts of Brittany. He could not help but feel the mark of time and those long dead who had once ventured into this underground world. He even thought again of Merlin's crystal cave, understanding for this moment how such myths are born. He felt the ghosts of those long dead, but where was the logic to explain such feelings?

Ariella knew he needed the truth. It was the only way to help as he adjusted to a world that, in his mind, should not and could not exist. She froze a bit of her heart, just enough to allow her to speak of pain so deep it bit into her with unmerciful memory.

"I have had a good many years to wonder about such things as how such vast catacombs have been kept secret by so many. What I know was told to me by Laura, her family in Venville, and by Rotheneuf.

"This is only one of many catacombs. Some date from an era of the Druids, as ancient as the cromlechs, others from the time of the Celts, the Romans, and the Bretons. Deep trenches in the ground were sided with stone slabs, topped with capstones, and then covered from the top. Time has added its own layers of earth and forest growth, and time has helped many to forget the very existence of the hidden tunnels of Broceliande.

"The ones who will not forget are those without recompense, without a champion. The unrequited spirits that wait remember when the forest was not enough. Not enough to save their sons from conscription by the French Republic or their priests and nuns from the guillotine. When it was not enough to save their daughters from the death women know when faced by men who claim the right to rape and murder in the name of war. Those who died here, I feel their souls within the earth, the catacombs, the hidden tombs, and the tunnels.

"Rotheneuf told me how the Celts hid to escape the Romans and the Bretons hid to escape the Normans. For a pirate such as Durand, you can only imagine how well such secrets served him. The tunnels are his ways. They lead him to a myriad of secret places and many he taught me. No one without such knowledge should ever broach the tunnels, for they would surely die. The pitfalls are numerous. Some true pathways are hidden, decipherable only by a chosen few.

"Durand broke with most of his clan. Only La Haie, La Bigne, and Chevreuil joined him to fight with the Chouans. The others, including two of his own brothers, dissolved the family, broken by hatred and greed.

"The clan fought against each other, both on land and on the sea, revolutionaries against royalists. Those who tried to escape were butchered. Many were women and children.

"The last battleground for most of the Rotheneufs was the island of

Benetin. Durand survived. We will speak with him soon, and you will learn a great many things about the planned siege of Quiberon Bay."

It was cool and dim within the tunnel, but still Ariella clearly saw the hard glitter in David's eyes. Fighting her own emotions, loving him had slowed her resolve, and she knew her loyalties were being tested. His brow tightened as he struggled to see her in the torchlight. The light had shifted, moving inward toward the passageway that beckoned them on. Time would wait no longer.

David had rarely snapped, but he did now.

"What is the endgame, Ariella? Spies are taught in the playing field of London's underground to never trust Pitt. Never trust the intentions of the country you war with, and England is at war with France! The kings, the lords, and the politicians always have their own guesses as to how the chips will truly fall. So tell me what you believe. Do the peasants, the women and children of Quiberon Bay or the Vendeans, have a chance in hell of surviving this uprising between the Royalists and the Republic?"

The words were on her lips as she almost said, "No, the children, the peasants will be the first to fall."

But the truth, she had learned long ago, was rarely meant for the ears of soldiers or in this case, for those who served the Crown.

"Those I can save I will, but nothing can stop the invasion of Quiberon, for it is this port that controls the sea.

"The Prime Minister directs us to destroy the munition stockade, but he has no care for the children you speak of. Most have already lost their fathers, for the men of Western France are now conscripted by the thousands. Many are forced to serve the Republic. Which side they believe in makes no difference, and if we blow up the stored gunpowder, destroying in turn the entire gunnery of the revolutionaries, they will burn down the fort. What is best for Pitt and best for England is to feed the fire of revolution to weaken France from within. You do not know of all the secret alliances Pitt controls.

Gloria J. Prunty

"Where this tunnel ends there are two rivers. One takes us back to Quiberon, the other to the seaport of Lorient. Two men wait for us, Durand and Charette de la Contrie. Go with me to speak with them, then choose. Follow the direction of Pitt or go with me."

CHAPTER 12

THE INN OF QUIPEN BAY

Charette de la Contrie and Durand understood what it meant to take power by the sword and the price paid in human lives. They knew no one truly escapes the darkness that descends upon the heart, the hold of death as the living walk away from the battlefield only to be pulled back by that darkness to look behind them and see the defeated and the dying. Yet both men shared a common belief.

Neither Contrie nor Durand would lend his sword to the evil they knew by the name of "tyranny," a master of power that knows no limit, usurping every human freedom, leaving nothing, not even the right to speak out. Neither believed in taking children by the laws of conscription, nor did they accept the burning of churches and the murder of priests.

Both had run the gamut of revolution. Contrie had fought for the Americans in their war against the British and then come home to find his own country in the midst of a revolution he could not support, not when it was led by men such as Robespierre and Danton, who spoke with lies. The worst of their lies was the basis of their power: "Freedom for All." Contrie watched as the ideal became a beacon, a call to the guillotine, death without benefit of trial. Both Contrie and Durand were guided by what they had witnessed: the deaths of good people, of in*ocents. They both knew,*

"Doubt all you see, all you hear, observe. Know when the code of morality is broken, then step back and see which side you stand on!"

Durand leaned forward, directing his full attention to the man he faced. Durand never spoke of serious matters to any man he could not watch while looking directly into his eyes.

Contrie's eyes were light grey, almost silver. Durand sensed a speculative deliberation and knew this nobleman was watching with similar reserve, but to his credit he showed no hesitancy. Dealing with a nefarious pirate was obviously not a concern, or possibly he kept any feelings well hidden.

Durand, without effort, appeared every inch an outlaw capable of taking a life without question of morality, the choice being instead about winning in a game of ultimate survival.

If he had been of the nobility as was Contrie, the two men would have been similar in acquired mannerisms. Those of dignity are practiced, learned by dictate of societal standards. Yet at this table where they sat across from each other, they were opposites. One was nobility by birth with practiced, rigid standards. The other was made hard, carved by the lives he had taken with no regard for the king's laws. What they both had learned well from the Reign of Terror was that treason, lies, and betrayal care not one whit which side of society's rules you stand on. Both sides are equally false in rewarding those who fight for justice alone. Justice is far too solitary and pays little regarding human status, political power or material wealth. Those who seek justice without benefit of power are doomed to fail.

Durand's face grew tight with an instinctive response. He shifted his position slightly, the same as he might aboard ship, to gain the best vantage point to look for markers, indications of danger. His voice was practiced, gaining certainty with each observation he made.

"There are few places where the two of us can meet. Taverns are always suspect, places where fates are sealed, where revolutions are born, but this tavern is not such a place. Its owner is Jardin Soveneau, and he and I share a great deal of history, making his concern for our welfare as strong as that he feels for his own life and that of his son, Philippe Soveneau. The man I speak of, Philippe Soveneau, is a master of deception and of walking the line between deadly political factions and maintaining an upper hand that always manages to keep him one step from the guillotine. Even now he is leading an uprising at the prison of Quimper. If he succeeds, we will be one step closer to crushing the remaining forces led by General Turreau, a man surely guided by the devil himself. His men are known in Vendee as 'The Columns from Hell.' One hundred and fifteen thousand soldiers from Paris were sent to destroy every man, woman, and child of Vendee."

Before Durand continued, he paused to take in the entirety of the room. He counted the men, noted where they sat or stood, and studied their weapons and attire. Three wore rough, worn baggy trousers and red caps. They were without a doubt sans-culottes. Their clothes marked them as Blues, men of the Republic. The remaining four were seamen, there for grog and beer and whatever was available from the common pot that simmered over the hearth. Durand's voice was quiet, but the intensity of hate he felt echoed in his words as he continued.

"Where we sit, this darkened corner in a room that curves inward, has been designed for men such as me. This booth is made of the same oak as that of the *Arrors of the Sea*, the fastest ships known, which were built by the Rotheneufs. Here, we are protected on either side by two-foot timbers, and facing outward, from here we can see any who approach. The windows are high near the rafters, and the oil lamps are centered near the long tables, easily seen from this corner."

Now it was Contrie's turn to speak, and he knew his words would

Gloria J. Prunty

be hard to manage. Because of his hatred, his thoughts were difficult to assemble. His memory seemed latched to the message he had read, the one intercepted by a conscripted Vendean soldier. In order to protect the soldier, the message, once read, was released and taken on to Paris and the Committee of the Republic. The words were those of Louis-Marie Turreau. The words engraved in Contrie's heart and memory were these:

As for the fate of the women and children I encountered in rebel territory, I found it necessary to pass them all by sword, to eliminate the brigands to the last man, there is my duty. I have crushed children under the feet of horses, murdered women who if left to live would give birth to more Vendeans. All homes, fields, livestock have been burned, slaughtered, their seed wiped from the earth!

It was impossible for Durand not to notice Contrie's hands trembling. Durand knew he was born in Couffe, and even though he had noble blood, he was also a Vendean and shared affection for the common people of Vendee. Contrie attended the same church and lived close to the peasants unlike most of the nobility, who preferred Paris.

Durand felt the numbing power of grief and knew Contrie's words would not come. Contrie's hand that trembled had once held the sword of retribution. He must take it once again, for the Vendeans were still being slaughtered, and he feared all that was yet to come. A peace agreement had been signed by Contrie, but all the Republic agreed to were lies, all was broken, and more young men woulb be conscripted and more would die.

Durand took the man by his arm and slammed it hard, timing his instinctive reaction, knowing he would have Contrie's full attention. Durand's voice filled the dimly-lit corner and reached into the main room where men sat at the long tables waiting for their pewter mugs to be refilled.

Lioness of Broceliande

"We drink!" The words spoken by Durand were just loud enough to be heard by the matron who served the tables.

Colette had been waiting. Quickly she returned to the kegs stacked in the back, away from customers' greedy hands and the heat of the hearth. Quickly she filled the tankards with dark bitter ale, almost black in color. Smiling at the men she passed and humming her own sweet tune as though all were well, and the night was for their benefit to enjoy, she walked lazily to the darkened corner, drawing no attention to Durand and Contrie.

When she lowered her body to serve the ale, her back turned to the rest of the room, she whispered,

"The two you wait for have arrived."

Chapter 13

THE BEGINNING OF THE END

Renard Soveneau had not always been an innkeeper nor a friend to nefarious pirates such as the Rotheneufs. Wars and evil men such as Faucher have a way of testing men's faith, bringing those of a chosen moral dignity together. It was not that the two men were free from the sword, but that they chose never to take the lives of innocents. They did not spill the blood of children, of women, or of priests.

Their own moral being tied them in with Ariella, for they too had memories of those they loved dying by the hand of evil, by the hand of Faucher. They believed in the magic of Broceliande, the gifts of hope and strength given to Ariella and her will to live for a debt owed, the debt of blood for blood.

Ariella stood now in front of Renard Soveneau, the man who had helped her flee France, a man she had not seen since she was a child. The look of him touched her soul

"*Mon sauveur!*" Her words filled the small room, and David watched as Ariella threw trembling arms around the innkeeper's massive shoulders, holding onto him as though he were all that kept her from drowning in a sea of death, as she must have done when she left her home so many years before.

"Ah, *ma belle*! *Ma* lionne" The innkeeper's words were sweet music, evoking her memories of once being the princess of Venville.

Renard gently held her from him, just enough to see clearly all her beauty: the violet eyes like no others, the black silken hair, and her face, the face of an angel.

"I see your grandfather, Durand, and your Captain McClure, they have transformed you, *ma chérie*." As he spoke, the gentle smile was there but also hard lines formed by the years of war that Vendee had endured.

"You carry the sword now, and the shoulders I hold are strong, ready to wield this sword within an instant. I feel the call of Broceliande within you, and I am ready, as is Philippe, to bring an end to Faucher. His atrocities continue, and no one stops him. He glorifies himself with the number of Vendeans he murders. It is time for retribution for those of Broceliande, for those of Vendee, and for the Duke and Duchess of Venville." These words spoken, he turned toward David with a forced smile. With controlled but biting humor, he asked,

"And this *anglais*, why have you brought him, *ma chérie*?"

Ariella caught his game the minute Renard's voice changed tone. *Ah, he wishes to play a bit, to test the intentions of my Englishman, and so we will!*

Before she answered, Renard could not resist asking his next question, directed at seeing what reaction he might get from David Grayson.

"Tell me, *Anglais*, why is a lord of British nobility clad in the clothes of a pirate, here on the coast of Brittany. War rages between the French, the English, and a hundred thousand peasants who I would think mean little to a lord of the British realm such?" Renard watched David's hands to see if he might draw a knife, but Ariella watched his eyes.

David's eyes were most beautiful, Ariella thought, when they were the color of the ocean at its most tranquil peace. It was the nature of

183

him to grow quiet when he watched everything around him or studied the men he did not know. She knew this color within his eyes, the color that hid a storm within.

He pulled her close before he spoke, his arm around her waist squeezing her just hard enough to say, *Don't play with me now, Ariella. Tell the man what he needs to know, and let us see to Durand and Contrie.*

David faced Renard, choosing words designed to end this show of manhood.

"Ah, you are as Ariella said: 'a man who does not trust until it is earned.' This I will tell you, and then you decide how quickly we move forward.

"What I do now, I do for Ariella, but there is more. "

His arm now brought her round enough so that he had a breath of her. Looking into her violet eyes was the key for him to unlock the mirrors of her soul, and there he saw clearly all that Broceliande had taught: the knowledge of what evil can do and the purpose of its destruction.

"You and I, Renard, we have the same enemy. Our countries are at war, yet the two of us choose whom we fight. I live within a realm of lies and political secrets, and I serve at the behest of the Prime Minister. He, like many who rule, never sees battle but follows wars at a great distance. At 10 Downing Street, a stone's throw from the palace and the king of the United Kingdom, he waits even now to hear of General Hoche, the number of soldiers he commands for the Republic, and if he is marching to the Bay of Quiberon."

David paused and looked directly at the Frenchman. He had felt from the beginning that Renard had been a soldier, and now as he watched Renard's eyes become tense and his shoulders broaden, he saw the responses of a man who knew battle well and knew the power of those who command and yet never see the slaughter. Renard reacted, and his words were a challenge filled with anger.

"Then you know your Prime Minister has given General Puisaye nine warships which wait to disembark at the Bay of Quiberon!"

Renard's hand was tightly clenched on the pistol just within his belted tunic.

David raised his hands to show his intentions were not to engage. His voice was thick with emotion, yet he chose his words carefully. He knew the importance of Renard's acceptance.

"Yes! I know that Puisaye has arrived at the Bay of Quiberon. Tell me, Renard, what do you think of the chosen landing point, the Ile de Quiberon? "

Renard was taken off guard. His hand eased, no longer reaching for his pistol, and the drawn lines on his face relaxed, yet not without obvious dislike for the necessity of meeting with an Englishman face to face.

"There is not a seaworthy man in all of Brittany that would choose the Ile of Quiberon. It is narrow, only a strip of land, with shoals blocking all ports of entry. Puisaye will dig himself a trap and be slaughtered or forced back into the sea. General Contrie and Durand know our coast, no man better than Rotheneuf. The Republicans have ordered fifteen thousand troops under the command of Hoche to push them back into the sea, and Hoche has begun digging a trench so deep and so wide they cannot cross without being slaughtered."

David's knowing smile did not go unnoticed. Renard began to understand.

"You know a great deal, *Anglais*. I wonder now if it is possible that the spies who infiltrate the underground of Paris might learn a thing or two from your informants." Renard looked at Ariella, and he knew what was there, everything, every lie, every deception the bastards of the high towers of London and Paris wished to employ.

"It is obvious to me now why you are not at Quiberon. The émigrés are doomed, and any support they offered to Vendee is gone."

Ariella watched Renard's face change. Remembered grief reflected the sadness he felt. She loved him and wished wars were always just, but they were not, and so her words were weighed in truth and only truth, which seldom equaled justice.

"Take heart, *mon ami*. We cannot save all of Vendee, but know a great evil will perish."

Chapter 14

SAGATH

The cry of the wolf reached above the forest toward the heavens; the last of the wolves of Broceliande had returned. Sagath stood beneath the highest cliff of the valley, his head extended upwards, his throat quickened, and he called to his pack. His call was heard throughout the valley. Here the *Chambre au Loup*, the place of his birth, knew his voice and celebrated his return. Above him were pieces of stone, rock formations defining the highest cliff of the valley. The image there resembled Sagath. It was *loup*, the wolf carved by time, and it gave its name to this valley of Broceliande. This valley was a source of many legends, the cry of the wolf from its highest peak became a cry for those who heard and knew the ties of family and what could be suffered by lack of justice.

Father Jacob was the first to hear the cry. The sound was hauntingly beautiful, and he recognized that his silent prayers had been heard and there was renewed hope for Vendee.

He stopped just beyond a copse of pines beside a running stream, clear and cold as ice. He was a large man, his clothes now filthy, stinking from the putrid ordure and squalor of the prison. His feet were covered in dirt, bleeding from sharp spines of the forest underbrush. Stepping into the stream he let its water numb his pain while cleaning the dirt from his wounds. For the first time in many months, he smiled. His thoughts filled with past joy, from when he was the priest of Venville, a parish so dear to him he felt blessed that he resided in this small village and that the seigneur was Jean Paul Lantenac.

Broceliande, the name was made of music, soft, like the sound of faraway church bells, filling the forest with magical beauty. Memories returned to him, brought through the call of Sagath. It gave him hope that the suffering of Vendee had not been forgotten.

"The dogs have his scent!" Pierre's voice trembled with desperate hope. Holding the dogs was barely possible for they were wild like berserkers gone mad with blood rage.

"The priest is close!" Joseph called as he took one of the dogs' leads, pulling back with all his strength. "I can't control the damn dogs. They will tear him apart if they break loose! We bring him back so's he can't speak, we're as good as dead!"

Joseph's words had barely escaped his lips when it seemed the earth fell beneath his feet. The dogs went still and silent, for at that moment they heard the howling of Sagath, a long, rising wail that seemed at first to come from a distant mountain and then closer, moving through the woods like the wind before a terrible storm. The spirits of Broceliande awakened, for they had heard the call of Sagath.

A low, guttural sound, thick with malice, stirred the darkness. The breath of the beast was in the air, close enough to prickle the skin, but where it came from was indeterminable. Something surrounded them, watching them, moving closer, taking the light from the forest and bringing shadows of darkness. There was no time to turn, to take a sword, or to even run. Fear touched every nerve, and as they trembled, the spirits of Broceliande watched.

The attack was fierce. One of the dogs was taken under the jaw, making his cry silent. The second dog's muscles flamed with intent, but before he moved forward, Sagath had him by the throat with an iron grip, thrashing him from side to side until his body grew limp, then he threw him at the feet of the men as though he was nothing of consequence. Joseph and Pierre, unable to move, trembled as they looked into the blood-red eyes of the wolf. For them they were the fires of hell, condemning them to death.

The shadows began to recede, revealing the surrounding trees, layers of fallen leaves, and partially-covered stones that banked the sides of a now-visible stream. The men saw nothing, still unable to move, still waiting for their impending deaths as the eyes of Sagath stared unto their very souls. Only when they heard the seemingly far distant voice of the priest were they able to return to a state of awareness.

"You move one hair's breadth and you will die!" It was Father's Jacob's voice, solemn, without pity, yet there was a reflection of knowing, knowing the beast in a way the guards could not.

Neither man yet dared to speak, but their eyes, dark with fear, said all their desire to live could convey.

"The wolf has a name, Sagath. He was named by a child I baptized many years ago in the village of Venville. The village was taken, as was the surrounding land, chattels, the monastery, and the chateau. The lord of the demesne was murdered, as were his wife and those who served him. This was done here in the domain of Broceliande, and the villain, the man who took all this, is your commander, Faucher. The wolf who decides your fate is waiting, not for me, nor for the two he is with, but he is waiting for the spirits of Broceliande, for only they know whether your hands are like those of Faucher, covered in the blood of innocent lives."

The guard Pierre had found his voice but barely, for his throat had tightened so each word rasped with painful force.

"Please, Father, we have no love for Faucher. We serve on threat of our lives. We were taken from the Royal Guard and forced to join the Republic or face the guillotine." Pierre trembled, looked at Sagath, and grew silent again as the giant beast had drawn back with uncertain intent and bared his fangs in a silent snarl.

The men, now on hands and knees, were swearing to run, to run from Faucher, to hide, to disappear, to throw down their arms and fight no more.

Father Jacob listened and knew. There are no safe havens for pawns such as these, nor for any who show themselves able to carry a sword, a gun, or even an axe. Men, women, and even children are murdered, imprisoned, or forced into conscription. Father Jacob felt a mark of sympathy, knowing even if Sagath released them, they would surely die. They were pawns and, in this war, there was nowhere to run, and what you believed was shifting sand beneath your feet.

Sagath moved forward. Broceliande had decided the fate of the men, and Sagath walked close to each man, close enough to cover the faces of both Pierre and Joseph with the blood that yet remained on his tongue, and then he stepped back and watched as they ran.

Within moments, Jock McKinney and Peter Cavanaugh arrived, breathless yet ready, with pistols in hand.

"You are Ariella's men." Father Jacob knew this even before Sagath was near the side of Jock, licking the sweat from his arm as Jock lowered his pistol. The wolf, only moments before a wild, snarling beast, was now enjoying the touch of Jock's hand brushing through his thick fur.

Jock stared at the priest, a man filthier than any he had seen. His clothes had fallen almost to pieces. His alb, once white, a color of purity worn for baptisms, was now grey, torn, and ragged. The other vestments he had worn were gone except for the chasuble, a tunic made of golden thread embossed with sacred hearts, now a ragged scarf that lay across his shoulders. Jock knew nothing of priests and little of God, but he knew from Ariella that this man had baptized her and most of those who lived in Venville. When he spoke to Father Jacob he did so with respect, knowing how much he had done over the years to save those he could in the village of Venville, for it had fallen into the hands of Faucher.

"And you are Father Jacob." Jock kept his voice low, personal. There was softness in his tone as his eyes met those of the priest. Not often did a pirate such as Jock allow kindness or even respect to show in his dark and somber demeanor, but this was a man he knew through the voice of Ariella, so he knew that for over a decade Father Jacob had served his parish under threat to his own life. He and Philippe Soveneau were the links that connected Ariella to information she had divulged to no one until she found purpose and reason, and made choices that led in one direction: to destroy Faucher!

Sagath stepped back from Jock's side, his head raised, his ears pricked, listening to the sound of silence as Broceliande spoke to urge him on. The spirits of the dead, those murdered by the hand of Faucher, grew impatient. Peter saw the impatience and felt the urgency of Sagath, and without hesitancy he brought an end to any exchange of words that lingered between Father Jacob and Jock. Tightening his hand on his pistol, he raised his arm as though to lead a charge, exclaiming,

"We cannot wait! Faucher will not. Even now he has very likely ordered men to the forest while we waste precious time. The priest is all we need. He knows the secrets to the prison's hold!" Peter's voice filled with anger as the trust Ariella had given him turned to fire within his veins.

Chapter 15

QUIMPER

The screaming was heard in every corner, echoing through the prison of Quimper, and somewhere within its ancient walls there were semblances of remembered pasts desiring vindication for the evil suffered at the hands of Faucher. His rage tore into everything within reach. He slashed at the air, at the guards, and tore the velvet drapery from the wall. The frenzy that had taken hold of him showed clearly the mark of Satan. There was no moment of calm in the rage that twisted inside him and claimed his sanity. His voice shook with it as he commanded the prison guard to speak.

"Speak! Damn you, speak!"

The man shook. A large man who had seen many battles and watched comrades cut down before his eyes, yet never had he seen such madness as this. Blood covered the brocade carpet, mingled with its rectangular patterns, and blended with shades of dark red wool. His friend, a man he had known for fifteen years, lay at his feet, unrecognizable with what appeared to be more than a hundred cuts. The final blow had cut him almost in half from shoulder to waist. The guard could barely stand for the shock of what he witnessed had rendered him powerless. No longer standing but stooped to his knees he heard the words only a madman such as Faucher could deliver.

"Speak! Before I end you!"

"My lord," the guard's trembling voice began as he tried to explain what had happened, something he could not believe himself, knowing he would surely die, for nothing could save him, certainly not if he told Faucher the truth. It was his hand that had opened the prison cells. Once he had seen Sagath, the priest had only to ask for him to open the cells.

"It was the priest, come back from heaven or hell! I know not where, for with him was a black demon. I thought them wraiths, appearing from nowhere, through the wall, like shadows of Satan. It was a secret wall, a tunnel, such a secret passage as was used by the nuns, and the priest knew of it. He knew. He brought the dark beast, and it was only me and three others, for the guardsmen watching the prisoners heard guns fired near the west wall and they left to secure the wall, but I stayed and guarded the prisoners."

Faucher, filled with madness, laughed bitterly as he gripped his sword, knowing the guard a fool. He felt the irony of how such worthless scum as this had cost him the loss of Philippe Soveneau. Killing him would not be like most, for those who fell before his sword were part of faceless masses, so many, not worth a backward thought, but this man he would remember, for he had cost him a valuable prisoner. With uncontrolled hatred he ran him through the belly, and those who watched were sickened as they watched the man slowly die.

Chapter 16

FULL CIRCLE

Philippe Soveneau led the group with unmistakable command, gained by knowing his enemy. There was no question Philippe was dangerous. He had killed many men and would do so again, but to know it was this man who had your back and fought by your side – that was the reason those who followed him did so with complete allegiance and fought in a manner intended to never earn his disfavor. Philippe spoke with certainty of purpose, like a man whose blood ran cold and whose eyes, though beautiful to look at, showed no emotion. He was a spy who walked the line between rebels and revolutionaries, who fabricated political loyalty and yet who, with uncanny ability, knew the machinations behind the battlefields and played them the best he could.

"We will separate at the west bank, near the woods of Pont Firmin." He watched the faces of Peter Cavanaugh and Jock. He knew because they were Ariella's men they could be trusted, but even that was not enough. He knew, had learned through the death of many, innocents as well as compatriots, nothing must be disclosed to anyone other than the intended recipient, and even then there was always a need for the master of the game to tie the final threads together. Ariella was one of the threads, but even she did not know how deep the circles of secrets ran. Philippe had received a small package, sealed, given to him by a guard moments before Father Jacob had managed the escape. Sketched on it in red ink was one letter, the letter L.

"Father Jacob and I will go on to the hamlet of Misdon near the village of Venville. Sagath will guide you to Ariella, and where we meet has not yet been decided, for the hands of conspiracy even now are changing, realigning."

He extended the small package to Jock but did not release it. Jock waited, without making the slightest gesture to receive it. Both men were silently weighing the other. Instead of handing it over as expected, Philippe threw a dagger, released, from his left hand, with such speed that it vanished between the men and by sound alone was measured to have been precisely thrown into a druid oak three feet away.

Jock stared at Philippe as though he were insane, and without emotion he asked, "Your purpose?"

Philippe, for a rare moment, smiled almost playfully before replying, "Touch your right ear."

And there it was: a touch of blood, nothing of concern, just a display, a promise of the importance of the package that Philippe gave to Jock, releasing it from his right hand.

"It is a thought, something to remember. You see what I am capable of when you watch the wrong hand. The same with the game you are now part of. This goes to Ariella on promise of your life. Remember you are always in danger, and from what direction your enemy comes, that you may never know."

Chapter 17

THE GAME THAT NEVER ENDS

David Grayson watched Ariella. She was a bewilderment, an impossibility, known in a society of the powerful and wealthy as a "diamond of the first water". Now, as he stood within the final circle of those she had brought together for one purpose, he knew Ariella Lantenac would never belong solely to him. Whatever filled her heart and flowed within her veins gave her extraordinary power. He watched her take the letters Philippe had sent. He saw her eyes grow dark, the soft lavender hues gone. All within her seemed to stop; she stood as though frozen in another time and another place. Sagath was by her side, and her fingers spread, as she ran her hand through his thick black coat, remembering the forest of Broceliande. The truth of evil, the power it has to destroy everything good within the world, that was what she remembered. She knew there was a veil that cloaked evil within the world and she had been given the ability to fight against it.

Whatever she had read and where these messages came from, she did not share.

David smiled and waited for her eyes to find his. When her hand relaxed, when her fingers no longer held tight to the dark thick fur of Sagath, she found the eyes of David Grayson. The moment was theirs, the exchange for them alone, words unsaid, and yet the message was clearer than words could ever express: "By your side, my love, now and always."

The room had grown quiet. The men – Durand, Contrie, Peter Cavanaugh, and Jock – had chosen not to sit. They were far from relaxed. All thoughts returned to personal losses the moment Ariella had taken the first letter. The men watched, each with different expectations, and not one had imagined the possibilities that had now emerged. None of these men nor those on the battlefields nor those who tomorrow would march to certain death knew the chances of their survival or knew that information such as this even existed.

Ariella took the measure of each man and knew the number of British and French émigrés, Vendeans, and peasant farmers who were at their command ready to fight against armies of the Republic, armies outnumbering them ten to one. She moved toward the stone hearth, where the fire had burned down to embers. Directly over the bright orange coals hung an iron pot. Ariella had expected Soveneau to prepare the room for the men and was glad for savory stew. It was what she and most of the men knew – cod from the Bay, sweet peppers, and garlic, simmered. On the long oak tables were black bread and tankards for ale. It was better to sit, listen, and find a bit of warmth, even if small, before thinking about the truth, the reality of what they faced.

The light from the embers burning in the hearth gave a soft blue shimmer to Ariella's raven-black hair. Silken strands framed her face, and the men were caught by her beauty, but, more importantly, they felt truth within her, truth that words could never voice. As she looked to them, they saw through her eyes the heart of Broceliande and a message for them. "Without warriors, the innocence of our world would die."

Her voice was calm, as though it belonged to another, who at a similar table, sat and broke bread with men of faith, men who lived for the "good that they could do" in the eternal war against evil. Before she shared what she knew to be the truth – predicted outcomes of each battle, the numbers that would surely die, and the villages that would fall – it was good for the men to know they were not sworn to serve or to obey without question. They were not servants directed by another's moral justice, and her words were chosen for this purpose.

"We are not servants of war and will never be such. When fetters are cut and chains of blind obedience broken, evil cannot exist in the world. When our eyes are open to truth and our swords cuts down false liars and tyrants, we are comrades, and as comrades what I know, you will also know.

"Renard Soveneau has provided for us. Through a bond that ties him to our common cause he gives us protection and secrecy for our purpose." Ariella turned toward the innkeeper. "Renard Soveneau. My life as always is entrusted to you. As the Blues walk the streets of the harbor, as Faucher even now commands an army of two thousand to raze the village of Venville, we remain your guests in secrecy and comfort."

The Lioness took a seat at the long oaken table and smiled at him with a look he knew so well, like her mother's face, whom he had known and loved for kindness and nobility. He gave her a nod as he sharpened his dark mustache, just to say, "For you, my princess."

Continuing, she pointed to an open door. "Please show the men the way out if we are discovered."

Renard had no shyness but humor enough to deal with times such as these. He lifted his own glass and motioned to the tankards set on the oak tables.

"First, we fill our cups and drink to the truth that unites us, that makes brothers of us in common purpose!" His words added to the warmth of the room given sanctity by the presence of good men such as these.

David took one of the tankards, filled it from a barrel in the corner, and handed it to Durand, then drew three more: for Jock, Peter, and Contrie.

Durand needed no invitation to take a seat at the long oaken table nor to pause for a moment as the last of the embers slowly turned to ashes in the hearth. It did not matter that his instincts were trained for survival, to be a soldier. The quiet pleasure of the hearth and a moment with comrades were valuable things.

His voice did not express any of that soft part within him, for he had mastered revealing vulnerability in himself long ago. When he spoke, the words were tight, practiced, serving the moment when battle is soon, death waits for many, and his own fate is unknown.

"Contrie! I drink to you. I learned much as we sat waiting for this gathering, and it is the same with all gathered here. We, as my Lioness said, are not men bound by tyranny, blind to the blood of innocents covering a battlefield!"

Durand's words were spoken without thought of his own death, for he was far beyond such wasted, soulless vanity of self-importance.

"I choose my enemy! I know the evil I fight! The evil I speak of massacred those I love, those left on the Isle of Bentin. The Rotheneufs were split into factions, each guided by their own self-interest. Their wealth had been in safekeeping, entrusted to the hands of the holy Order of Saint Benedict. This ended when the Republic stripped the churches of all property. The destruction of the Church gave opportunity to Faucher. The changing political order served him well, creating chaos so complete that all were vulnerable, for allegiances changed with the wind, and faith in the church and belief in God no longer had favor.

"Faucher had no resistance when he with his army razed the town of Bentin, slaughtered those without defense, and took everything. Tomorrow he will meet resistance! Tomorrow Faucher will feel my sword!"

With lightning speed, he raised his right arm, sword in hand, every muscle flexed and his hand clenched, readied by instinct to take the head of any who stood against him.

His fury was that of a warrior who had looked into the eyes and the soul of evil and knew the truth of the world. He knew all good, all justice would end if warriors such as he put down their swords, for evil would never stand down. It would exist as long as the world of men craved power. It would grow forever stronger, held at bay only by the sword.

His words were felt in the hearts of all there. Sagath, like an unnoticed shadow, perceived yet not acknowledged, ventured close to his side, so close that Durand, by instinct, relaxed the arm resting at his side, opened the palm of his hand, and let the black fur of Sagath touch between his open fingers. *Broceliande was within the touch, within Sagath.*

The night was descending. The light which filtered in came from the high window, above the view of any who would see into the room. Twilight deepened, bringing with it a deep purple hue. When the sky turned black the stars began to come out.

The men were seated. Renard walked to the door and closed it, taking a key from the lining in his cloak and securely locking it.

The room was private, long equipped to protect secrets. Those who entered, entered in secrecy, and their leaving was the same. Even now as the men watched Renard, they questioned their safety, for they knew twelve armies, each an "infernal column" of twenty thousand men, were approaching the last of what remained of Vendee. They knew the orders of the Republic:

"Leave nothing but scorched earth: farms, villages, forests, every man, woman, and child. Render all to ashes!"

Renard had returned the key to the hidden pocket of his cloak.

"There are two doors for the room and one key. The door you entered is locked, and the key is with me. The second door is jibe with the wall, invisible to the eye. I challenge any man here to find the keystone and put his hand squarely on the push lever that opens it." Renard stepped back, watched the men and the direction of their gaze, and smiled. Not even one looked at the compass wall. That the wall was distinct within the room, went without question, but once regarded and admired as a unique and highly visible map of the entirety of the Bay of Biscay, it was accepted as a functional asset, valuable to seamen.

The wall was decorated with the skill of a master mapmaker to show with nautical perfection the Bay of Biscay. The chart detailed the coast of western France and northern Spain, detailed the sea with depth soundings in fathoms, small letter composition only a trained eye would recognize as the seafloor, where to drop anchor. Hazardous shoals and reefs were indicated, those responsible for the graveyard of ships that lay on the seafloor. A sixteen-point compass with a fleur-de-lys was drawn upon the map, decipherable only by a skilled navigator, with lines of magnetic delineation determining currents, wind directions, even treacherous mists, capable of destroying visibility. It was the knowledge compiled by the Rotheneufs.

The value of what the map revealed was the difference between survival and dying at the hands of a treacherous sea. "The Valley of Death," the name given hundreds of years ago, described it well, and the maps created by the Rotheneufs who had lived within the treacherous bay explained why they were master navigators and how easily they had bested ships that had chosen to venture into the Valley of Death where hurricane winds were unpredictable, shallows and reefs undetectable, and an unrecognizable abyss dropped into an eternal sea to a depth no sailor had rope enough to measure. This was the Bay of Biscay, determined to be one of the most dangerous passages in the nautical world.

Renard, without waiting for any man to respond to his challenge, walked to the wall, spread his hand, and with exacting measure touched the third, fifth, and seventh points of the fleur-de-lys. The door opened, masterfully hidden within the drawing, navigational artistry had concealed the door with amazing precision.

Durand sat back in his chair, smiled, and enjoyed another drink of the dark malted grog. He was slowly savoring the drink as he watched Renard, knowing all he would do in exact detail.

Once opened, it was apparent the outer wall had an extended arch, a space just large enough to house the entrance to a subterranean tunnel that branched into two separate underground passage ways. The first led to a small inlet and a passageway to the River Oust. Here, it was simply a matter of direction, south to the open sea, the best choice for escape from the Vendean battles raging to the north. The second choice led to the hinterlands of Morbihan, a wooded valley of pastureland, divided into small fields of gorse bushes, yellow as bright sunlight and spiky enough to tear a man's flesh. Mixed with purple heather, the untamed beauty of the gorse had a magical enchantment, the kind Ariella could never forget, for this was home, where the one path she knew so well led to Broceliande and the village of Venville. Ariella's memories filled her with passion, heard clearly in her voice when she spoke.

"You know my loss, all that was taken by Faucher, an evil man, one of many that destroy the good that gives light to our world. I live because I was saved by that light within the heart of Broceliande. There breathe the stories that never die of a kingdom guarded by the spirits of warriors and of a king who fought tyranny.

"Within me is that strength. I died there in hidden tunnels beneath the earth, but I was not given the peace that death is thought to bring, for I was not the first to watch the hand of evil take innocent lives. The powers I have, to see where evil abides and to hold a warrior's sword with a warrior's strength, those were the powers that gave me life. What I will tell you now and what I show you are for you to believe as you choose. "

David watched her, saw her dark eyes lighten, listened to her voice. He knew her the way a lover can, but this woman he watched was not the one he had made love to only days ago. He did not know the woman he saw before him now, and when he heard her words, he listened and remembered what it was to be a soldier on the battlefield, guided by instinct and prayer. He felt what she felt: spirits that saw and knew things beyond the scope of today's battles, knew the past, saw into the future, and stood by such warriors as seek to destroy evil to protect the good within the world.

Ariella centered herself at the table, placing the oil lamp close, for the light in the room had softened. A bit of twilight leaked through the high windows, and the embers of the fire burned low. David sat to her right, Renard to the left of her, Durand and Contrie across, Jock and Peter at either end, and Sagath at her feet.

The lamplight was sufficient for all to see a small parcel she held in her hands. It had been folded into a rectangular shape the width of a hand, a knife hole through the center, and there inserted was a small strip of the same paper cut from one end, looped and tightened, creating a spiral lock. No wax or adhesive was used. The men watched as Ariella took a small dagger tucked in her waistband and cut through the spiral lock, unfolded the paper, and found inside not only the message but a golden ring.

She said nothing of the ring but placed it on the third finger of her right hand without pause or noting that the ring was far from ordinary. David watched, wondering how much he did not know and whether certain secrets would ever be his. He saw the ring more clearly than anyone else since he was seated to the right. The exquisite craftsmanship needed to form such a ring was a rare gift and to recognize the skill – possibly only a spy such as himself would look so closely at such things, always expecting hidden meanings. He knew immediately it was four rings interlocked and held by a split bezel so fine, so meticulously perfect that each ring joined in the formation of a tree carved from the darkest ebony, lacy black branches fitting together as one form on a golden ring. None save a gifted eye would ever know it was four perfectly bound rings Ariella wore on her right hand.

Ariella held the message slightly up from the table, just enough for the light of the oil lamp to make the words visible.

"The siege of Quiberon Bay is failing. General Hoche pushed nine hundred émigrés back into the sea, and Puisaye fled back to England with them. Seven thousand remain and fight and hope for the support of the Chouans of Vendee to come to their aid."

Each of the men knew, understood the message well, knowing how it feels when the battle is lost. The soldier either dies or surrenders. These men were warriors of their own making. In other times such men had been called by other names, but whether cavalier or knight or simply a protector of freedom, each man remained for the moment within his own silence to pay homage to the brothers in war who awaited certain death.

For David the message released unequivocal anger, anger for those in high towers who made decisions bringing death to thousands of soldiers. His eyes met Ariella's with cold, icy steel. She knew David's bitter reflection was on the Prime Minister of the United Kingdom, William Pitt, sending prisoners dressed as British soldiers. Always it had seemed to David that those who sit in the high towers, such as Pitt, wash their hands of blame, for he sent no British soldiers. What he did send were cannons, ships, and arms he could spare, and they served his purpose, for the aim was the same. Either way it was Frenchmen who would die, not British.

The silence waited to be broken, for there was more that must be read. The light of the oil lamp flickered, a reminder that the oil had burned half down. Ariella wet her lips, enough to give her breath a moment to cool the fire inside her. The next words had been memorized by a Vendean sympathizer from a message sent to Houche. Such words opened the wounds of memory as Ariella thought of Faucher and knew, "These orders have been forged in the furnaces of hell and will be carried out by men who have given their soul to evil." Her voice did not quiver nor show even the slightest hint of emotion, for warriors were not allowed to convey their pain before battle.

Now, for the first time, she remembered her papa smiling with pride holding her. Perhaps she had been four or maybe five. Her papa was such a handsome man. She remembered asking, "Papa. You are my Papa?"

"*Oui, ma chérie.*"

"And I am your *chérie*, your own Ariella."

"*Oui.* You are my own, *ma chérie*, and my Ariella."

"Tell me. Mama calls you Jean Paul, Laura, Duke Lantenac, and Jeanene she will say, 'Your Grace.' So, Papa, tell me your true and only name."

Now her heart fell, and she knew the memory was not for comfort nor to see her father's face once more. Her papa's answer changed everything she might have wished for but could never have. She remembered every word now, words she had long ago erased which now came back to her with the irrevocability of fate, written on the wall of eternity and sealed with the hand of destiny.

"I may be called by many names, *ma chérie*, as are you, names from those who love us and those who serve or respect us, but the one name I keep for myself was given to me by my father. I think someday you will know the name, but it is a long story to tell now, so I will tell you just a part."

He took her small hand, and he said, "This hand is part of me, for I am your papa, and that is a truth between a father and a son and, as for me, a father and a daughter. Maybe, my sweet child, someday you will remember the words I say to you and maybe never. If you do not, do not worry because you will never have need of them, and that will be good, for then life will be far simpler, but this is what I tell you now. Your name is Ariella, Lioness of God. Ariella was an archangel who protected innocents, and you, *ma chérie*, may remember or forget if this is a good name for you. If you remember, know you are not alone, and if you forget, then I am sorely happy the burdens of this earth will not find your heart to tie themselves to."

His voice stopped. The memory stopped, and she breathed deep into her chest and closed every word she had remembered tight within her heart. The weight of what she remembered was steeled, and so she filled her voice with the strength of such weight, and her voice echoed it through the room.

"The Directory is sending a hundred thousand men from Paris with orders to kill every man, woman, and child who live within the region of Morbihan, within the forest of Broceliande and the villages of Vendee."

Ariella's words conveyed the worst. The power of consummate hatred had now been achieved through the tyranny of the Directory, for they would destroy all who did not share their hatred. The crux of all that made Vendee and Broceliande their worst enemies lay in one truth. They were a land of peasants, farmers, and families who loved their churches and lived in peace with the landowners, nobles who, in most cases, worked alongside the peasants. To allow them to live was like spitting on the revolution.

These men, this room were now ablaze with the same eternal flame that brings light to the world when the evil of darkness descends. The men were not beaten by such impossible odds, for they felt strength as never before.

Ariella, Lioness as her father had named her, turned her eyes to the light of the dying embers, and as if by magic, bright flames burst forth from the hearth of ashes. Throughout time, protectors had stepped forward – knights and cavaliers, priests, and warriors of conscience – and now the Lioness would choose as the others within the room would choose one part, one village, or one army of Vendean Royalists out of all that were marked for destruction, one part which could, by their efforts, be saved. Every child, every woman, every priest, and every man, whether noble or farmer, who could be saved by their sword would live. Innocents must survive, their memories must survive, for they have seen the evil of tyranny.

Contrie was the first to speak.

"I am ready to march to Quiberon! One thousand Vendeans, my men, good men, are waiting for my orders. We have sworn to fight with the Royalists, and fight we will!"

He stood strong. The information freed him from the lies of the Directory, from the bitterness of signing the Treaty of La Jaunaye with the National Convention. Within a day it was broken. Boys, not men, were taken by conscription and forced to fight against their own people and most to die. If he did not join those who still fought, his village of Couffe would be burnt to the ground, leaving the earth so scorched nothing would ever grow again.

Contrie was hesitant no longer. Knowing what he faced, knowing that fight or surrender, either way Vendeans would die, he spoke, and the fire of hatred burned in his chest. His voice embraced the iron of his hatred, and he said what all evil men should hear and tremble before God to hear if their souls had not long since been sent to hell.

"Those that kill unborn babies, alive in their mothers' wombs, that drown priests and guillotine children, these are men Vendeans will not surrender to. Our countrymen will not face them alone." Contrie stood back from the table, lifted his sword to his face with the blade directly in front of his nose and his lips pressed to the hilt. As he looked forward toward those seated, the crossbar of his sword served as the symbol for the crucifix. His gesture was clear, the same as it was for the knights who went to war for their faith. He would not run from his enemy nor wait for them to bring death to Vendee.

Contrie returned to his seat. He would wait until all were finished speaking, and then he would lead his men to Quiberon.

Ariella stood. She knew what she said now would be a determiner for the rest, all but Rotheneuf; he would return to the Isle of Benetin. There were still hidden treasures there, and Ariella knew this was the last chance to salvage the remainder of the Rotheneuf fortune. But for David, Jock, and Peter, she wished to be clear, to leave nothing unsaid of her intentions and her chances of success.

The moment she stood, Sagath was by her side. Something within the room had changed. A presence, a hand upon the shoulder, felt but unseen, had entered. Spirits of Broceliande, warriors of past lives lived now within the energy that filled this room.

Ariella's hand touched Sagath. Her fingers held his dark fur. David saw the ring, the ebony branches, the tree of Broceliande disappeared into the black wolf coat, but it was there interlocked by four rings.

Each man anticipated the next words, which would tell of the battle that Ariella would choose, whether she would follow the orders of the Prime Minister and go to Quiberon or choose a place for spies but not for warriors, a place, such as the Isle of Jersey where a matrix of lies and truths was tied to threads of political forces, where master spies of both Britain and France could be found. In their hearts they knew the answer, even before her words rang loud and clear.

"Faucher will go to Broceliande, and he will die there by my sword! His lies, deception, and the blood on his hand will take him to the one place he must go without his army, and that is where I will go!"

Sagath's head fell back as his neck arched, bending upwards. Ariella stepped even nearer to the orphaned cub who, like her, had known this moment was coming. Her long coal-black hair, fallen from her dark felt cap, fell back behind her shoulders as she anticipated the cry.

Like no other, the voice of the wolf reached a depth of loss, far-reaching, touching the hearts of those who knew the greatest of pain and meant for all kindred spirits who waited for payment of debts owed.

Chapter 18

RETURN TO BROCELIANDE

Philippe listened to the sound of the sparrow. The melody was a broken memory of home, a reminder of the forests and meadows of Vendee, places with secret tunnels, rings of fairy stones, trees a thousand years old, and lakes made legendary by stories of Viviane. He knew nothing could be more secret, more silent, and more savage than those things the forest did not freely disclose. Here the inhabitants of Vendee had the power they needed to defeat armies four times their size. It was easy to disappear within the thickets, the masses of briars and twisted vines, woods thick enough to hide behind, and then there were the wells, masked by stone coverings, many leading to the tunnels that spread into underground mazes. A glade close by concealed a cave he referred to as Le Grotte, a dark chamber dating from the time of the Druids. This cave had been shown to him long ago by Father Jacob.

Philippe pulled his own horse to a dead stop, paused, and listened again for the sound of the sparrow.

From the message he had received at Lorient, he knew one thousand

Vendeans had been shot to death at Angers. In Les Lucs-Sur-Boulogne over five hundred were burned to death while seeking refuge in their church, one hundred of whom were children under the age of six. What hope remained lay in the hands of one man, Georges Cadoudal, and that was the reason he and Father Jacob were going to the town of Muzillac.

Father Jacob pulled back slightly on the reins of the grey gelding he rode. His cloak hung low on his shoulders, and his hair, long and unkempt, was no longer covered by the hood of his cloak. His hair was fully silver, making him appear older than his thirty-five years. He had a grim cast to his grey eyes, and his grip on the horse's reins showed that he was ill at ease waiting for Philippe's lead.

The sound Philippe waited for lifted into the wind, then paused. The same sound repeated itself, a quavering sound, rapid, spaced notes, the sequence almost mechanically spaced but unmistakable, the song of the bush sparrow. At least to any ears but those of a well-trained Vendean sentinel.

Father Jacob steadying his horse, now focused on Philippe, as he waited for him to answer the call.

Philippe, pressing his fingertips together, brought his hands close to his mouth. His hands curled together with his thumbs pointing down. The quavering notes were a welcome memory for the priest. He had taught the song himself to a young Vendean lad of twelve, one he had prayed would never find use for it, God's gift, the song of the sparrow, a warning of impending battle.

Insurgents were well hidden within the surrounding forest. Many were strategically placed closer to the road, well camouflaged in the tall grass of the pastureland and the surrounding hedges and field brush. The call of the sparrow and the pausing of their horses made the difference between being shot by a sniper or passing safely. Father Jacob and Philippe would have no difficulty from this point. Philippe had given the expected signal and within a few miles they would meet one of Cadoudal's men to guide them into the village.

No one but Philippe, and possibly Father Jacob, could have traveled from Quimper to La Rouche-Bernard and escaped capture by the armies of the Republic now gathering in the Vendee. The horses they rode were farm horses, used primarily for the plow, but they were a godsend from an old friend of Father Jacob, a parishioner who had known him well. Henri Courbet had been gamekeeper for the Duke of Venville. He survived the savage massacre, for he had not been there when the family was murdered. He was only one of possibly a thousand Vendeans who would risk their lives to stop the Republic from taking their sons and murdering their priests.

Only now, a few miles from Muzillac, did Father Jacob ask the questions burning inside his heart. He had always known Ariella would return to Broceliande, but even so he had prayed there would be no need for her to do so. Philippe had anticipated Father Jacob's question, so the moment the gelding slowed his pace and Father Jacob eased the rein, an answer was on the lips of Philippe, for no one survives the inner circle of warring political factions, no one survives the turns and balances of power without anticipating exactly what happens next and what questions he must be ready to answer. Philippe would have been guillotined five years ago when the revolution began if he were not a master of knowing the results of all the words he chose to reveal. What he now knew was the crux of all that encompassed the death of the Duke of Venville, the savage destruction of Venville, and the blood debt owed to Faucher, but even that was only a part of the truth, and that was what Philippe would tell Father Jacob – only part of the truth.

Father Jacob's voice was brittle. His words sounded strong and matter-of-fact, but Philippe already knew the answers would fall in his heart like broken glass.

"How much does Ariella know? The message she received – how much did it reveal?" Father Jacob asked, kicking his horse forward, just enough to be side by side with Philippe.

Philippe's silence as he stared straight ahead was more powerful than any words. Father Jacob knew then that Ariella had been given her father's ring and that her blood was now and forever linked to the Guardians of Broceliande, but he needed to know more, to know the fate of the only child of the Duke of Venville. Philippe's response was cryptic but enough to convey that Ariella's meeting with Faucher would be a battle with only one outcome: her death or his. Philippe's response was wrapped in a shadow language of warriors, a precognition of things only fate can determine.

"This was decided when she was a child, and it will always be her path. She alone is the one who must end Faucher. There are some evils in the world that are so strong they can only be destroyed by an eternal flame of light that only a few are given the power to wield. Ariella is now a keeper of that flame."

As Philippe spoke, he never once looked at Father Jacob, for eyes can reveal more than he would ever wish to share. He gave a sturdy kick to his horse, riding ahead with one thought that he voiced aloud to Father Jacob as he cleared his mind to prepare for the next battle.

"We are within a mile of Muzillac, and I have information vital to Cadoudal!" His voice was loud enough for any who wished to hear, and then he turned for a moment and looked back at the Vendee pastureland surrounded by forest. There was no other earth such as this. It was his home and the home of eight hundred thousand Vendeans, maybe half of whom had already been killed by the Republic, and here in this field and forest he estimated maybe as many as twelve thousand waited, hidden. He listened once more to the sound of the small shy hedge sparrow. *Innocents*, he thought, as memories of his sister Laura and the Princess Ariella warmed his heart for a moment before he thought once more of the twelve thousand men hidden here and wondered how many would die before the passing of two days' time.

CHAPTER 19

MUZILLAC

Cadoudal was in both heart and soul Vendean, the son of a farmer, born in the small parish of Kerléano. The same as four hundred thousand other Vendeans, Cadoudal loved his homeland and rejected the tyranny of the Republic. He became, within the first three years of the Vendee wars, a hero, a leader who rode at the forefront of his men. Only after Savenay was burned to ashes and half of the Vendean army was dead on the battlefield or had faded into the shadows did he cross back across the Loire to the Morbihan. Now he fought under no one's command. He fought under his own account, general-in-chief of the Chouans. Philippe knew this was the only man who challenged, in leadership ability and the devotion of the men who served him, the Corsican threat, Napoleon.

The first visible indications that the village of Muzillac was held by Chouans were the simple, loose-fitting shirts, trousers held by suspenders, and broad-brimmed hats the men wore, clothes of farmers who labored in the fields of Vendee. No blue uniforms or red hats of liberty, no forced or recruited soldiers or hired mercenaries, just Vendeans who knew little of any other part of France. There was no other home than here, with the great ocean to the front of them and the forests behind and the hundreds of years, the many lifetimes the blood of their own had covered this land, to hold it, to keep their memories and stories, and find the magic in the telling until the souls of all who lived and fought became their legends, and their home became unlike any other, a place of beauty and magic.

One of the guards moved away from the building that faced the narrow street, gave Philippe a nod, pointed in the direction of the road from La Roche-Bernard, and directed him.

"He is waiting. The brown thatched hut, five houses down, on your right." The guard spoke matter-of-factly, but his spirit was resolute, with the courage a man holds when he believes that victory is given to the righteous. His voice grew louder and filled with passion, for he recognized Father Jacob, a priest well known for his devotion to the people of Vendee. The guard moved quickly, ordering the foot traffic to the side of the road to leave a clear path for Philippe and Father Jacob. He turned to Father Jacob.

"Do you not remember me, Father?" With that said, the heavyset man pulled the wide hat back, swinging it and his arm down to his side. He looked up, and his face could be seen clearly. The right side of his face was terribly burnt. The flesh had melted, tearing from the right jaw and then reforming into a mass of scars. By whatever miracle was afforded him, his eye had been protected, possibly by the large brim of his hat. "You see, Father, God did not let them bastards take my eye nor my will!"

Father Jacob was already aware of the savage executions. Seven hundred had surrendered on the promise of being released. They were shot to death or drowned, women and children as well as the men. It took eight days to kill them all. Yet Father Jacob said nothing but gave this man his blessing and listened to words of sorrow, the memory burning within him as he spoke.

"Brought their own guillotine in by wagon, marched hundreds, children even, and cut off their heads, one by one, the same as those had done in Paris. They brought their evil to Vendee! Forgive me, Father. I want them bastards dead and their souls to rot in hell!" Tears now fell, for the man was crying with his final words. "God bless you, Father. I know you are here to help protect our children. God bless you!"

Father Jacob immediately noticed there were no children and the women who were there each wielded a hunting knife or carried a rifle. He felt the stillness in the air, an unspoken calm that soldiers knew, waiting for the impending storm, and he asked Philippe, "Where are they, the children and the feeble, those who cannot fight?"

Philippe sat tall and alert on his horse with Father Jacob close enough to easily hear the message he intended for Cadoudal.

"Cadoudal is preparing for an attack from the fourth army of the Directory. Faucher will be there, leading a *fédéré* battalion from Quiberon. It is imperative that Cadoudal blow the bridge and force Faucher and his battalion into the Vilaine Valley.

"As for the children and others who are in hiding, that is the reason I brought you." Philippe looked directly at Father Jacob.

A faint wind blew over the bell tower of one of the churches. The peasants watched as the banner of Vendee waved over their heads. It was a silken cloth of pure white. Centered were deep red emblems of the sacred heart, and within the center of each emblem was the cross.

Father Jacob knew. The flag from the highest spire of the village, the signal to the men and women waiting, twelve thousand ready to meet the Republic. The cavalry would carry either muskets or sabers with thirty-eight-inch blades. The cannons had no lack of mortars. The shots would be heated to a temperature that would destroy the forest and burn the towns to ashes, the same as they had done in Savenay.

It took Father Jacob a moment to comprehend Philippe's words, but when the understanding came, the anguish and the fear left his own eyes.

"I will find them, those seeking sanctuary in the forest and take them to Le Grotte."

Philippe, who rarely allowed himself to look deeply into the eyes of any he truly cared for, spoke of things deeply hidden, things only a very few left in his life would feel as he did and understand.

"Father, do you remember, before it all began, three children to whom you taught the secret places of Broceliande? You said to us,

'There are magical places upon the earth, places where spirits live, very special spirits that choose brave and loving souls to reveal themselves. Broceliande is such a place. There is a soul of God's love within the heart of Broceliande and magical beings who keep such love alive. When evil ascends, as it did long ago in in a garden such as ours, the spirits I speak of hear the cries of those whose hearts and souls have been shattered, those who ask for the power to find the evil in this world and destroy it. Broceliande is filled with legends of such heroes, and they are called by many names, but one secret I will tell you now. They do exist and the power they have is kept within them, used only when it is called on, they are called 'The Keepers of the Flame.'"

Philippe turned away once those words were said. He had thought it would be easy now, before they separated, to ask Father Jacob why he had been chosen, but the question froze in his throat, and he could not bring it back. None of the three children, neither Laura, Ariella nor himself, had been taught the same secrets by Father Jacob, for each was different, and each had a different story of when their world fell apart and their own soul was dying. For Ariella it had been in the tunnels after the deaths of her mother and father. For him, it had been in a past just as brutal which had left him, it seemed, without a heart to love, at least not in the way that Ariella and David loved each other. He was a shadow of invisibility who traveled within a world of secrets and lies, who gained knowledge that could turn battles from victory to defeat, but he was never given freedom to fight or die in such battles. His destiny was that of a messenger, a shadow always listening, always aware of where the serpent of evil grew strongest.

Father Jacob was watching Philippe, very aware of where his thoughts had taken him, and he knew what it was that had brought Philippe to that long-past memory.

"Philippe, my son, I know the day you spoke of." Father Jacob's voice changed now, for he summoned into himself truths that seldom reveal themselves because few can understand the depth of human suffering when it refuses to surrender to evil.

"We know the children waiting in the forest wish to hide from the soldiers, and we know that without my help they will be found. Why were you chosen, Philippe? Why are your innocence and the happiness of childhood gone? It is simple in words but beyond the scope of hundreds of thousands who live on our earth. That is why the legends of warriors never die. It is so we can hold on to hope and know there is an invincible will in human beings that can never surrender to evil. Why, Philippe, were you chosen? It is because your heart and soul can do no other than hold to the power that burns within you. You will never step back. Even if granted a hundred lifetimes, each would be the same. You will always stand and fight. You were not chosen to be a Keeper of the Flame. Your heart and soul chose it for you. Without warriors all innocents would die!"

CHAPTER 20

THE SERPENT

All of France was ablaze with fires of war. There was nowhere to run or hide, no safe sanctuary. The émigrés had fled to England, Portugal, Spain, even as far as the colonies of North America, one hundred thousand and more. In Paris, those who did not believe hid behind the colors of the Revolution. To do otherwise was to be imprisoned and then sent to the guillotine. Now was the height of the reign of terror, and now was the time for evil to gain its greatest dominion over the human soul. Evil was embraced by tyranny and humanity was forsaken.

Faucher stared straight ahead, his lips tightened, his jawline extreme, set with rock-hard control, and his eyes unrelenting in their intensity to see every man and command every point of the battlefield. He was seated high on a black stallion, its sleek coat covered with sweat, for the huge animal was in a heightened state of frenzy. Faucher's hands yanked the reins of the seasoned warhorse, and the Morvan threw its head up so that Faucher had to reseat himself quickly in order not to be thrown violently forward. Faucher pulled the right rein tight, forcing the horse to turn inward, forcing him into tighter and tighter control, and with the strength of his legs and unrelenting control of the rein he forced the stallion into submission, an act of great pleasure for Faucher, for this was no small feat. The horse was bred to battle and trained to attack head on and trample a human being to death. If it were possible to read the fire in the dark eyes of the stallion, it would be hate, broken to bitter submission by Faucher's grip.

Faucher's anger was far from vented. His face was blood-red from it. Even the grip he kept on the horse did nothing but feed into the passion that swept over him, pushing him towards rage. He was in the forefront, in command position of one of the twelve columns ordered to the Vendee. The unexpected command by the Directory confirmed his suspicions. He had an enemy, one he had not anticipated but one he would discover and destroy.

He quickened his grip, keeping himself in total control. Sword in hand, he prepared to give the command to move forward to secure the bridge in the village of Muzillac. The first assault was well planned. He had sent twenty of his men to confirm the village was not expecting a seize. The men had covered the entirety of the village without finding any indication the Chouans were preparing for an attack.

Faucher had long ago made his pact with Satan, the Devil, or the Powers of Darkness, whatever name Evil had chosen to call itself. As any who have become soulless, who have worshipped, desired, and invited evil to possess them and carry them body and soul into its darkest secrets, Faucher had found the way. Through his debauchery, his indulgence in buying and selling African slaves, marketing them in the port of Saint-Malo, and paying enormous sums to the French king for the privilege to do so, then plunging himself into the India Trading Company with a brilliance of deceit and a quiet death for any who hindered his success, he became very powerful.

Darkness had descended on him in his dreams. Sometimes in the shadows he sensed himself hand in hand walking in the footsteps of something vile, evil, and soulless that whispered the blackest of secrets, all the secrets he needed to turn friends against friends, to take the shining light of truth and promises of brotherhood and cover the land first and foremost with the blood of the innocent. He served Evil well and in return received power and wealth.

He never questioned the demons he heard. He killed because he was commanded to. He killed those chosen by the darkness, chosen by the blood of their forefathers. Why the powers of darkness had whispered the name Lantenac to him, he did not know. The blood lineage of Lantenac had not ended and would never end until the last child had been killed, until the line of their blood was wiped from the earth, until the throat of Ariella Lantenac was severed by his hand with the sword he carried.

King Louis XVI was not a bad king, but he was a weak king. If he had taken up arms and stopped the storming of the Bastille, events would have unfolded very differently. Revolution was much easier to ignite against good and benevolent rulers than tyrants. The King was not a tyrant, but what unfolded was the hand of evil making mockery of the noble-sounding words, "Liberté, Egalité, Fraternité." Faucher, in league with the Darkness he had given his soul to, took great pleasure as he reveled in his power. He could turn the conscience of a man on the phrasing of a sentence, planting a thought in his mind that turned him from a peacemaker to the voice of a tyrant. He smiled remembering the words of Robespierre, a man who began the Revolution with words of change by peace, taking no lives but ruling with reason. Robespierre's grandiose self-righteousness was the key to his destruction. As reason failed so did Robespierre's words of peace. Darkness surrounded him until he shuddered with fear and then all changed. His friends turned on him as he had turned on them.

Monsieur Desmoulins began the chant of liberty and freedom and easily took the Bastille, for only a handful of soldiers were guarding it. The prison was stormed by insurgents, peasants, some who believed, and many who did not but were filled with anger and hate. Liberty and Fraternity and Brotherhood did not grow, but the fire that was fueled by hate, and anger began to rage. Desmoulins was executed, declared a traitor to the cause by his friend and schoolmate Robespierre, and in turn Robespierre met the same fate. His own friends, seeing the terror grow, knew their only chance of survival was to act quickly. Faucher watched Robespierre place his own head on the altar of the guillotine, knowing the terror would grow even stronger.

He did not miss the opportunity to attend the execution, for there was little to compare with the passion that fed his soul as he watched the lust for blood grow, feeling that this was a passion that knew no satiety. The crowd had seen a hundred noble heads fall beneath the guillotine that day, and Faucher watched from the Place de Grève, beneath the platform of the guillotine. Such places were much sought-after. He watched as head after head fell beneath the blade, without caring that he became covered with the blood of the executed. He watched as the women who drove the carts disposing of the bodies fought over the golden locks of hair and made bargains with the executioner for the best of the aristos' silver and golden hair as their heads rolled down to the waiting carts.

Faucher had paused. It was the moment before he would raise his sword and lead the Third Column as commanded by the Directory of the Republic, and he froze.

He had never felt fear, not the kind of fear that takes you suddenly, as though a premonition, a warning from something that sees you, knows you and is watching, waiting for an opportunity to repay you for a debt grievously owed, but now he felt it in the wind, the air, and the expanse of sky reaching beyond him. There was an edge to his awareness that made his skin cold and clammy. Each day of the journey toward the east, toward Broceliande, had been worse than the day before. Each day had taken him further from Quiberon, closer to Venville, and he felt a presence. He knew something was waiting for him, something he had never faced before.

The howl of a wolf pierced the thick dampness and froze the morning light. Faucher felt a thousand shards of finely-cut glass rake into his skin and pierce into the darkest caverns of his soulless body. He called to his second-in-command, needing someone to focus on, something to return him to the impending battle.

"Royce!" Faucher did not shout as he called the name but raised his voice enough to be heard. The fierce musketeer was just under seven feet tall, a mountain of a man no one challenged. Royce crossed his arms and leaned forward on his horse's neck to be easily, but more privately heard as he gave attention to Faucher. Faucher's voice awakened concern but not that of a caring nature, for Royce hated the man.

Royce watched Faucher pull a woolen cloak onto his shoulders and shiver as though the warm summer wind had turned to ice, and then he listened.

"Can't you hear it?" Faucher asked. "Listen to the darkness, to the wind and the rustling of the trees. A wolf howls, and its cry is like a keening, a death knell!"

Royce heard nothing but watched as Faucher remained frozen, and he considered whether this moment was the opportunity he had waited for.

Royce was there to make sure Faucher did not return from the attack on Muzillac for the same reason Faucher had been placed in the front command. His power and influence had begun to eclipse that of his enemies.

Faucher had lost his iron grip, and before he regained his strength to command, the timing was perfect for Royce to force the attack and push Faucher into a deeper sense of uncertainty. Royce raised his sword to signal those directly behind him, for they knew a charge was imminent. Seated on a giant warhorse that was draped with a great cloth of red and gold, the embellished colors of the Republic, he raised his sword and shouted with clarity and strength,

"Liberté! Égalité! Fraternité! Kill them all!"

The front men shouted the cry, and those beside and behind repeated the charge. Like a roaring beacon of death it was repeated two thousand men strong, and they marched forward in a line that stretched to Cosquer. The Bay of Biscay was less than a league away, and Quiberon was now hours behind. It was in Quiberon that the émigrés, the British, and what remained of the Royal Vendee Army were fighting to the last man, praying for the five thousand men Contrie was leading from east of the Loire River to arrive in time.

Muzillac was a key between the two. Take Muzillac and destroy Contrie.

The order was given, and now they charged.

Royce could hear the rumble, the distinct pacing of the beating drums, the heightened yells of the men repeating the orders of charge, exclamations of "Death to Vendee." Awakening to the reality of what they faced, the men thrust their minds into thoughts of hate, of injustices by their enemy, and finally into blood rage, the key to killing, to murdering women and children, to committing acts of evil. There was such power in their cries, in their frenzy, that it beckoned the demons of hell and roused evil spirits to enter into the thick of it.

Royce prepared himself to take Faucher, to cut him down. Royce had seen the confused state of his mind and counted on this moment, before Faucher regained conscious awareness. Royce raised his sword, shining, naked in the light. One stroke to unseat Faucher, and then the warhorses would do the rest, trample him to an unrecognizable bit of human flesh.

Seconds before Royce unsheathed his sword Faucher reclaimed the demon within him. As though Satan had thrust himself into the deep and cavernous heart of Faucher, Faucher breathed into all the evil of the world and took willing within him demons so strong and so massive that their presence within his body was undeniable.

Royce looked into the eyes of Faucher, and he saw the pits of hell. A flash of light and then his own head fell, sliced from his body and crushed by the charging warhorses.

Faucher had faced the only enemy that had ever truly been a threat to him, not the stuff of Royce or even the Directory, for they were nothing to the demons he aligned with, but he had heard the cry of Sagath, and he had been forewarned that Ariella waited for him in Broceliande. The moment had challenged him, but it had also prepared him. He knew exactly what he had to do and held his lance high as he rode his warhorse toward Muzillac.

CHAPTER 21

DAVID AND ARIELLA

"Spare no one! Women anhd children will be shot. Houses, farms, villages – set all of Vendee on fire. Babies will not be spared. Let their mothers watch them die, and the young girls, drown them all."

Ariella stood with David. Her thoughts replayed the words over and over as though she were the child again who watched as the same evil commanded the death of her parents. Now she was back once more but no longer the child.

Where she stood by the stones of Monteneuf, those that time could not date, was the beginning of the moorlands around Broceliande. There were seven rows of monoliths, lichens covering each stone in random colors of silver and grey. At their feet, covering the space where she and David waited, were myriad patches of purple schist. The stones ran east to west, significant for following the path almost hidden by the gorse and short grass that covered most of the forest floor.

"This path will take us to the ruins of the Chateau de Venville," Ariella said as she loosened her grip, her hands relaxing as she held the reins of the silver-grey filly she had ridden from Questembert. David dismounted before she was aware and stood close, waiting for her eyes to lock into his own. He could hold her now, at least long enough to put his hands on her waist, to feel her near him as she slid from the saddle. He lifted her down as though she were a small child. Ariella stood there, uncertain for a moment. He stroked her face, tracing the curves of her ears, running a finger gently around her mouth. When his lips touched hers, she felt their warmth, their tenderness, more than she had imagined of life's splendor, and she allowed herself this moment to feel love so deep that it was the breath and soul of what could be if the world were not so heavy upon her heart. When she stepped back from his embrace, it was not what either wanted, but it was the only way. When she spoke, she forced her eyes from his, to look instead to the highest point of the ridge. She spoke with remembered innocence of childhood.

"There at the top of the ridge is a great sentinel, a tree tall enough to see leagues away. It was a place to challenge your courage, at least for a child. Philippe, Laura, and I, we would dare each other to see who could climb the highest. The bravest would claim to see as far away as the ocean. That was our truth until another climbed higher, and then the story would change, but always the aim was the same: to see beyond the woods and valleys. My claim was seeing the highest cross in all of Broceliande, atop the church of Saint Marcel."

She looked at him now. Her memories returned her to their purpose. It had taken them two days to travel the distance she had imagined as a child from the coast of Quipen Bay, past what had once been villages, some no more than a small parish or hamlet with only a church and four or five farmhouses, all governed once by their priest or seigneur or part of a larger demesne, but now divided into communes and governed by the Republic. The trees of the forest or the bocage of the fields made them seem far apart, but they were not. For most, only a few miles separated them. Many small hamlets had been burned to ashes. The voice of the National Convention ordered that all of the "Vendees" were to be burned, wiped from the face of the earth. Louis Marie Turreau, commander of the *Twelve Infernal Columns of the Republic,* had begun. He moved across the countryside from east to west. Yesterday it was Bournezeau and tomorrow Saint Hermine, with each column commander given orders to burn villages, farms, forests, and put all Vendeans to the sword.

Ariella looked up at the cloudless sky. It had turned to a deep purple, fading slowly to black. Already the stars had begun to appear, and the half-moon rose. A shadow emerged from the dark woods. Ariella knelt, her arms raised. Sagath was there within moments. She embraced him fiercely with a need to feel the communality between them, a dual destiny formed by loss and restoration and given to them by Broceliande.

"Sagath!" she cried. She pulled his face close, staring directly into his eyes, then bent her head forward and waited for the huge beast to nuzzle her forehead. She took comfort from his presence, smiling as his wet kisses covered her cheek.

Jock was barely a league behind the wolf, and Peter held the rear, keeping a clear watch on the path behind, making sure no one followed them. Without Sagath the forest would have been impossible, for there were few paths between villages. Those once existing had vanished beneath the overgrowth or turned to ruts, washed away when the spring rains filled the mountain creeks and streams.

Jock, close enough to be heard, could hold his hatred for the Blues no longer and shouted as loud as he dared, the sweet taste of every word filling him with righteous contempt for the murdering bastards.

"Between us and the sea, thousands of blue coats, Satan's bastards every one of 'em!" Jock cleared his throat, pausing, taking enough time to deal with what he had seen. "Only the Devil himself would give such orders as these men had. How many towns they burned. The children ripped from their mothers to die at the end of the spear. We seen enough and had little to do but stay if it was dying we were wanting, and that we knew well was comin' for the poor bastards, same as me and Peter, him Irish, me a Scotsman. All we once had, our own families, taken and murdered by the English."

Neither Ariella nor David had seen Jock show emotion, not like this, clearly affected by the slaughter he had witnessed. As a seasoned seaman he had seen more than his share, but that was men fighting men, not soldiers cutting down women and children with the sword and raping by orders given. That was beyond anything he and Peter had imagined, for they were not evil men, not men who could ever do such things, by order or not. The one Irish, the other Scottish, one tall and handsome, the other not so tall nor handsome, but neither would yield in a fight, and neither had ever lost, nor had they reason to fight each other. That Peter was more flushed and breathing harder was no surprise; a deep priority to the fiery Irishman was being a few steps ahead of Jock and being the first to address and report to Ariella. He had failed. Jock had beat him once again, but even so he was the first to give an account of Faucher.

"My lady, Faucher is a full day's ride south, making his way through the lower valley. The Oust River is to the west of him and the valley to his east. Cadoudal's men, hundreds of Chouans, are well-positioned riflemen who know the woods of the Vendee. They occupy every tree and ridge that gives them vantage. Before Faucher reaches Beignon there will be few of his mercenaries left. Most have turned on him or deserted. The men have no reason to follow Faucher. Most hate him, and for those paid to fight or forced into battle by conscription, this is their chance to desert the bastard.

Ariella was silent. Sagath walked to her side. His great wet tongue licked her hand, nuzzling there until she opened her palm and ran her fingers through his thick black fur. He lay by her feet, and she spread her woolen cloak next to him and sat, waiting without a word. Nothing was going to happen until she shared secrets she had long kept buried.

David watched as she turned the ring around and around. He watched as she placed her right hand once again into the dark velvet fur of Sagath. The ebony branches of the tree designed to hold the four spirals of the ring in place disappeared in the black coat of the wolf. Golden specks of movement were seen as her hand, guided by a subliminal purpose, continued to softly caress the wolf.

"Please sit." Her voice mixed with the quiet sounds of the forest. The last of the sun's light had begun to fade, and she spoke without fear, even knowing she would soon meet Faucher.

David spread his own cloak to the left of Ariella, seating himself close enough to feel her presence within the scent of her, something lovers invariably know. Whether it is a catalyst that draws like a flame or learned from the intimacy of bodies connected, it was his to know, lavender and lilacs or musk, the sweet smell of the earth. Her nearness touched senses of desire. Something physical within him now belonged to her, and he knew no other woman would ever fill his soul, not as Ariella did. David had learned as a soldier when battle is near, breathe in all of life, as much as possible before you join the battle, and now he did exactly that. Without a pause, he breathed the love between them as he sat next to Ariella.

Peter and Jock had spent most of their lives at sea. Their home was their ship, and their world was those they knew and fought for on board that ship. They were here now because this was where their world had taken them, and when it was time to listen, to trust, and to follow commands given to them, they did so without regard to living through the next battle or dying, sword in hand. Now both sat back comfortably, feeling the earth beneath them, and listened, waiting for Ariella to speak. Five sat and five waited, forming their own inner sanctum. Soft, warm, misty rain began to fall, touching the broad leaves of the trees that closely surrounded them, covering them, protecting them from discovery.

Ariella turned toward the flickering lights, bright bits of stars that sparkled, appearing and then disappearing like the wings of a thousand fairies, creatures so small they were invisible except to her, revealed by the magic of Broceliande. There was more here within the voices of

Broceliande to guide and protect her than anywhere else she might go. A voice, real or imagined, touched her. *Trust the forest, trust Broceliande. It knows you. It knows who you are. Trust the ring.*

She turned the ring once more around her finger. It now fit her as though made for her, never to come off by anyone's hand except her own.

"Ariella." David's voice drew her into the very center of him, and she met his eyes knowing love was there. She allowed the warmth to hold her, she allowed herself to rest within his hold, like the cresting tides of the sea, she held the touch, of heaven's reach and the moment held them both. She did not look away. She wanted him to see that she loved him.

"Yes, David, I know. It seems time escapes us, that Faucher and those with him are even now just beyond the last valley."

David's brow tightened, and he pressed the palms of his hands flat against the woolen cloak, the strength of the earth beneath him. He now shifted his previous thoughts, for he had assumed, the same as Peter and Jock, that they should prepare for an attack in which the odds against them would ensure the certainty of their deaths. He simply looked at her and smiled the same as though he were once again an overly handsome rake of the privileged and extremely pompous British nobility.

"Ahh! It seems by the look of you there is a great deal the three of us do not know. Although I think we are indeed a band of soldiers, too small to do a great deal of damage to the columns we face but yet willing to fight to the last line of defense without complaint."

She watched him, knowing every bit of him. His eyes changed when he looked directly into her eyes. He often chose to avoid such moments, and she knew that this was not a moment when he would look away. It stilled her heart to see the completeness of love's hold, rendering a man so strong, so silent as David into utter surrender. His words now sounded far away, and yet they were written within her, more dear than she had ever remembered.

He said, "Spies such as the two of us, who serve the rulers of nations at war, have really only one expected outcome. Ride the tide on the highest crest, for the waves of war may reach their greatest height just before a fall. That, my sweet, that is where we are. We have always been caught in a web of lies, deceit, and betrayal. It is the fate of all spies."

He shifted his weight so his body was close to hers, and his eyes directly met her own before he finished.

"So, I see that you do not plan to win your own private war with just the three of us, as willing as we are to lay down our lives for you." David's voice carried a hint of levity, but his words were true. He was telling her that today he expected to die and, as a spy and soldier, had always envisioned this as the endgame of the choices both she and he had made. She faced all three of the men who had pledged their lives to her. With more beauty and depth of soul than any ordinary man or woman could possibly conceive, she laid open the palms of her hands, inviting into herself a transcendent flame of light. It burned bright, and its power and its meaning were imagined in the hearts of those who saw. It was that image of her alone that gave truth to the words she spoke.

"You will not die for me, David. It is not my plan. I think there is much to learn, so much we do not know." She smiled. "Between Muzillac and where we stand now, all the bridges are cut off, boats sunk, wagons broken, and as for paths open to men who ride warhorses, that is impossible. Without cutting the thickets, they cannot go through the impenetrable bocage that blankets the field between hamlets. The forests and villages remaining must be burned if General Turreau is to uncover the thousand men who hide there. Who do you imagine is winning the war, the hundred thousand Vendees or the Infernal Columns that vastly outnumber them?"

It was Peter now who spoke. He had lived in Ireland long enough to know all that he lost when he chose the sea over the barren land left to him.

"I know what they fight for. Every village, every man, and every woman is a willing servant to their cause. They carry messages of the enemy, relays from village to village, through the forest of Bisdan and the woods of Misdon. They have the means to tell each other everything. No one is not informed. Each farm, each cottage waits and watches. A peasant I passed, his message for me he had hidden in a hollow stick. Their messages, their secrets are guarded by four hundred thousand Vendeans or more. Their devotion to their homes and parishes is such that they guard them with religious vigor." Peter stopped himself as his voice began to fill the air, reverberating with the intensity of emotion. He saw the expressions of those who watched and listened and then realized that the plight of farmers and peasants, women, and children he had met had touched his heart, but he knew *"the heart was not enough to win a war."*

Ariella bowed her head as though in prayer, her raven hair loose, the silken strands fallen, covering her face. A moment blinked within the conscious state where men dwell and shifted. As Ariella listened to the voice of inner being, she heard the guiding spirit of the flame of light. The war of France, a revolution that was killing its own – priests and kings, peasants and nobles, women and children – had climbed step by step to the highest pinnacle of evil, for now, without thought to the suffering man could inflict upon his own brothers and sisters of earthly creation, the highest command was "Kill them all, wipe all of Vendee from the earth." What she saw was incarnate evil, unleashed. She saw the terror that had become an infectious disease. She lifted her head, and her dark hair fell back, softly touching her shoulders, like silken ripples made from the touch of a raven's wing, soft flames of ebony enfolding her, and she knew all that must be done. Her dark lavender eyes saw the world not as one but as three: that of tangible being, that of spirit, both good and evil. She spoke.

"Until the demons that drive the forces of evil are destroyed, the pinnacle of good will be torn asunder by those with power to destroy it."

David was aware of the binding the ring had now formed. He watched her hand, watched her slender fingers as she again began to turn the ring. He was concerned, baffled by its source and by the control it seemed to have. The ring had become so much a part of Ariella that he wondered if it had given her the power to see the future. He listened with an intent desire to uncover the mystery. Her words were softly spoken yet gripping in their ring of truth when she said,

"I have been listening to the bells. You can hear them clearly in the hamlet of Beginon. Their knell of hope, of faith is one that only the bells of Vendee can sound. The meaning is clear. Monsieur Henri de la Roche-Jacquelin has joined the Catholic army. He is well loved, and soon all the church bells of Vendee will be sounding the tocsin. Within a day's time, Isernay, Corqueux, the Echaubroignes, the Aubiers, Saint-Aubin, and Nueil will bring ten thousand more men to join the Vendean army. Before this revolution is over, one million will die."

David, as well as Peter and Jock, heard every word, every detail of what the future held and stared at her for one long, incredulous pause as each attempted to understand. It was David who asked the question. The tension he showed as his jaw tightened and his eyes darkened was easily detected in his voice, strained and troubled with confused anger.

"If this is truly the future of France, then what you see must come from the ring you wear, and that, my lady, tests my faith. If so, many are destined to die, what is our purpose? I find myself lost by the sheer weight of it. "

David was a soldier. He as well as Jock and Peter had seen terrors that could not be forgotten. They knew war begets more war. Submission by forced terror hides under a pretense of peace. For these men, peace was an illusion.

The next words were those of Ariella, and she spoke as though every thought, every feeling the men had experienced had been said aloud.

"What is our purpose? We cannot save Vendee, and we cannot bring evil men to peace.

"Peace among men is impossible as long as evil exists. The defeated and dying know nothing of peace, and the victorious do not pause to hear the anguish and the hate that still breathes and whispers for another war, another opportunity to conquer, to command the world from their own realm of power.

"I have brought you here for a reason. This place is filled with memories, memories of men who chose death before surrendering their freedom of will to darkness. Believe as you choose as to whether the world you know is cloaked within a veil conceived by the minds of men but judge your faith by what you are shown."

Her dark raven hair shimmered by the silken light of a thousand silver wings that cast a net of diamond threads over the earth where they stood. Sagath, an ebony totem of the invisible realm beyond conscious power, stood on the primal footprints of the forest and gave the cry of awakening. Vibrations of sound filled the air and began the opening of the veil.

David felt the forest, the air he breathed, and the sky above melt into nothingness. Dimensions of time and space were lost, and he knew the world was not as he had thought. Dreams dismissed by his conscious mind, legends and myths of good and evil, unseen spirits – all he had rejected for lack of substance he now saw as miraculous wonders beyond the scope of ordinary humans.

He stood on the edge of a crimson sea where an endless array of shadow lights moved like rippling waves. The air turned sweet and cool as red tides of lifeblood washed over the earth, then receded into a disappearing myriad of endless horizons. From this holy water emerged twelve figures that David thought were dream images of knights in shining armor. Jock saw priests in flowing robes of silver, and Peter, he saw clearly angels with wings of fire.

Jock had reached for his sword, but as the twelve figures came closer, the weapon fell to his side, and he stared at the eyes of men that were blacker than midnight, knowing these shadowy figures saw deeper into his soul than he could conceive.

It was Ariella's voice and the understanding of what she said that returned the men's attention to her, and they did not move as she spoke to one of the shadow figures.

"Father! You are my father, and I am your Lioness, your Ariella. Will you call my name? Will you take me with you to the land beyond the sea, where there is no more blood and death as I begged that day I watched you die in the garden, and you left me behind, alone without you?"

Lantenac was a knight in armor who towered above the other eleven. He wore black boots, black woolen pants, gloves, and shining black ringmail. The cloak that covered his broad shoulders was sable, thick and softer than the finest silk. When he spoke, his words were filled with love and regret but also fire and judgement.

"Daughter, blood of my blood, soul of my soul, you have been chosen without consent, awakened by the evil within the world, and now my heart, which once bled for the path you have been given, has been made whole by the blood of human love, a love that sacrifices all to protect the eternal flame. The light that will never go out as long as heroes and warriors remain, the light that recognizes evil. That is now your path: to embrace the eternal flame and slay the evil you are shown before it blankets the earth. By the light of Heaven's realm, in the guiding light of tomorrow's rising sun, we bring the swords that will claim you to their power and burn within you. These swords you will use to destroy two hundred devils that live within the human form of Faucher."

Three of the shadow figures standing behind Lantenac now stepped forward, each with a sword held directly to their breast. As they approached David, Peter, and Jock, they drew the swords out to full length, the points toward their own breasts and, holding the blades within their grasps, directed the hilt of each to Peter, to Jock, and to David.

These were men accustomed to weapons of all kinds, and as for swords, all three had held a blade that had taken lives, yet the hand of Peter trembled as he took the sword and asked in a rasped swallow, "What is it you want of me?"

The response was immediate. Immersed in a depth of sorrow yet also unbreakable force, the angel with wings of fire asked, "Whom do you love?"

The words sank into Peter, setting his thoughts to the home he had known, to his mother, his father, and his sister, those he had loved, taken by those who wanted the land but not the peasants who farmed it. Then, as if no thoughts were needed, his right hand raised the sword he had been given. He held it with a grip of steel, and his voice grew with a blood fever that bared his memory of love, broken into a hundred thousand pieces by those who have no soul. He raised the sword, and he swore with the fury of a berserker and the feel of angel wings of fire touching his shattered heart.

"It is the sword I love! Above all, it is only the sword that protects the blameless. The blood where I stand will never be that of the innocent."

He turned the sword upwards and then with one stroke turned the blade inward toward himself and sliced the heart line of his left hand. It was unspoken, the reason, but the act and the blood now tied him to the twelve shadows who had once lived as men upon the earth and who now were all that kept the crimson sea from burning to ash.

A sudden silence descended over the hallowed ground chosen for such as this, and without the question breached, that "of love," both David and Jock raised their swords just as Peter had done, and blood flowed from their heart lines onto their swords. They sheathed the crimson blades into dark black belts that held to their waists and waited for the voice of Lantenac.

Ariella imagined the feel of her father's arms once more holding her close to him. That did not come. The presence of him brought a quickening to her mind and soul, but comfort such as a child wishes for did not happen. It could not happen in worlds turned asunder, a world that was not whole and could never be as long as the hearts and souls of human beings were mere pawns in a game waged by the sins committed.

Ariella breathed in the dampness of the air, filled her lungs with the air of Broceliande. She dug her fingernails into her palm to feel her own pain and her own heart line. She watched her father reach his hand into the earth. It opened with fire, and he pulled from it a sword covered in blood blacker than the darkest night, a battle sword with a blade of blue iron and the ebony tree of Broceliande carved into its pommel.

He said, "From the life blood of the earth, I give you the sword to save us all from evil's power."

Ariella held the sword, and as she did the veil between them closed.

CHAPTER 22

ONE HUNDRED DEMONS

Once Faucher had crossed the bridge at Muzillac it was blown to bits by the Chouans. He was forced through a gauntlet of waiting Vendeans, their subterfuge flawless, for their cannons and best riflemen had been well hidden. The reconnoiterers sent by Faucher had blindly misdirected him, and now he was trapped. He had no supporting infantry behind him, and going forward without his ground soldiers was suicide.

Dawn had barely broken, yet the light began to reveal the men and women who had hidden themselves. They now began to emerge from the shadows, the thickets, and some from the banks of the river now littered with splintered wood, ash, and burning timbers from the blast. The number of hamlets and small villages represented was over one hundred. They had come across fields of rye, climbed fences, and walked through meadows separating neighboring farms. To escape the eyes of Republic scouts, some had slept in hollow tree trunks, others had covered themselves in the impenetrable thicket of the forest. They had in common their knowledge of the woods, every inch of the land they were born on, and what they wore: wide brown felt hats and sabots. The weapons they carried were sabers, scythes, or poles with sharpened edges. Some wore beavers or brown caps with attached white cockades. Those that had them carried rosaries or sacred amulets. They began like a great dark wave breaching the ocean surface to move forward.

Shots were fired, and Faucher's horsemen began to fall. He watched as seven horsemen, previously gendarmes of the royal French army, men of noble birth who were forced to join the Republic or face the guillotine, began to desert. Sabers in hand, they cut into the flesh of any who tried to stop them as they headed their horses south toward the Gulf of Morbihan, their only possible escape. Faucher knew what he had been given. He knew the favor of the Directory had been lost.

Closest to him were five men who would not run, for they had seen him unleash the demons, the devils that came at his bidding, a fury they had watched as Faucher in a blood rage hacked men to death before any of them could put hand to blade. The five envied the deserters, not only the gendarmes but the German mercenaries. The Directory expected them to die, knowing they had no proper training to fight against Vendeans. Running, deserting had not been an option before the bridge blew, but now they had no one behind their backs to push them forward. Their chances, though not great, were far better than fighting for a Republic which doubted their loyalty and would as soon shoot them in the back as trust them.

The men closest to Faucher waited in terror, knowing if they showed any movement that was misunderstood, they would die instantly by the blade. They watched not only the saber but also the musket. If he chose to kill the fleeing gendarmes, they were as good as dead. No man, no matter how skilled, could fire twenty rounds from a musket in one minute's time, and only a true devil could kill thirty. They watched the devil and waited.

Faucher saw the Vendeans screaming forward, appearing from every vantage point. There were no regiments, no properly trained soldiers who marched forward in format. The men carrying hunting guns were skilled far beyond the training of soldiers. Their accuracy took down soldiers of the Republic with each shot, defending their homes, their families, and their God. Such faith was within the fiber of their souls; they would not run.

The bitter chaos began to fill Faucher, to feed the demons taking delight in the death of human beings, a battle waged where the banner of God could be covered in the blood of both the sacred and the unbelievers. He knew his way was best carved through a path of death and depravity, an opportunity, such as this. With the face of a crazed berserker he commanded the men closest to him, those that knew he was the devil. He screamed his own cry for his own battle to begin and only end with the death of Ariella.

"By my side! Kill all in my path! We ride north to Broceliande!"

He knew none would follow, for now they were all consumed in chaos. Few men were left that fought for the Republic because, such as they were, their great republic had destroyed the church, drowned and guillotined both priests and nuns, and begun a Terror that had waged out of control. Even for them, the words: "Fraternity, Equality, Freedom for all!" carried the truth of a guillotine and blood of a hundred thousand lives.

Faucher rode north with less than a hundred men, but that was not important, for the demons inside him screamed in his ears.

Kill the Lioness. Wipe the blood of the Lantenacs from the face of the earth and you shall be rewarded tenfold. You shall be arrayed in robes of crimson and rise to the highest towers to see clearly the death of all mankind, and you shall be among the kings of the earth.

Chapter 23

GOOD AND EVIL

The crystal-clear water of the pond shimmered with light, reflecting the beauty of the morning sky, and the songbirds with the same endless melodies of their magical presence brought peace to the gardens of Lantenac, or so the gods of heaven looking down wished it. Peace, freedom, and equality - words chanted by those of good intent and by those of evil were a beacon, a promise that rested on the blade, the sword of the victor, for that was always the way wars were decided.

The garden had not changed, not in the memory of Ariella, and for the moment that she thought so, she felt the same as she had long ago, the same as she had when she was the princess of Venville.

She knew what depended on her, and she knew before she faced the demons that rode even now toward the village of Venville that she must see to her heart and soul, pause to watch the mirror reflections of the crystal water, and let memories wash her in purpose and strength. The memories she sought within the garden, those were of her father's love, love that time could never erase.

David watched her. He, Peter, and Jock were part of this now. They had witnessed the unbelievable and found truth that gave them purpose. Killing men in battle, soldiers such as themselves, weighed heavy on the soul, and the sense of it was impossible to discern, for he knew not all that died were truly evil. They were all token pieces, some with souls and some without. Knowing evil, the evil he had seen, knowing evil plays with human souls and is a master of the game, and that it holds those it can, captures the weak and vulnerable, and moves them by its will like pawns on a board where death pushes the fallen aside to be replaced, and thus the game goes on. He had seen behind the veil to the source, the power that wished utter destruction of human souls, and now, to carry such a sword as he had been given, to kill demons to fight evil,

this was purpose!

"They are here! Prepare your heart! Believe! Have faith in the good of mankind! Take that strength and with the power of all that is good, draw your swords!" Ariella's voice rose into the morning, awakening spirits of the dead that had awaited her return. She commanded the silent watchers just beyond the veil, and she reached into the heart of Broceliande, into the crimson sea, and pulled back the veil that covered the truth of legends, the spiritual realm that existed and had existed since the beginning when the Creator's hand shaped the earth and breathed the breath of life.

Without pause, Sagath's voice rose to meet that of Ariella, his cry raw, haunting, of primordial substance, rising above the garden, above headstones of unmarked graves and the remains of the grey stone chapel where a princess once sat next to her papa and mama, a child who believed all was good within her magical kingdom and within the world beyond. The cry of the wolf did not stop. It filled the now-empty streets of the town once called Venville, and it echoed through the Valley of the Wolf, ascending the Val sans Retour, the Valley of No Return.

Faucher and his men, the hundred that had sworn their souls to him, rode their warhorses straight through the deserted streets of Venville directly to what remained of the garden wall, and there they waited as they stood witness to what remained of the demesne of the Duke of Venville, once a kingdom of Brittany and now lost to ruin and defiled by the blood of those who died here. What had been protected and treasured by those born of this land whose lineage began with the first beginning was sacred. Their bloodline was sacred, their legends and stories were part of them, and it was their seigneur, the Duke of Venville, who valued them as he valued the sacred land of Broceliande. This was the love, the pure heart that had brought the devil to Broceliande. Broceliande was their land, freeheld for as long as their bloodline remained. This righteous act, land given by the Duke ov Venville, gift for the greatest good, had brought the devil into the garden of Broceliande, and now he returned, for he had failed to take the one soul he coveted most, the last of the blood of Broceliande, Ariella!

At the garden gate was evil manifested by the brilliant light of self-love. The men who rode by Faucher's side were emblazed by the power that evil gave freely to hollow men who have no souls. Their eyes were deep and cavernous, dark holes of empty life, and they were bearers of shining swords wrought in the furnaces of hell.

Sagath was first to attack. This moment had been burned into his first breath, for he was born with this purpose and had lived each moment knowing whom he served, for he was the last descendent of the *Vallon de la Chambre au Loup*.

He had chosen the highest pillar of the wall surrounding the garden. Here, on the capstone of the garden gate, he looked down from a position that flanked the line of Faucher's attack, and he waited, watching every movement with a will that carried the blood fire of a hundred thousand wolves who lived through him, a sentinel, a protector, the last of his breed.

When Sagath leapt from the highest pinnacle of the wall, he did not do so alone, for now the veil was open and the good as well as the evil were at war. With him were the spirits of one hundred wolves with the size, the strength, and the fire to match his own. The impenetrable fury of the fire beasts descended on the horsemen of Faucher.

There was no joy in taking down the horses, stallions bred for strength but guided by the hands of evil. The raging wolves were there at the behest of good, but here was the crux of humanity's fall: evil begets evil with instinct to kill.

The wolves went for the horses, maiming, crippling, taking away their ability to carry the men who rode them, men who forced them forward with spurs and pain. They fell, the beautiful black stallions fell, dying in agony and heard through the forest in the throes of death. The wolves moved forward, holding the horsemen at bay, and the demons within Faucher spread the width of two legions charging forward.

Faucher held his sword far above his head, untouched by the wolves, for the men who guarded him had taken the first onslaught, and now he rode in the lead, screaming with blood rage, for he had not seen the thousand knights, bearers of the flame of light, that now stepped forward, for they had been waiting just beyond the veil for Ariella's command.

Faucher seemed to falter for one long moment, realizing evil did not have dominion on the earth, even in the throes of revolution and the atrocities committed. The soul, the good within men still existed. The moment of realization vanished, and in its place was screaming, almost human, a long piercing ululation that could have been a war cry from a hundred thousand warriors, but this was a sound from hell that followed the demons to earth.

The numbers were not even. This was a perception for soldiers such as David, Jock, and Peter. Only when the wolves began to tear through the demons as though they were fodder to be crushed and trampled did the men realize that the demons were not the greatest hell had to offer. This was but a skirmish for the greatest of battles were yet to be fought.

A winged creature four times the size of a mortal man emerged from the throes of the battle. The first of the warriors flanking Ariella's right side stepped forward, and with a blaze of fire thrust into a cavernous socket a burning sword that, if this had been a man, would have penetrated his eye, piercing through to the brain. His head crushed and his neck fallen forward, his unnatural cries were a signal for the greatest mass of creatures, not unlike himself, to come forward.

Now the battle began in earnest. David, Peter, and Jock fought back to back, with all eyes forward. The winged devils now came in pairs, their wings spanning more than a spear's length, but the difference was in the power of the swords given to the three soldiers, for their power was tenfold that of the talons and razor teeth the devils attacked with.

Ariella watched but stood firm, for she knew despite all the chaos unfolding around her, there was only one battle of importance.

Those with her kept the demons back so she would face Faucher on even ground.

As Ariella stepped forward and began to walk directly toward Faucher, she again saw the carnage left by Faucher and his men, she heard the last words of her dying papa as he reached to hold to the hand of her mama one last time, and she remembered a child dying inside as she was pulled away by Laura.

She had not expected the absolute, immaculate ecstasy that filled her, the certainty that she had been born for this, that her bloodline would go on for eternity. As long as there was evil, there would be good, and her mama and papa, their love for her, and the beautiful world of human love were eternal. With sword in hand, she would make it so.

This knowledge propelled her forward, brought a peace that swept through her as each demon that escaped through the swords of David, Peter, and Jock fell to her own. In the still moments between the death blows that took down one devil after another and in the long spaces between heartbeats when her flaming sword rested, waiting for the next demon to fall, she breathed exalted breaths, knowing she was one breath closer to erasing the face of Faucher and his diseased evil from the face of the earth.

When she was there, finally facing Faucher, she screamed with the name of her father. She gave voice to all the innocents killed without remorse, and in the name of Lioness she lifted her sword and ran at Faucher with the heart of a warrior.

The demons pulled back to watch as did Sagath. The warriors called from the crimson sea and the three who were here, their lives given to the Lioness, lowered their swords. For this was the final purpose, to wait now and watch the final battle.

As the noise of battle died away, a hundred thousand demons clashed swords on their shields and shouted in deafening synchrony. If the Devil himself had sent the thunder of hell, the noise could not have been more deafening, yet the sound was nothing, for the only sounds those who loved the Lioness heard were the sounds of Broceliande, and all they saw was the Lioness clad in a binding of steel made of threads that sparkled with diamond light and reflected the color of ebony as dark as her silk hair. Her beauty overwhelmed them as they watched her wield the sword given to her by her father, and the final battle began.

Here was a battle between humans, one good and one evil. This was no longer a battle between demons and the knights behind the veil, for they were no longer of the human world. Now they watched as all eternity beckoned for the final outcome.

Faucher held fast, waiting for the power of her strike. His own inner strength was not as he thought. What was left of the man he once was, known for the lives he took, the power of his sword, that man now fought without the benefit of demons, yet he had evil, and that had no less transformed him and filled his mind and body with hate. What he drew from still spun him into a mighty foe no ordinary swordsman could defeat.

He screamed with the conviction of his own invincibility as her sword landed heavy on his shield. The cry on his lips was never uttered, for faster than his mind could conceive, she switched the sword, and the second blow, ten times stronger than the first, now came from her left hand. She had bested him with an understrike, learned on the corsair and from the blade of Durand Rotheneuf.

Faucher had no respect for caution nor for believing she was a better swordsman. His hand began to twitch as he turned and blocked with his shield, feeling the blood flow from his right side. His first thought was to call the demons inside him. Remembering they were not there, he reached beneath his belt sheath for a hidden blade, one he had used to kill again and again.

Ariella knew her skill exceeded his. She had learned that within the first strike. The seconds he lost in directing a blow and the fault in not expecting the undercut told her his weakness, but skill was not enough. Even without demons he was a master of deceit and of the hidden blades he carried and the poisons that would kill her. The swordplay with Durand, the battles engaged by the corsair, they were fought with one rule: kill by any means necessary. She had been cut, forced to the gunwale, and thrown into the belly of a trading ship, but never once had she thought she would die. Always in the back of her mind was her grandpa or Durand, but in this place, the spirits of Broceliande had no dominion, nor did Faucher's demons. Now was not the same. She would die if she faltered. She would die if she did not find the poison he would use and the hidden blades. Fifteen years she had been given to prepare for this moment, to show whether her father's blood flowed through her veins. This was the test.

She watched him. She watched his left hand even as he prepared for a strike with his right. She saw the fine blue powder that covered his left hand, and she knew once it was in the air, once she breathed the powder, she would die. Durand had taught her this, the immunity from ingesting small doses of deadly poison, the ability to use it as a deadly weapon.

Faucher was immune, and he had gained position. Now he was within a sword's reach. His right hand went toward her face, forcing her to turn into his left side. The moment she turned toward him to block his sword, his fingers began to open to release the powder.

She knew. She had been taught and practiced the motion a thousand times. The mesh steel she wore flowed to her wrist, the beauty of slender arm covered by fine ebony threads. One flick and her wrist was free. Faster than a heartbeat she released a Kilij blade. The diamond razor found its mark before Faucher's fingers opened to release the powder.

He made no cry, for he did not believe what he saw. His fingers, all four, were cut straight through to the bone and the powder rendered harmless, for it was covered in blood.

Still, she knew it was not over. Evil would not die until it was matched with fervor unlike any it had ever known, in a heart such as Ariella's that carried the soul of her father within her own.

She did not know where his pistol would appear, but she knew. She remembered her father. He had broken the ties that bound his wrists, loosening them with his own blood. She had watched as Faucher daunted him, coming closer as his men cheered him on, and she watched, knowing her father would kill Faucher with his bare hands the moment he was close enough. Faucher was slow to approach, for in his eyes there was fear, and he was afraid of Jean Paul Lantenac, Duke of Venville. Faucher's first shot was intended to maim. To slowly kill a great man was more exquisite than any pleasure a demon such as himself could ever imagine, and so he got close to see the pain. Her father freed his hands, and her heart had beat with hope. Frozen in her mind was the memory of the face of Faucher, its sordid and wretched ugliness, the scar that ran the length of his forehead to his jaw, black against his ashen skin, and his tricorn fallen from the misshapen head of a devil who knew if he died, he would burn in eternal hellfire.

She had waited a long time for this moment, anticipating, planning her every move.

He drew the pistol from within his coat. One shot to end the bloodline of Jean Paul Lantenac, and Faucher would be given a reprieve from hell's gate.

He aimed for her heart, and he fired. The blast, then the bullet, tiny fractions of a second between, for Ariella it was the space that separated heaven and hell.

Fifteen years, every moment with purpose, learned through a shattered heart that, piece by piece, reformed, awakening to suffering beyond her own. A thousand died each day in wars that never stopped. Only when evil was defeated, when diseased men such as Faucher were wiped from the face of the earth, would they stop.

When she moved, she did so with extraordinary power, achieved through human will.

With precision, she judged her distance and executed a turn, a movement, within her, part of her made so by those who had taught her and the thousand times repeated until she was the power, a force greater than the velocity of any pistol in the hand of the devil.

She was there, a blur of motion, perfectly positioned. The entirety of her momentum struck him from the height of her leap. Her kick sent him to the ground, falling forward on his face.

She braced herself, palms down on solid stone, left leg extended back with power building into the right, waiting for his move, waiting to strike him.

She knew he had no more poison, no more hidden blades when he grabbed a chiseled rock, sharper than razor edges, and threw it at her.

She pushed off the forest floor, taking her energy from the solid ground. She flipped the knives from their wrist guards around to her palms. With an effortless motion, she slammed a spiked boot into his groin. Then, with the knife blades pointed forward she rammed them into his throat, not waiting even for a word before she turned them deep, his throat opened and emptied itself of dark blood that flowed slowly, thick and vile.

Faucher was dead, nothing now but a stain of darkness on the earth's surface.

Sagath's voice sounded in triumph, his cry rose into the heavens. The rising sun shone through the branches of a thousand trees, leaving no shadows, no darkness from what had descended upon Broceliande.

The men were there waiting for the Lioness, willing to march into the furnace of Hell if that was to be her next command, but her words as she turned to David were sweeter to him than an imagined reprieve from Hell itself. Her voice found his heart and she said,

"We go to the Bay of Biscay. There is a pirate there waiting for us and a long-lost brother of Laura's. David, your family is waiting for you, and my grandpa for me. We all know the wars are far from over and that men we love as brothers still fight and some will die today. The battle we won will only be remembered by us, but the evil defeated will never again wage war on the earth and we have claimed a great victory. Today we go home. Tomorrow is another day."

GLOSSARY

Ariella – "Lioness of God."
Beau Monde – the fashionable world of high society.
Blues – soldiers of the revolutionary government.
Broceliande (bro-SAY-lee-ahnd) – a legendary forest located around the village of Paimpont in the department of Ille-et-Vilaine in Brittany, France. The ancient forest is connected to myths of King Arthur, Merlin, and Vivien.
Cadoudal, Georges – leader of the Chouans.
Carnichot – a large hole dug underneath a tree's roots and covered with branches. Used as a place of hiding.
Chouans – led a revolt along with the Vendeans as anti-revolutionary.
Committee of Public Safety – a political body created to oversee the defense of the French Republic from foreign and domestic enemies. To achieve this goal, the Committee implemented the Reign of Terror (1793-1794).
Cotters – peasants or farm laborers who occupy a cottage.
Danton, Georges – a leading figure in the French Revolution who spoke out against the Reign of Terror and as a result was executed.
Demesne – a royal domain of land ruled over by a lord of nobility.
Émigrés – French men and women, mostly aristocrats, who fled France during the time of the French Revolution.

Infernal columns – columns of soldiers, were led by Louis Marie Turreau in the War in the Vendée. The National Convention stated that the goal was to exterminate "brigands" in the region south of the River Loire. Twelve columns were formed and sent through the Vendée to exterminate the local anti-Republican population.

Jacobins – left- revolutionaries who aimed to end the reign of King Louis XVI and establish a French republic.

Noblesse – members of the French nobility.

Pitt, William – Prime Minister of Great Britain from 1783 until 1800.

Quimper prison – Quimper is a town in Brittany, a few miles from the Odet River. The prison was originally a Catholic convent, but the nuns who formerly occupied the building were evicted after refusing to take the oath of allegiance to the Republic; at least one was executed by the guillotine.

Quiberon Invasion of France (1795) - The Battle of Quiberon was a major landing on the Quiberon peninsula by émigré, counter-revolutionary troops in support of the Chouannerie and Vendée Revolt.

Rake – a man who was immoral, a womanizer.

Reds – Revolutionaries.

Republican Marriage – during the mass drowning in Nantes, between two thousand and four thousand people were drowned. The "marriage" involved tying a naked man and woman together and drowning them. Jean Baptiste Carrier, who ordered this atrocity, was later guillotined for his cruelty.

Reign of Terror – September 5, 1793 to July 27, 1794. The Revolutionary government decided to make "Terror" the order of the day. Nobles, priests, and hoarders were main suspects. Three hundred thousand were arrested, seventeen thousand executed, and ten thousand died in prison without trial.

Robespierre, Maximilien – was powerful in driving the Revolution and instigating the "Terror." His policies regarding the "Terror" led to his own death.

Rushlight – miniature torch made from a plant by soaking the dried pith in fat.

Sans-culottes – poor people in France who enforced revolutionary laws.

Ton – Who's who of British high society during the Regency era.

Vendée – An area in western France, south of the River Loire. Estimates of those killed during the rebellion vary, possibly four hundred and fifty thousand out of a population of eight hundred thousand. Whether this can be called a genocide remains questionable.

SEQUEL

The sequel, <u>Bloodline of Lantenac,</u> follows the aftermath of the French Revolution. Evil feeds on the ever-growing desire for power as innocents caught in its tyrannical grip die in vast numbers. Ariella and those now sworn to serve the Keepers of the Flame depart from France. They have seen behind a veil that is so vast it defies their attempts to challenge its power, and as they discover, it waits for them. The Scottish Highlands are in a bitter struggle. Their ancestry the birthrights of the greatest Scottish lairds are being challenged, and vast numbers of Scottish peasants and farmers are being driven from their land. This is only one of the atrocities Ariella will face, for the Napoleonic wars, just as the Revolutionary Wars, will reach the pinnacle of evil, the call to slaughter a million people, a genocide, a cleansing of the innocent that stand in evil's path.

Please share your thoughts on <u>The Lioness of Broceliande</u> by leaving a review on Amazon.

Thank you, Gloria J. Prunty

Made in the USA
Columbia, SC
23 October 2024